This is a work of fiction. The characters, locations and storyline are drawn entirely from the author's imagination.

Mabbs-Zeno, Carl C.
    Neige Noire / Carl C. Mabbs-Zeno
    ISBN 978-1-7331262-6-7 paperback
    ISBN 978-1-7331262-7-4 e-book

Other novels by this author:

A Pale Shade of Honor

Birch Bark and Blackberry Thorn

A Witness Too Silent

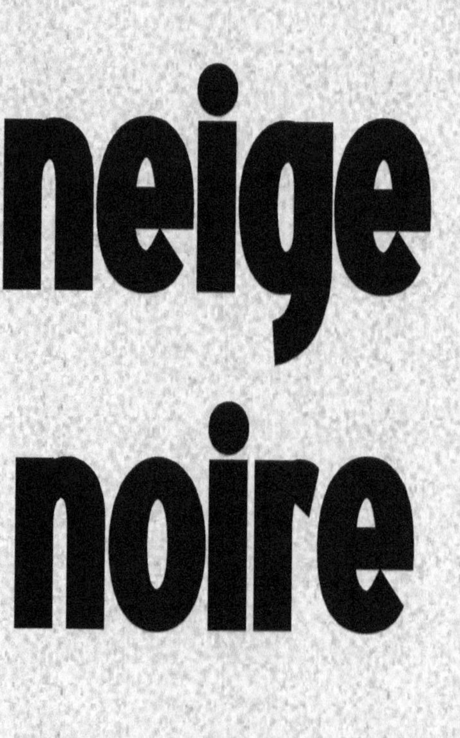

Khotso Publishing
2019

Neige Noire

Contents

"Neige noire" is French for "black snow."

Neige Noire

Chapter 1

MAXIE'S BAR

How many hours had the man with the crooked nose been seated in front of his computer screen, reading, expanding, summarizing, rearranging, and otherwise chasing clues to whatever was wrong about the data file on his client, Pulter, Inc.? He had a feeling he was getting close to something but he could not say exactly was what wrong with the account. It was the feeling of being on the edge of an insight that kept him focused. He did not want to lose whatever germ was birthing in his brain and he was looking forward to finally solving this knotty problem. Suddenly he became aware of the pain in his back. He leaned forward to stretch and the pain stabbed up to his neck like a deep cut from a scalpel, and then dulled to a general ache along his spine. He looked at the bottom-right corner of the screen to see the time: ten-thirty. The last time he had checked, it was not yet nine o'clock and he was worried then that it was getting late. He needed answers before the working stiffs started out on Monday. If he had no plan by then, he would lose his edge and might lose the trail completely.

He stood up and stretched some more without feeling any better. He was wide awake with the fear of failure looming closer. It would not be his first failure, but it would be a dangerous one, one he could not afford. He was a long way from knowing what step to take next and he suspected there would be plenty of steps before he would be ready for the evidence on the computer to start telling a cogent story.

Without thinking about why, he went to the closet and pulled out a scarf and a knit cap to cover his ears. His coat lay on the old easy chair. The gloves were in its pockets. In less than a minute from leaving the computer, he was outside and feeling better. The cold air slapped his face like a woman who had been insulted too close to home, but he did not mind much about it. He had wrapped the scarf around his neck while going down the steps from his apartment house and felt the bulk of his pocketed gloves while striding quickly up Walnut Avenue as if he had someplace to go. The only plan in his head for the short run was a hope to get lost in the city, to find a street he had not trod before, a quiet street, where his thoughts could get out of whatever rut was keeping him from getting anywhere with Pulter.

After a couple blocks, out of sight and feel of his apartment, he slowed down and looked around. It was all too familiar and if he walked straight forward, it would be familiar all the way to the end of the city. He looked ahead to consider where he might never have been before. He stood next to a lamp but was too charged to lean against it. He wished cigarettes did not kill you; it would have been good to light one now. He became aware of the snow on the sidewalk. There was not enough to cover the surface; just enough to lighten the street's tone a shade in the pool of light under the lamp. He looked back to see his footprints lead up to the ends of his shadow. When he raised his face to the streetlamp, the light hurt his eyes so he closed them while he tried to feel individual flakes settle on his face. Closing his eyes was good. He had not realized they were stinging after all that staring at the internet for far longer than is healthy. Once, and then again and again, he felt cold flakes land. He counted them up to ten and then opened his eyes and looked before him as far as he could see. The snow improved his sense of distance, flakes looking smaller and slower a hundred yards down the street and only a grey backdrop farther away than that. His body was back to reality and his brain was outside the computer where he preferred it to be.

Though he felt returned to the real, his next step was beyond his conscious volition. His foot went in front of him and his thigh pulled his weight over it. The momentum of that shift carried him past the point of balance and his other foot went on ahead. He was walking again. A few flakes blew onto his throat and he pulled half his scarf out of his coat and wrapped it around his neck, covering his chin at the same time. Then he reached into his pockets and happily found his gloves were were dry inside. He was walking with purpose, or so it would have seemed to an onlooker, and he adopted the perspective of an onlooker just to be sure he was moving well.

He noticed when he blinked that his eyes had been cold when open; not in a painful way, just in an interesting way. And then he remembered that the light had seemed too bright when he stared earlier which was an odd thing at night. He looked up again. Without a streetlamp above him, it was not too bright, but it was brighter than he expected at night. The city was reflected in the heaven although the image was not focused into an actual upside-down picture. Seeing a vague, blurry reflection of the city was possible, he figured. What was unlikely was that the opposite would occur, that heaven would ever be reflected in this city.

He looked to left and right, and decided it was darker to his right, so that is where he went. At each cross-street he looked to the right to see if it looked unfamiliar. At a distance of eight or ten blocks from his start, the view to his right looked as strange as a foreign country and he made his turn. He was now walking into the wind, a wind that he had felt before only when he came to a cross street. In those open squares, the snow swirled, especially on the sidewalk, making it look alive. Elfin snowdrifts accumulated at the edge of some buildings. He was disappointed the snow was too dry to settle into a layer that would accept his footprint everywhere, leaving a history back to his starting point. In his present mood, it would have been reassuring to look back and see evidence, however ephemeral, of an impact on the world.

The cold penetrated his thin coat and attacked his core. The pleasure was suddenly over; it was time to go back. Fifteen blocks, 45 minutes at a good pace he estimated. He wished he had walked a circle instead of an ell.

And yet he did not change direction or slacken his pace. He would not go back until he had gotten someplace. He needed some sense of accomplishment from the expedition. After two blocks of dark residences and shuttered shops, he saw a red glow ahead that might mark something distinctive enough to count as a destination. He did not set a high standard for his destinations.

Up close, the red glow said "Maxie's Bar." The sign was inside the bar, shining through the window, but the buzz it made could be heard from the sidewalk. He looked admiringly at the single, complicated neon tube, at how it had been bent to form the letters and painted black where it connected the letters. He wondered where someone learned the skill to make intricate glass shapes. And he wondered that someone with such skill would work for the cheap price a marginally successful neighborhood bar could afford. And yet the sign was typical of such small businesses. Maybe they made more money than they appeared to make. He knew nothing of such businesses beyond what he had seen in television dramas. He had never been inside a local bar although he envied the people who seemed to find pleasure in taking a drink in the company of strangers.

Julie had said she wished he would get drunk sometime. He had understood her point but there was not much he could do about it. She thought he would become unrestrained, wild, naughty, or some combination of similar attributes. He knew from some experimentation in college that if he drank and kept drinking he would only become increasingly uncoordinated until he fell asleep. He did not explain this to her because he wanted her to retain the hope that someday he might be just as she wanted him. He did not think of himself as restrained. Surely *she* was never wild, not that he had witnessed anyway. She was highly disciplined in her personal habits. She liked to serve a drink before dinner, hard liquor only. He took it and pretended to like it. He sipped it slowly to get rid of it with the least pain possible but if she happened to look when he was about to sip, he nonchalantly knocked back whatever remained in the glass and then shuttered with a forced smile. It was not an important barrier between them, yet enough, he knew. She wanted a more manly man than himself and he strove to keep her from learning this fact. When he was least inhibited, he was childish, and she did not appreciate such behavior so he was careful around her and came across to her as restrained. She was right in a way, but not in a way that drink could help. He wanted to stop remembering Julie-bird. She had flown away and was not coming back.

He looked around him and saw no one else on the street. He put a finger on his right nostril and blew the snot from his left side onto the sidewalk. His right nostril was already open and he went innocently inside to get out of the cold before returning to his apartment. He had a handkerchief in his pocket, clean and neatly folded. He always had one, proud of fulfilling at least this one of his mother's admonitions about what determines a gentleman.

He was too proud of his accomplishment to soil it. Someday he may need to offer it to a lady.

A warm blast hit his face from a heater hanging on the ceiling and facing the doorway. He quickly stepped farther in. He was standing too close to a woman who was facing the jukebox. She turned her face toward him and smiled. The smile surprised him so much he was past her before he could react. He would have smiled back. She did not look like a hooker, dressed in a soft sweater with a high collar and wool slacks. The slacks especially looked expensive and fit well; comfortable, they seemed, on a night as this. She had a beautiful oriental face lacking any obvious makeup on her eyes or mouth; it looked beautiful in the glimpse he had under dim lighting, but he may have been seeing mostly the smile. Why would she smile at him? He was neither good nor bad looking. His face had more angles than Pythagoras and none of them lined up. Sometimes people had a first impression of him as handsome. It came from a view of his whole rather than his details. He was all even numbers: a full 40 years old, a short six foot and a firm 200 pounds, a solid mesomorph with the mottled skin and sharp features of his remote north European ancestors. She had the briefest moment to see him before starting her smile. The smile must have come from her personality or her mood. ...Unless she were looking in an amateurish way to be picked up tonight. Past eleven o'clock, anyone needing company might be getting desperate. It was, however, not the first time an interesting woman had unexpectedly smiled at him. The outcome was always the same: he always hesitated and thereby missed his chance at even so little as mere courtesy.

He quickly surveyed the small room and walked to the bar. Somehow, it seemed important to appear decisive, probably because that was the characteristic he most lacked at the moment. In fact he usually sought indecision; he sought freedom from making any decision.

There were three men sitting in a booth and two more at a table. He calculated the seating capacity of the room at 24 in addition to six stools at the bar: counting himself, an occupancy rate a tad under 25 percent, or better, a smaller tad over 23 percent. For this night, he was living in the moment as a way to escape the drudgery of decision after decision in his work, but he could not turn off his numeracy.

He unwrapped his scarf and pulled his coat off, placing them on the second stool before sitting on the end one. It was part of looking decisive. He did not plan to stay, but he was not planning anything so that was not a constraint. Putting them on the stool was not part of any plan either, yet it seemed to him a gesture signaling that he wanted no company. He did, in fact, want no company. It would have been nice to imagine the oriental woman sitting there and talking to him while he looked at her more closely, but he could not imagine anything so unlikely. She probably was not beautiful anyway. His brain always interpreted rapid or incomplete views of females generously.

"What'll you have?" asked the bartender, a young fellow in a t-shirt and jeans. He wiped the bar with a damp rag in the classic movement of his profession accompanying the classic inquiry. His clothes reflected the heat in the room; the dry hot of baseboard electric panels, clearly distinguishable from Arizona desertlands in summer by the frat house scent of stale beer and overweight males.

"Hey." Buck paused. "Buck" was the name used by the man with the crooked nose. "I'll have a Chevas Regal," wondering if he should have just said "Chevas," and then continued, "neat," and he thought "don't ask me for any more detail than that 'cause I am only guessing that was an appropriate thing to say." The bartender nodded very slightly and sat a small bowl of peanuts on the bar before turning behind him to get the drink. The warm air was bringing a flush to Buck's face, but his fingers remained stiff with their internal cold. He formed each hand into a loose grip and blew slowly into them, one by one, grateful for something to occupy his movements until the drink arrived. He would have lit a cigarette if he had one although he was not sure he could light one or smoke one with aplomb, having never tried it other than a couple evenings in college 20 years ago. He wondered how many sweaty, 28th Street fingers had been in the peanut bowl on the way to gripping too many drinks after wiping dripping noses on their owner's flu-ridden faces. He scraped a dozen peanuts into the palm of his hand and tossed the nuts one at a time into his maw.

The drink arrived quickly. He sipped it, but not too cautiously. It tasted like poison and caused his throat to spasm. Why would people choose to drink this; even to pay for it? No wonder he had been unable to please Julie. He just wasn't a drinker. He took another sip and set the glass back on the bar. In a slow movement, he wiped his eyes with the napkin. They were tearing in reaction to the warm air after being frozen, not from the whiskey. He folded his arms on the bar and leaned on them contemplatively. Without staring at the shelves, he read the labels on the bottles lined up on the wall behind the bar. His throat burned slightly, perhaps pleasantly. He formed a plan: finish the drink and go home.

He was disappointed that his thoughts were tending back on the matter of Pulter, Inc. It was like a song he could not stop replaying in his head, earworm. If people went to bars to get away from their everyday stresses, he should have lost track of Pulter for some time. His boss was considering partnering with Pulter on a major project, maybe even a merger, and asked Buck to look them over. The man with the crooked nose, known to his friends and most other people as "Buck" even though it was not his name, had looked and everything was fine, everything but the itch on the back of his neck.

Their records all added up just as they should. He was sure they would pass any audit, but something was out of kilter. Their accounts were a degree more complex than needed. Were they just incompetent on that minor aspect of their operation? Buck guessed they were but it did not look exactly like incompetence to him. He had looked at everything available to him and found nothing really wrong. He could let it go, but it would have felt much better if he could confirm the complexity was not set up to hide something. He had reworked all the records and was frustrated that he could find nothing certain. As he searched for a new angle in the evidence, he always found a need for more evidence, evidence of the sort that did not exist. The only thing he could think to do with a chance of success was to create new evidence by asking questions of the Pulter honchos. But that was not a path Buck would take. He looked at the books and never spoke with the client. In meetings, he was always the guy sitting against the wall, nodding to his boss from time to time, no more than that. Sitting in Maxie's, unintentionally thinking about Pulter, he framed questions that might trap or free the Pulter execs, questions he would never ask.

He was about to reach for the glass again when he heard a voice drawl, "Why don't you sit down a minute?"

It came from one of three guys in the booth. He nearly turned his head to see if the question was directed at him and then he realized it was not likely at him since he was already sitting. The only people not sitting were the bartender and the woman. He could see the bartender did not lift his eyes toward the questioner.

"Hey, we have room here. Sit with us!"

Buck listened for her answer and heard a faint, "No, thank you." Then he looked back at the booth. For the benefit of the three men in the booth, he was establishing himself as a witness, not an invisible part of the room. He decided to keep the path between himself and the door open. He looked to the back of the room to see if there was a back door. He was not sure whether the door he saw was the men's room so he figured it was best to rely on the front door. He turned back to his drink and heard more sounds, too indistinct to eavesdrop effectively.

He had another sip of whiskey and again avoided making any facial response to the poisonous taste. He looked at the glass to calculate how many sips remained. He did not mind dragging it out, at least until his body had forgotten the cold. He was surprised to hear a female voice nearby and nearly flinched.

"Are you cop? I mean, policeman?"

She had some kind of accent, not a native English speaker. He looked toward her slowly. She was not smiling.

"Me? No. Of course not." At least he had a chance to smile at her this time. It was not too broad, not leering; only as friendly as possible without being threatening. He looked back to his drink and clasped it with both hands but did not lift it to his mouth.

"Those men over there, they say maybe you are."

He looked back at her just quickly enough to see which men she meant. It was the three sitting at a booth. They were not looking toward the bar.

"They were just teasing you."

"No, they nott know I can hear them. It's what they believe. Maybe you don't want people to know you're police."

"If you want the police, it is easy to call them. I'm an accountant. I just know numbers." This time he continued to look at her. "That is, I know money numbers, not phone numbers, but I can find a policeman pretty quick." The light was not good, but he was getting certain she was very attractive in a 40-year old way. Without moving his eyes away from her face, he shifted his attention to her body and graded it highly. She was very slim, not curvy at all in the clothes she was wearing. "Healthy" seemed a fair description. She stood straight and confidently. "I don't suppose you need an accountant." No one wants to meet an accountant outside the office. "Would you like me to call the police?"

"No, no," she answered very quickly. "Don't call no... don't call anyone." She continued to look into his face as she backed away and sat on the stool next to his coat. The bartender was watching a television beside the cash register but he was also casually monitoring the conversation. The only explanation for her behavior was that the woman wanted to be picked up. One time in twenty years he goes into a bar and a woman is after him. Is it that easy these days? Maybe she was going to follow up the policeman question by saying he looked physically imposing or smart or mysterious, and that would get a conversation going, but instead she had accepted his answer. He had smiled but in a way that showed no special interest in her. He lifted his drink with two hands and sipped half of what remained. He watched the bartender who watched the television.

One more sip... The whiskey had not tasted good and it had not warmed him noticeably although the room had cured his frostbite. He formed another plan: to wait at least twenty more years before drinking another whiskey.

He heard the sounds of the three men in the booth getting up, and walking over to him. He continued to study his glass with its final three-fourths inch of glistening brown liquid.

"Did you two have a fight?"

Buck cast the speaker a wry smile in complete answer to his rhetorical query.

"No? But she's still alone? But you guys ought to be together, her with that scar and you with that nose. Maybe you already had your fight, huh?"

"I don't know her," said Buck and he looked at her briefly with yet another small smile before turning back to his drink. He wanted to finish it off, but did not want to appear rushed by the drunk's intrusion.

"So ma'am, where'd you get that scar? Bad night with a customer back when you were young or a gift from your pimp?"

She looked down at her hands on the bar. Buck looked for a scar on her but could not see one in the dim light. He looked to the bartender who did not turn his head away from the television.

"You a cop? You get that nose in the line of duty?"

"I'm not a cop. Just a guy who stopped by for a drink."

"You need a drink. How did you get so ugly? I bet I know how you got that nose. Anything to do with a woman who thought you was too ugly for her?" The drunk smiled but mostly faced his friends, like a teenager who has discovered he has grown some muscles and thinks they place him on a higher plane.

"I'm sure you don't know," Buck answered before hearing any more of the drunk's conjecture, "because I got it from many different breaks. I claim seven, but I don't really know. I don't like sticking it where it don't belong, but it seems to get there from time to time and obviously I don't take it out of the way too fast. You see, a good looking guy like yourself has something to save, but my face is already broken up so it doesn't matter to me anymore. But I was ugly before I broke my face. It came natural. My mother was ugly and her mother before her; my father too. I think I have one cousin who is not ugly, but I'm not sure 'cause I never met her."

The drinking buddies laughed but the drunk thought he was being humiliated in some way.

"And even with that headstart on being ugly, my broken nose is not all of it. I've broken plenty of other bones, some in the face and some all over the rest of me. You can see I'm irregular in lots of ways. Of course, I shouldn't say I've broken my nose and all those other bones. Pretty much every time it's been someone else that broke it."

The drunk was confused about whether he was being insulted. "Did it ever take three guys to break that beak?"

"No, it never took more than one. I never had to keep my nose away from three at a time and I don't expect I ever will. I've been too mature for some years now to fail to appreciate the obvious lack of potential good in brawling. Too many things can go wrong and nothing right can come of it. Don't you agree?" He switched eye contact back and forth between the two buddies. Neither of them would meet his look.

As he spoke, Buck rotated on his stool so he could slide off quickly away from the drunk. He monitored the drunk's friends and saw they were not part of the discussion, not yet, but they crowded the woman's space. Before the drunk responded, Buck stood up and stepped around the stool with the coat and nodded to the woman to take his seat. That would leave him standing between her and the three men.

He leaned on the bar and called to the bartender, largely to get him to come into the situation,

"Thanks. How much is it?"

"Four bucks."

He put a five on the bar and reached for his coat. The bartender took the bill and went back to the cash register.

"Taking her with you, nosey guy?" The drunk lowered his volume, maybe from losing some nerve; maybe to keep the bartender out of range. "Would you like to lick that ugly scar on the old lady?"

Buck kept his scarf in his hand, thinking it was not a good idea to wrap a handle around his neck. He addressed the drunk's friends. They had not stepped forward when the woman moved away and they looked uncomfortable. They were just the sort of friends a bully accumulates. They were unlikely to get involved, but he asked them anyway, "Your friend doesn't need to insult me or the lady. Why don't you advise him to relax?" They did not move. "Now would be a good time."

Finally one of the wingmen reacted, "Come on, Dave, the beers are getting warm. Let him go." That suggestion, that the drunk was the one in charge, fed his ego enough for him to relent a tad. It was clever enough, or just lucky enough, to merit a conspiratorial nod from Buck, but that might have threatened the fragile truce, so the nod was not given.

Buck turned back to the bar and tossed down the last of his whiskey in classic fashion, more concerned about not turning his back from the drunk for long than about looking like Bogart.

In a low voice, not quite a whisper, he asked the woman, "Would you like me to walk you home?"

She still looked uncomfortable. Seeing her from her other side, he could see her scar, a jagged mark that ran up her neck onto her cheek. It did not look like a surgical remnant, but it did not look bad. It was thin and colored about the same as her pale skin. It might even have been a bit sexy, certainly making her distinctive from a certain direction.

"No," she answered and a moment later added "thank you."

"Would you like me to wait here a few minutes after you leave to be sure no one is close behind you?"

This idea caused her to smile very nicely and she nodded her agreement with that plan.

The bartender came by to pick up the glass and return the change from the five which Buck waved away. When he turned back to the woman, he saw her hand resting on the bar beside him. His first thought was an appreciation of her hand. He had always identified strongly with his own hands, seeing them as tools that were always available and nearly always able to do what was asked of them. Her slender fingers and graceful position aroused a sympathy in him for her beyond what had been present before.

Beautiful women are not very rare. They are on billboards and television and magazine covers visible every day. There are two or three beautiful woman on each block of sidewalk in the central part of the city at lunchtime on a working day. They had no more effect on him than well executed architecture on a building. On those rare occasions over the years when a woman's appearance had affected him deeply, it was always due to some tiny detail, a simple gesture, a lilt in her voice, or a gleam in her eyes. There was no explanation for the attraction that surged through him now beyond some evolutionary wiring in his make-up, wiring whose effectiveness was normally subdued by a lifetime of cultural obfuscation.

While he hesitated, looking at her hand, her fingers opened to reveal a cocktail napkin which she patted carefully and then withdrew. He nodded quickly in the negative and pushed the napkin back to her. He said "Good night," and sat down with his back to the bar to watch the room while she left.

The drunk was watching them. Buck walked over to the juke box by the door, shielding her from the drunk's attention as she went out. The drunk said something loud but it was unintelligible.

A song cost fifty cents, which seemed like a lot but at that moment would be well worth it to distract everyone for a few minutes. Most of the titles were unknown to Buck. They came from a time after he listened to popular music but this surprised him because Maxie's Bar seemed a holdover from the era of his own youth. He recognized the names of a few artists, none of whose recorded songs he knew. He thought it might be a good gesture to suggest a title or two to the others in the room, but decided it was best to minimize interaction.   What if they disagreed on the selection? Then he saw a title he knew well and pressed E24: "Piano Man."

"...Sing us a song tonight
Well we're all in the mood for a melody
And you got us feeling alright."

He knew Billy Joel sang the song but he wondered who it was who first said "Music hath charms to sooth the savage beast," while he watched the room go silent but for the jukebox, and all tension drained away. The phrase sounded like Shakespeare who said many things for the first time, but Buck slowly remembered, in a manner typical of his quirky capabilities, that it came from a later playwright and that it was originally soothing a savage breast. The writer's name would not come to him except for the letter "C." He suspected he might recover the name if he worked on it, but it would have been work to do so and useless work at that. He stuffed half his scarf inside his coat and wrapped the tail carefully around his face, knowing the cold would require a big adjustment from the warm bar.

Outside, the snow was falling faster than before. More than an inch of the stuff was underfoot, ensuring he would leave tracks on the way home. At this hour, they might be the only tracks along some stretches of the way. On the other hand, at the rate of new accumulation, his tracks would be soon covered. He visualized the old footprints filling in a block behind the new ones. He wrapped the scarf over his face partly to protect himself from the air and partly to direct his breath down into his coat. He did not own a heavy coat, relying instead on the poor man's system of wearing layers. While he was usually satisfied by this system, it was not good for spontaneous walks on wintry nights. He would hurry to generate heat from the exercise.

Before starting for home, he looked again at Maxie's Bar. It had been an interesting place to visit. Then he looked up and down the street to remember the scene; not to ever return, but just to preserve the adventure. There was a figure on the other side of the street, standing under a streetlight. It was odd to be waiting on the street at this hour in this weather. He looked hard into the blizzard, hardly able to be sure it was a person and not a mailbox or some other urban furniture. It moved and he knew it was alive, and probably thin. She waved at him and he was sure it was the

woman from Maxie's. He waved back and she walked off.
In a few seconds, she faded into the storm like a TV image
lost in static.

Chapter 2

WINTER MORNINGS

The terrifying din of the alarm jarred Buck more than usual. Worse, it would not end when he fumbled with the usual buttons. It was not the alarm; it was the telephone. Why did he leave that on? Also curious to his muddy mind, why was there so much light in the room?

He tried to express himself in a perky voice: "Hello?"

"'Morning, Buck. I take it your day's not off to a rousing start."

"Hi Rich." Buck jumped out of bed and looked out the window, seeing a world heavily clad in snow with even more snow dropping rapidly from above. "Yes, rousing... Beautiful day we're having."

"The office is open but I can understand if you can't make it in. I'm worried about that Pulter file. Did you come up with any ideas on that yet? Are the buses running in your neighborhood?

Buck hated to acknowledge that he could not make it in. He could if he really wanted to. He was less than three miles from the office. No matter how deep the snow was, he could plow through it. He was fit and capable of great determination. Besides, it did not matter if the buses were running in his neighborhood as long as they were available somewhere he could reach them. However, he was not, in fact, determined to get to the office this day.

"No way, Boss. The plow's been by but there is no traffic now."

"I was thinking you might be waiting on the curb somewhere or walking to the subway."

"I'm not near a subway. It'd be better to walk all the way in. I could get there in time to turn around and come back. But I don't need to go outside to see the street is not in use." As he spoke a pick-up truck went past.

"And no conclusions on the Pulter case?"

"You know I am worried about that too. I have an inkling of an idea. Sitting out a day may be the best thing for incubating it." Buck heard a skeptical grunt come through the telephone. "No, really. I have an angle that requires focus. The office is not the best place for it. I may have to do some research to finalize it, but working the angle does not depend on the details as much as on having a good concept."

"That's a lot of BS for a snow day. If you can't get in, you can't get in. We need an answer to Pulter soon. If you work on it today, we'll call it a work day."

"Let's see if this angle works out. I don't care about the hours." Buck was insulted at the suggestion that he would want to account for his time this day or any other."

"Well, how good is this angle you think you might have? Should I be expecting relief tomorrow?"

"It's not done until it's done, Boss. If it was easy, you'd be doing it, not me."

"Well, give me a call if you figure something out. I won't be able to relax."

"Sorry about the weather, Rich. I'll leave the phone on."

"I appreciate that you left it on this morning. See you tomorrow."

"Yeah, if that stuff stops coming down on us first."

"Yeah."

Buck stared lustily at the accumulating snow. It promised an unusual day, a day outside the rut, a day of pleasures without responsibility... to pursue his pleasures he had received an unrequested and unplanned license from the heavens for freedom. As he ran the water in the shower to get it warm, he wondered at his undeserved good fortune. He had slept through his alarm due to staying up excessively late on a work night. In particular, he had failed to reach the office on a day when he might really matter to the company, that is, with the Pulter case in play. And then it turned out there would be no repercussions for being late. Instead, he had the rest of the day off as well. It was nearly enough to believe in luck.

Bad times had been heartily deserved for the most part. Mere chance had favored him many times more than it had harmed him. Too often he had challenged fate and that it sometimes caught up with him was inevitable. But how had he been lucky enough to cheat on every math exam in high school and never attract any suspicion? How had he managed to escape being caught on the dozens of times he had trespassed with his college pals in abandoned houses, stealing worthless junk, but stealing nonetheless? And why had no one ever noticed his petty shoplifting? It had become so easy to commit these minor crimes, he had stopped committing them. He had hated himself for doing them and wondered why he did them since he was gaining so little from them and then one day in a drugstore, with a pocket full of batteries, he thought he might have been spotted. He thought he might have missed a camera or a mirror, and there was a man who might have been a store employee going to the front of the store. On that day he quietly returned the batteries and walked out looking as guilty as possible to test whether he was under suspicion. No one stopped him and he decided it was time to grow up. From that moment on, he had never cheated, lied, trespassed, or stolen. He was never even tempted to return to those acts. He had a strong sense that he had not been cleverer than the world, but had been lucky. And he knew enough of statistics to doubt that luck came to people consistently over a lifetime, but he saw the price of an arrest was infinitely greater than the value of a package of batteries. He felt this was largely a rational decision to accept some of the rules of society rather than a moral one, but he held out hope that his earlier self-loathing might have been driven by an underlying morality. And what of the vast majority of people who had rolled the dice less often than he and yet had been forced to pay for their misdemeanors? Were they more likely to drift to greater crimes, having been marked for their sins by society? Were they compelled by that additional experience to view themselves as reprobates? Chance had allowed him to grow up unmarked and he marveled at it and intended to enjoy being forever in the right.

As he toweled off, he wondered what to do with his freedom. At his root, he wanted to be ten years old on a day when school was cancelled and the neighborhood would be collecting, unbidden, on the hill by his house for sledding. With his ablutions completed, he would rush outside to test the snow to find its consistency and depth. If it was powdery, the sleds might be able to make their own way down the hill, tracking any way the driver wanted. If it was thicker, he could build a track like a toboggan run, and put in some ramps to send the sled into the air if it is going fast enough. If the snow was light, it might blow into deep drifts where he could dig a cave. And if it was not powdery and was really deep, and today may be getting to that point, it would be good for building a fortress and using it as a base for a snowball fight. Any of these options would be excellent, driven by the nature of the storm; apart from his not being ten years old, having no hills in his present neighborhood, knowing none of his present neighbors, and having no sled. But he was anxious to test the snow anyway.

What does an adult do on an urban snow day? Mainly, he gets into the snow. Until he knew the nature of the snow, he reasoned, he could not plan on how to use it. So far he knew only that it was welcome and it was cold. He dressed in layers, wearing extra socks, extra pants, and a sweater under a sweatshirt under a jacket under his coat. He tromped happily, heavily and warmly down the steps of his apartment hearing only one viable idea: go somewhere for coffee. That would do for the start of the day. He wished he had brought something to read. There might not be newspaper delivery in this weather, but there would likely be no place to sit anyway on a day with people like himself cast out of their routine.

The walkway from his building to the sideway had been shoveled and had already accumulated an additional inch of snow. Buck felt badly that he was a late arrival to the snowy universe, that he had missed the first part of the day. Nonetheless, it was probably best, since he had needed the sleep. Other walkways had been cleared and portions of the sidewalk were more or less clear, depending on when and how well they had been shoveled. The street was white with a fine layer on top of the soft salty mush left behind by the snowplow.

He picked up a double-handful of the snow and squeezed it into a ball. It was not a firm ball; half the snow blew away when he threw it at the streetlamp and the remainder was not heavy enough to fly true to its target. So, in the first analysis, it was too cold. He felt the sharp air on his face and realized he would soon need to wrap his scarf to minimize the exposed skin. The snow would be sticky one day before it melted away and he could build a snowman then. Maybe snow "sculpture" was appropriate for someone in his age group. He pushed his arm into the snowbank and noted its depth, using his arm like an oil gauge. At least twelve inches had accumulated already and more coming as if there were no end to it. He walked into the untracked show on his neighbor's small lawn and dragged his feet to exaggerate the track into something an exhausted explorer might make on the way to the South Pole. No, the South Pole was too unreasonable; say, like an exhausted explorer might make in Siberia. He fell forward, twisting as he went down so he landed on his back. Lying there, recovering from his trek, he was comfortable, feeling only the danger of being so comfortable that he might *allow* himself to freeze to death. But so far, he was warm. His layers played their roles as planned. He could see only gray clouds and falling flakes as the sides of his bodyprint were high enough to block his peripheral vision. The wind blew a little powder onto his face, chilling the skin further.

ɤɤɤ

There had been a day when he was in high school when he walked alone into the woods during a blizzard like this one. Fifteen was a great age to be; old enough to be a man in some societies, but in modern America, young enough to have no pressure of imminent independence. His body had done most of its growing but little of its shaping. The present was for pleasures and the future was full of promises, some real and many merely plausible dreams. Deep snow was a challenge to be appreciated by the young and fit and free.

He rose early that Saturday, fixed himself a full breakfast of eggs, sunny-side up, with toast, and dressed in long johns, double socks, double pants, wool shirt, sweater, scarf, hooded coat, knit cap,

28

gloves, over-mittens, hiking boots, and gaiters. No one else in the family had risen early enough to be aware of his early meal, so he felt the virtue of taking better advantage of the day than anyone. He over-heated from the effort of dressing the final layers after breakfast while being unable to emit any of his heat through the clothes he had already put on. He cleaned his dishes quickly and then adjusted the straps on his day pack to fit over his new bulk. He turned off the lights in the kitchen, leaving no sign of his early rising; only his tracks on the lawn would be evidence to the late rising members of the family that he had left.

The sharp cold on his face was thoroughly welcome when he first went out the back door of the house; temperature, wind, and large flakes the size of weightless pennies combining to cool the skin like dipping a finger into dry ice. He enjoyed the pain of it as long as it took to make his track across the lawn to the start of the woodland; and then wrapped his scarf across his face and drew his hood tight so only a hole the width of his two eyes was exposed to the air. The path was not visible under the snow but he knew it well and could follow its course by the touch of the familiar trees that bordered it. He followed the path, or walked where he know the path to be, to the point where it was farthest from the house and began to return. This, he knew, was at the edge of a swamp, but the swamp was not a barrier on a day as cold as the present one; the soft muck and open water were as easily traversed as a golf course. At this point he needed to decide where he was going; 'til now he had only wanted to be outside and alone. Yet as he considered his options, he knew a plan had lurked in the back of his mind all morning: he would find the ice cave.

He did not believe in the ice cave. It was a tale too fine to be true, told by older boys some years before. The story said that far back in the forest behind his house, on the vast tract rumored to be owned by the "water company," in years when the winter was worst, a cave made of ice would form. The story did not give any more information about its location. It was just the sort of vague glory certain older boys without the pride to earn their authority boasted to younger ones. Buck had kept the image in his mind whenever he was exploring the woods. In all seasons he was alert to topography that might support cave formation but he had not explored the cliffs much in winter and he felt badly that he had not kept up with the seasonal variation in his woods. It was hard to get into the woods in winter with schoolwork during the week and the shortness of the daylight, poor excuses for his deficiency. He would set himself the goal of finding the ice cave but, more realistically, would explore the cliffs to see how the season had changed them.

It normally took an hour to reach the start of the big cliffs. In the snow he would move more slowly, but more directly, not needing to skirt the swamp. It was hard to drag his feet through the deep snow and he dreamed of the day when he would try out snowshoes. He did not mind plodding; having no agenda was an important part of any Saturday's merit, an attraction he would learn to appreciate ever more as he got older and accumulated more detailed agendas than he could not have conceived when he was fifteen. He was slowed too by the effort to keep track of where he was going and where he had been. As he got farther from home, he was in less and less familiar land and all of it was changed by the look of snow. He had never used a map or compass in this forest, having explored it over the years at ever increasing distances. There were no landmarks in the swamp, where he had rarely ventured anyway, but he had the wind direction to keep him oriented and he reached the higher ground on the other side without feeling lost. Then he kept out an eye for familiar terrain and stared long whenever he thought he had found some. His exploration had always been intuitive but was sufficient even in winter to keep him in the general direction of the cliffs, knowing the pine woods on higher land would be to his right at least until the start of the cliffs and a gentle rise to the left signaled he was going parallel to the cliffs. The heavy snow, mixed with some fog, kept visibility short but the worst he could do was to drift too far right and reach the pines where he would know how to adjust his course, drift too far left before the cliffs started where he would see the road, or drift into a circle and head back into the swamp.

He had no watch and certainly saw no sun to gauge the hour, but he estimated he reached the cliffs by 10:00. He had not drifted off course at all and felt, out of all the places on the planet, he belonged just where he was. He had played on these cliffs countless times when a small boy. A couple times he had camped with some friends near them. In recent years, he had not been here often; there being so many places to explore in his state, but he still felt ownership of the woods behind his house. Even the more familiar cliffs were different in the snow. He felt well rewarded for his efforts in getting out early in the storm.

The cliffs were festooned in icicles in addition to the snow on the horizontal surfaces. He looked for his favorite ledge, a place he discovered two years before he was big enough and brave enough to climb onto it. It was his favorite spot because of his eventually conquering the failures to reach it and because it was tucked under an overhang, giving the feel of a cave. The geology of the cliffs did not favor cave formation and no cave had ever been reported to him in this region although he knew of a minor cave a few miles away in cliffs that looked similar to him, so he had always held out hope of finding one.

He did not go onto his favorite ledge. With the snow and ice, it was too dangerous. A few icicles hung in front of it and he could see how it might be called an ice cave, if one were generous in his definitions. This was as far as he usually went in the summer. He had gone on to other cliffs a few times, enough to satisfy himself this was the best place along the escarpment. He walked cautiously as close as he could to the bottom of the cliff. He was fifteen or twenty feet below the ledge, standing on loose boulders sometimes coated in ice beneath the snow. He grabbed the bottom of a long icicle and broke it off. It was heavy and he nearly dropped it when the weight shifted from the cliff to his hand. He held it horizontally with both hands and threw it at a row of icicles beyond his reach. They crashed and tinkled in a most exciting explosion. Buck worried for an instant that he had broken something natural and beautiful but soon subdued his regret, knowing all he had broken was doomed to fall soon and would likely never have been seen or appreciated by anyone. He had made the place more valuable by visiting it, by enjoying it. He had not destroyed a piece of it, only used it.

He marched along the cliffs smashing icicles for a quarter mile, learning techniques for ensuring they crashed more noisily. He left a path of guiltless destruction mentally framed in starring roles as a soldier, a monster, an alien, a superhero, and other images not fully formed into more or less human figures.

Finally he reached the place where the cliffs ended in a field of boulders. It was time to cook his lunch, here in a wild place on a wilder day, far from and free from the prospect of meeting anyone. He looked for a protected place among the boulders, clambering over them carefully, knowing a slip could hurt his mobility, and feeling all the more pleased for the danger, but not foolish enough to make it any larger. And happily he soon found a small nook into which he could crawl to get out of the wind. When he squeezed down into the nook, he found there was a large space under the boulders, almost a cave. It was damp and irregular but roomy. He sat comfortably and set his pack beside him. His legs tingled from relaxation after a morning of scrambling about while carrying the extra load of the winter clothes. He removed the scarf and opened his collar, letting steam from his sweaty torso rise in front of his face. There was no horizontal surface in his false cave, but there was a way he could sit comfortably and lean back on a flat rock.

He took out his small gas stove and small pot. He melted snow to make tea, and then melted some more and boiled some hot dogs. It was a slow process to get enough water for cooking. He ate the hot dogs with his gloved fingers and felt his stomach accept the heat of his meal. After finishing the hot dogs, he wanted to take a nap. He imagined freezing while he slept and doubted anyone would find him unless the reek of decomposition happened to reach someone well off any trail, probably in the spring. There was a comfort in being so free of all humanity.

He began to cool down when he stopped feeding on his hot lunch and was too bored to await a frosty loss of consciousness so he packed up his gear and rewrapped himself in his damp clothes for the trek back. When he scrambled out of his hole, he was stiff from the hour of sitting on the rock. He was especially careful in climbing out of the boulder field and emerged safely on the side farther from home.

As on all explorations, he hesitated to return without one more look in the less familiar direction. Through the falling snow, he imagined he could see a large, solid white area in the distance that made no sense. As far as he knew, there were no houses or other building anywhere near. And there were no open fields or hillsides. But he was on the edge of his former trips and those trips had been some years ago so he went a little farther to work out what he was seeing, if anything.

He walked through the slim gum trees found in that part of the forest, staring ahead to work out what he was seeing. The fog had dissipated or been left behind, but visibility was very poor and he would not have been surprised if the white patch turned out to not exist except as the random juxtaposition of small elements of the landscape, near and far. He had just about decided it was real and was likely a building, maybe a shed, when he reached an opening in the trees and could see the clouds met the horizon on both sides above the white patch. He was looking at cliffs. And they were covered in ice. They might make a crash suitable as a grand finale for the day's trip.

When he was closer he saw the ice was thicker than on any of the icicles he had broken. At the bottom, it was five feet thick and twenty feet wide. He was seeing the frozen remnant of a slow waterfall. He maneuvered to the right to get closer. From his new position he saw the broad sheet he had first seen was hanging fifteen feet from the cliff face. The ice cave existed! It was here this day and with so much bulk, would remain like a glacier well past the snow covering. He had no interest at all in proving its existence, as by bringing anyone out to see it. It was better to remain a tall tale; it would be a vanity to claim having seen it and to be disbelieved.

He climbed to the edge. The floor of the cave was protected from the snow but was slippery from ice patches and very irregular. Buck feared to go inside, having seen lesser ice sheets crash all day, knowing how brittle the ice was in the deep cold. Nonetheless, he scooted just inside the perimeter, officially inside. He did not trust being able to keep his balance if he stepped on the ice floor, so he sat down. He slid along, holding his position by putting his feet against the ice wall until he was all the way to the inside end of the cave. Light was passing through the wall, showing where it was thickest or thinnest. He did not imagine waiting to die here; it was a place too exciting to die peacefully. If it all came down on him, which he knew was very unlikely, he would be washed out into the open woodland floor below and when his broken body was found in the spring no one would be able to figure out how he got there or what had crushed him. He sat for a minute and made a slow movement as if he were throwing a rock at the wall to break it apart. The cold reached through the layers of pants and long johns, reminding him it would be much more comfortable to be walking, and still he sat in the place that no one but he knew existed.

And then it was time to go. He slid carefully back and escaped with no more harm than a wet spot where his body had sat on the ice. From below the cave, he looked up and wondered if he threw a rock large enough and hard enough he could break the wall, leaving it for no one else this winter. If it came down all at once, it might sweep him away. The idea was idiotic. He thought of waving back to it as if it were a friend, but he was no poser and he headed back with a casual saunter.

He followed his own track, as much as possible. It had not filled in with new snow, but had been blown away in a few places, not enough that he could not pick up the trail again. His concentration on finding the way in the failing daylight diverted him from reliving the day's adventures but he was contented to have them stored away for another time.

ɤɤɤ

Yet that time had not ever come. The day was not lost to him, but he had never savored it as he thought he would, not until the second day of the big storm twenty-five years later when he purposefully fell into the soft embrace of a drift and was reminded by the blown icy dust of his adolescent discovery of the wonderful truth in a myth.

Despite the comfort of his snowy bed and his memories, Buck was too excited to linger anymore, so he rose to seek new adventure.

The coffee shop was two blocks off. He walked in the street. A few cars went by but it was easier in the street than on the sidewalk, much of which had not been cleared since the snow began. Many people were out, shoveling their personal walkways but, sadly, relatively few bothered with the sidewalks. In the second block, Buck came to a car spinning its wheels. Buck ran up to lend his shoulder to the driver's purpose. He wanted to help, of course, but he also felt sorry for the car, which was being unskillfully commanded. Some dark slush splattered Buck from the knees to his boots as the car rocked backward, then, with Buck's earnest efforts, it went a few inches farther than it had gone before, hitting fresh snow and gripping enough to get entirely out of the icy rut its spinning tires had carved. Buck felt powerful. He waved to the car and saw no acknowledgement in return. It was possible the driver was unaware of the help he had received. Buck hoped for another car to help, and the messy roads would support that quest, however there were too few people trying to get anywhere. Buck wondered if the citizens of his city were intimidated by the storm's rare size or if they were simply sleeping in.

No one was in the coffee shop. There was no sign on it explaining that it might open late, just the one-word sign hanging on the inside of the door that had been flipped last night to read "closed." Buck remained encouraged by the occasional traffic (and the certain knowledge that his neighborhood was not the center of the city) to believe there was some place open to serve him coffee. He headed toward Market Street. If any place were active, it would be Market.

He could not remember another coffee shop nearby, but he came upon a drugstore that was open and thought he recalled that it served food. He looked in the window and saw the lights were on. Towards the back, he saw a row of booths with tables. Doubting the coffee here would be any better than was typical of America in the days when drugstores served ice cream sodas, he looked both ways along the sidewalk and seeing no one, snorted the snot out of his left nostril. As he wiped his face with one cold glove, he stole a glance at his watch, ten-thirty, and went inside.

He was pleased to see the café portion was not crowded even though that constituted a further poor recommendation on its fare. There was only one diner at the counter, a slender woman eating a waffle. He noticed her form when he first stepped inside as if it were shouting for attention, although it was not clear how he could tell she was young and fit when all he could see was her fully clothed back and some light red hair. He attributed his positive impression to his fortunate habit of anticipating generously whatever parts of a woman are yet unclear to him. Despite his habit, the red hair put him off. He denied favoring any "type" but redheads rarely got good grades from him. Nonetheless he chose a stool close enough to allow him to see her without being close enough to confront her. He did not look at her immediately but his attention kept on her even while his eyes looked everywhere except at her. She was eating cozily, anonymously, like a jaguar in the deep Amazon, fit and fine and fast and dangerous.

The waitress gave him a menu and he asked her if the drugstore sold the newspapers. She said it did not have the paper, leaving open the issue of whether it never sold the paper or just was not selling them today because of the storm. He said he was glad the café was open and she nodded that she heard him.

The last time he had eaten breakfast at a drugstore counter was with his grandfather. In fact every time he had eaten at a drugstore counter was with his grandfather on those mornings when they had gone deer hunting. He spent several summers with his grandparents in Colorado in the years before he was too young to get a summer job. About once a week, his grandfather would get him up early to go deer hunting. The two of them would leave the house in the dark and reach town when the light was building but the sun was not yet over the horizon. They went to the drugstore and ate pancakes and bacon. His grandfather sometimes knew the other old men having breakfast and he knew the waitress. They went hunting regardless of the weather. At the drugstore they usually met a friend of his grandfather's who would be hunting with them. They never took a gun. They were hunting deer, not killing them.

He opened the menu but looked at the women before reading it. He was surprised at what he saw. She projected fitness in her posture. Perhaps he had noted that in his first glance, but it was more apparent from her profile. She wore a snug sweater with nothing to cover the soft flow of skin from throat to cleavage. She was fortunate the café was well heated. Her face had the fine bones of a model. Her pale skin was the sort that did not usually look good to Buck, but it was so flawless, it did not suggest the poor health that paleness usually did for him. She turned her head and looked at him almost directly. He lowered his eyes too late to disguise that he had been looking at her. Seeing her face in full had shocked him, it was not a face like the ones he had seen all his life; it lacked reality. He noted with surprise that it was three dimensional and capable of movement. It could have served Hitchcock with its icy perfection but that it was rusty rather than blond. She had the pale green eyes and dark, thin eyebrows of a soap opera actress. It was a supple mask that made him feel odd; not intimidated, he thought, but unable to ignore her physical attributes. It would have been easier to accept a dwarf or a giant sitting beside him. He did not feel a desire to possess her, but he needed to see her again. He casually drifted his head toward her, thinking she would not look his way again, but she turned back quite soon, again quickly, knowing he would be facing her.

"What are you looking at?" she asked, adding some personality to her face in a way that diminished his appreciation of her pure beauty but increased his respect for the person behind it.

"I was rude to intrude." The rhyme hung aggressively between them, challenging the direction the conversation would take.

"Do you think you are clever, saying something like that?" she asked, a beat too late to be her most frank thought.

"Once in a while I am clever. In this case, I enjoyed having that little phrase come to mind, but it came to mind first of all because it is true."

"Do you think this is the way to meet women?"

"Not in the real world, it is not. Especially not in the part of the real world I inhabit." She looked back at him with slight curiosity.

"I say that with certainty based not only on my 40 years of having never picked up a woman under any circumstances, but more than that on having heard from women I knew well, both beautiful and ordinary, of the resentment they feel from being watched by men when in public places."

"And you ogle them anyway."

"Ogling versus appreciating as scenery is in the mind of the beholder. I do not ogle. I haven't the imaginative powers for that. And I do try to be polite and appreciate the human scenery with subtlety. I was lazy this morning and [pause] 'rude to intrude'. I was not crude."

"Too slick." But she did not look away.

"Not one of the beautiful women I have known has enjoyed being told she was beautiful by friend or stranger. Most of them feel insulted to hear it as it reduces them to their shell. I understand this since I do not care in the least what someone thinks of how I look; it says more about the speaker's superficial nature than the nature of the person being assessed."

"You talk too much."

"Sometimes. Not always.' He turned to the waitress and waved his hand toward a booth, "I'll take it over there." He smiled grimly at the beautiful woman and went over to the booth and sat with his back toward the counter.

The drugstore café was not in the diner tradition and had no jukebox at the table. He would have liked to select a song. It did have a supply of cheap paper napkins in a tin box on the table and he extracted one to wipe his dripping nose. He extracted a couple more, folded them in half and put them in the left pocket of his coat to use as tissues. The cold always made his nose drip even though he was not sick. He reserved the right pocket to hold the used napkins until he came to a trash can.

The menu pleased him with its generic offerings. He considered ordering waffles. It might lead to something he could say to the woman, except he knew that conversation was permanently ended. He considered ordering pancakes and bacon in memory of his grandfather. But those pancakes had always been trimmed with huckleberries and this urban, wintry drugstore could only offer a weak imitation of the opening to a hunting trip. So he decided to honor the memory of his mother by ordering steak and eggs. She had not normally made him breakfast except on Saturdays when he had a track meet scheduled for the afternoon. She never came to any of his meets, never asked how he did or commented on one when he told about it, but she knew when they were scheduled and said nothing about why she was cooking steak and eggs on those mornings. He did not explain his reasoning to the waitress when he ordered although he thought she might find it interesting. Wouldn't she like a little story out of the ordinary? At least she would not worry that he had some prurient interest in her as she was clearly no candidate for ogling.

His cell phone rang. Before he dug it out of his pocket, he began thinking of the Pulter file. What more could he say about the angle he had visualized for dealing with it? Could he even recall his idea? Had he written down enough to recover it? Before clicking the button to receive the call, he noted the caller's name. It was his pal, Walid.

"Walid, I need a woman."

"Damn right you do, Bucky. What are you waiting for? Are you calling me to say you are doing something about that?"

"Did I call you? I don't remember it that way."

"You practically called me. You left your phone on. You never do that unless you want to be called."

"I did not want to be called. I left it on so Rich could reach me. I didn't go in to the office."

"You stayed home? You never do that! Aren't there any buses out your way? I wouldn't think that would stop you."

"What stopped me first was I rolled over after the alarm went off and slept until Rich called."

"So what are you doing now?"

"Having breakfast with a beautiful woman."

"Uh huh."

"Really."

"You don't eat breakfast."

"Today's an odd one. The beautiful woman, and she really is one, is not at my table."

"It's starting to make sense. I'm not going to work. Where are you? Can I get my coffee there?"

"Yeah, come on down. I'm not sure exactly where I am. Let me get the address."

Buck went to stack of menus to see if the address was written on them.

"Come by for another look?" she asked.

"Not exactly. My buddy is coming by for a look [holding up the phone so she could see it and he could hear it] and I need the address of this place."

"You don't know where you are?"

"Today is an odd one; right, Walid? We're at 5610 Archea Street. It's not far from you. And Walid, wear layers. It is really cold out. Wear something with a hood and a hat. And a scarf."

"Is that your son?" she asked without looking up.

He held his finger up to suggest to the woman that he was about to answer her.

"Did you hear that, Walid? Right. I am sure others have wondered the same thing. See ya soon." He held the telephone up to show that he was ending the call. Then he moved the finger he had been holding aloft and pointed it to the woman. "First, let me apologize for subjecting you to my conversation. I hardly ever use my phone but there is no excuse for intruding on your privacy again. To your question: no, Walid is not my son, he's my best friend."

"But he doesn't know how to dress himself?"

"He's Algerian and this is his first winter in the North."

"Algerian? Is he dark?"

"Walid? Dark? Not at all. He is about the most innocent and upbeat adult I have ever known."

He considered winking at her and decided against it as he was not flirting with her. He might have had the same conversation with anyone up to this point. He added "Excuse me, ma'am" before he returned to his booth. Buck allowed himself one more look at her. She was still beautiful, but she did not interest him anymore.

Chapter 3

USE OF SNOW

Buck's mouth watered at the sight of his breakfast. He liked eggs, but never cooked them back in his apartment because Julie thought they were not good for him. Of course, Julie was no longer in charge of his inputs. Nonetheless, he never cooked anything that left odors except baked things, so the rare taste of eggs sunny-side up was especially good. They disappeared as fast as a New Jersey commuter at five on Friday even though he tried to slow himself down with a few bites of toast. He nursed the steak more graciously, reflecting with every morsel on how warmly a thin steak had impressed him every time his mother brought one out for breakfast.

"Where is she, man?" asked Walid as he slipped into the bench across from Buck. "I thought you'd have her at your table by now."

Walid was tall and slender, with hair that tended toward large curls. He tried to keep it short, but did not pay attention closely enough to prevent its frequently growing into the appearance of a salon creation. With his long eyelashes and even features, he might have appeared feminine except that he also wore an intentionally unkempt beard. In sum, his appearance matched his intelligent, gentle personality.

"It was going fine until I mentioned you were coming and then she blew out of here like a bat outta hell.

"You going to see her again?"

"Not a chance. Not even in my dreams. She was so far out of my league, I would not even waste the energy to throw her a pitch. Besides, in our little interaction, she already doesn't like me."

"Doesn't it usually take longer than that for a woman to hate you? There wasn't even time for you to have a story to tell your poor married friend?"

"I didn't have a chance from the start and I knew that the moment she turned to face me. She was not coy; she had all the confidence of last year's MVP. It was a kindness to glance my way as if I were a candidate for conversation."

Walid shook his head slightly and responded quietly and seriously, "You ought to be a candidate. You always think women care as much about looks as a man, but damn few do."

"I acknowledge you meet women far more easily than I do so I should respect your assessment, but you are good looking so you don't notice that it matters. Maybe you even like to presume it does not matter since you can know first-hand how superficial it is."

"You are more what women want to see in a man. You are tall, athletic, articulate, well dressed and white."

"Articulate matters? Oh, friend Walid, do not let any woman ever learn of this exchange we have had this morning. Neither of us will meet another one worth meeting."

"Does the waitress know her? See if she knows her name. Just tell her I'd like to test your description for accuracy. And, you know, it wouldn't even be a lie. There's nothing better to do on a day like this with everything closed down but the drugstore."

"I would not be averse to tracking her down if she were a woman of interest. She was not interesting; she was just beautiful. Honestly, I do appreciate that, but she was a long way from interesting."

"Missing what exactly?"

"On the positive, she was very forthright. I love a firm backbone. But that movie star face and figure don't feel real enough to get exciting. I don't favor a particular type, but some females are thrilling and some are not." Like the one at Maxie's Bar, Buck thought, but he did not want that additional experience examined. They sat quietly for a few moments and Buck felt dishonest for saying nothing about the previous night.

"I met a woman last night, more sexy than beautiful. She gave me her number but I didn't take it." He drank the last of his coffee.

When he did not continue, Walid objected. "That's it? You want me to beg for more? Alright, I'll give you your question. Why didn't you take it?"

"When a woman offers her phone number and she does not know you, she is either too loose or too desperate." He paused. "Besides, she worried me. She was scared of something and I don't need drama. Still, I could use a woman."

"You're leaving a lot out. How did you meet this woman? What do you mean she worried you?"

"Aw, it was a strange night. I felt edgy and went for a walk." He grabbed the salt shaker and spilled a small pile of salt on the table. Then he placed the shaker in the pile and balanced it on one edge. He blew the extra salt away, leaving the balanced shaker, held in place by a minimum of salt. It was a trick he had not done since college. Walid watched silently. "It was a good experience, but I'll not do it again."

"Yeah, you wouldn't want to have any more sexy women giving you their phone numbers."

"You've got Masha. She's a rock and she's a rock star. I really don't know how you found her, but you can't expect it's easy to get hooked up."

"You're a smart guy at work, aren't you? Anyway... you convinced Rich you are. Can't you attack this woman question like an assignment?"

"No, I can't do that. That would be admitting I need something."

"But you just said 'I need a woman'."

"That was talking to you. You already know it anyway. I can't be telling myself that stuff."

Walid touched the salt shaker lightly and it stayed in place.

"The beauty was not my failure. I did nothing wrong, nothing imperfect. When I need a woman, I need a woman who is compatible with me. Sure, my first glimpse of her made me think that was unlikely, so unlikely it made no sense to investigate the possibility. But I soldiered on; I took my shot. I did not try to get her to sit with me or to take me home with her or let me caress her supple body at any venue. No, in complete honesty with myself, I checked to see if the disparity between our outer appearances did in fact parallel... Not appearances again... In complete honesty with myself I checked whether there was any prospect of fitting together. I was prejudiced against her for her appearance. I would have liked her to enjoy being with me, but it would have been very hard to convince me that she would. I was strong enough to grant the possibility for the duration of a half a sentence ... no more. By the time the sound of my voice had reached my own ears, my mind was decided against her. It would have been too bizarre. You know what it was? It was Groucho Marx not wanting to be in any club that would accept him as a member. No, it wasn't that. I could easily be in a club that would have me; I couldn't be in a club that she wanted to be in. She could not be a companion of mine."

"You don't need to explain it to me. I know what you mean. You're looking for Julie's twin sister."

"Nice of you to offer sympathy, but you do not offer a very sympathetic model. You have a complete fairy tale princess in your bed every night. I bet you forget for long periods of time how gorgeous or smart Masha is but then it always come back and you remember it. When you remember it you look again and you enjoy it, not just because it makes you feel accepted by an attractive woman but also because it is just so great to be close to someone so good.

"Good? You think Masha is good? She is smart and beautiful; no one could miss that. She is everything I would put on a list of what I want in a woman but she is not all the woman I want. I'm really, really lucky to have her..."

"I don't need to wring out what reservations you might have. It is way outside my right to know. This rule we all have that love should be all that matters and it is possible and mandatory that you exist for just one companion; well it leaves me out for one, right? But what I have been wondering ever since you got here: how do you like the snow, man?"

Walid did not answer right away. When he finally answered, it was not immediately obvious what remark he was answering. "Bummer, isn't it? ...Except for getting a day off."

"How can you say that? It's the best day we're going have all winter! Sure, people bitch about it, but everyone likes it underneath. They like the change. Did you see how many people were outside on foot this morning? They're doing something physical and useful. You won't see that on the best of spring days."

"But it so damn cold and dark! Look outside. It's almost noon and the cars are driving with their lights on."

"You were never a kid in the snow. It's time you learned how to use it. Let's go sledding."

"You worry me, Buck. You won't get yourself a woman and you want to go sledding. Do you have a sled? Can you rent one? Is there a place to do this?"

"I've got this. Let's get going."

Buck was tired of discussing his woman problem from the moment the conversation began. He had thought the matter through many times and reached no good answers. He saw no point in going into it again, even with the variation imposed by involving Walid. He would wait for something to develop. Things change. Things move on. Not everything changes of course, but there were women out there for him, he knew for certain. Would the thing change in which he was too proud or too shy to seek out a decent woman? No, he was not too shy; he must be too proud. So it must be his fault he did not meet someone, but not because he was unworthy, just quietly, almost unperceptively arrogant.

The two friends stood together on the street outside the drugstore, Walid waiting for direction from Buck. "Cold as a Hitchcock heroine," Buck suggested, pulling up and buttoning Walid's collar.

"What?" and answered Walid who was no movie buff.

Buck had an idea, a good idea, come to him in a flash. It was so strong he nearly ran off with Walid to implement it, but he stopped himself in time to recall the fun it was in seeing the storm through Walid's eyes, through Walid's adult, but inexperienced eyes. Buck looked him over.

"We're going to be in this snow and you need to be dressed better than this. I am, myself, overdressed. I was expecting to wander around casually. The plan is now more active. Take this." He removed his coat and a down vest, giving the vest to Walid. "And take the scarf. My collar zips up over my chin. You need to protect your throat, at least."

Walid objected mildly, but could scarcely prevent Buck from dressing him more warmly. Buck unbuttoned Walid's coat and beat the slight accumulation of snow off his shoulders before slipping the vest on him. He shook the scarf to be sure it had no cold flakes to drop down Walid's shirt and wrapped it around his neck. Walid felt like a doll being dressed by a human.

"Are we going to make a snowman? That should be cheap and should be possible somewhere in the city."

Buck wanted to give his friend the enjoyment he sensed in the exceptional snowfall. Making a snowman would be a great activity as an adult if a woman were with them. It was innocent and creative and there were some tricks he knew to impress the woman if she had not made snowmen before. A snowball fight would only be good with kids, and experienced ones at that. The tricks he knew with snowballs would enable him to be much more aggressive than he allowed in his adult persona. With kids, he might make a snow fort. The tricks he knew for this had come too late to him to be used much in childhood. He could let some kids in on techniques he would have adored learning from an adult. If he explained these options to Walid, he might have been told, as he often was told, that he would make a good father since he could be playful with his kids, meaning since he could be a kid again himself. But that is not what makes a good father and Buck was not tempted to procreation by his capabilities for childishness. No, if he were a father, he would impart the lessons learned from his personality and generally preach against the ways of his own youth.

"No man. That's a good idea but it's for kids or we could do it with some girls but we don't have any with us right now. And this isn't the right kind of snow. Not yet. It will be later."

"Are we going to ski somewhere in the city?"

"I have never been skiing. From an early age I was afraid of it, that is, afraid of the cost. I am certain I would have loved it so I stayed away from it."

"Sure, that makes sense. It makes sense coming from you. I know you feel a major need to husband your financial resources. I imagine how poor you would be without that constant attention. So is it snowballs?"

"No, of course not. It wouldn't be any fun with you. You'd be terrible at it. If the snow is bad for snowmen, it's bad for snowballs."

"I don't know what you mean about the snow being bad for one thing and good for another. Is it too deep for snowballs?"

"You're right, some things are better experienced than taken on faith." Buck decided to punish Walid for doubting his advice. "You stand here beside that beautiful drift..." Buck positioned Walid facing into the wind. "...And I'll stand just a short way off. Snowballing is competitive and violent, so that's why it is not for you, regardless of your age, but you know that I have never outgrown these things."

"You hate violence."

"Certainly I do, and yet I have it in me so I give it no room to show itself. I will not throw any snowball, but I offer myself as a lesson for you. Please do exactly as I describe,

Walid. Put your hands far apart like this and then bend forward toward the snowbank and pull your hands together to hold as much snow as you can, like this. Good, now I will not react, but you must throw your snowball as hard as you can at my chest."

Walid hesitated.

"You see that you have no violence in you? It is only snow; hard as you can now. No more hesitation."

Walid threw the snow, but it was only a double handful of unpackable powder and it blew into his own face in a frigid cloud. Walid sputtered with the shock of it in his nostrils though it had done him no harm.

"You see that I have violence in me?" asked Buck. "Take off a glove to wipe your face. We're off to the hospital, but not to repair your frostbite. I can't explain why we're going there just yet."

Walid was not dismayed by the mystery. Buck sometimes took charge and usually led them into something interesting. He had gone to the drugstore exactly because he was hoping Buck would entertain him on this inconvenient day. He did not yearn to be taught American things but he was pleased to be seeing the snow though Buck's eyes.

They did not speak on the way to the hospital. Walid was more or less forced to stay behind Buck. Some places the sidewalk was open only by the width of a shovel and some places was not open at all; in those places Walid stepped in Buck's footprints.

The hospital was not far from the drugstore. The road was nearly clear in front of it, although a salty slush was piled more than waist high along the edge. Inside, Buck asked Walid to open his coat. "We won't be here long but it will feel better when we go back out if you can bundle up a bit." Buck did not merely open his coat, he took it off entirely. Buck asked the attendant at the desk how to get to the cafeteria. Walid smiled to himself, aware he was the object of whatever odd thing Buck was about. When they reached the cafeteria, Buck motioned to Walid to stand by the door. Then he went into the food line. He put two apples on a paper plate and put the plate on a tray, slid the snack along the metal track and paid for the apples. When he got back to Walid he handed one apple to Walid and suggested he put it in his pocket. On the way out, Buck tossed the paper plate in the trash. Outside the hospital, the snow was falling as heavily as ever but Buck did not put on his coat. Nonetheless, he advised Walid to button up.

After a half a block from the hospital, the cleared space on the sidewalk opened up and Walid moved alongside Buck. "What the hell am I supposed to do with the apple?" he asked.

"Eat it, save it, or throw it away. If you see a hungry guy, you might give it to him," Buck answered as he started to put on his coat. Inside the coat were two cafeteria trays. "We'll return them when we're through with them," he explained needlessly and he handed one to Walid.

"What the hell am I supposed to do with a tray?"

"Sit on it. But not yet."

Walid shook his head. He now had a good idea what Buck had in mind but he was not impressed with his faux sled. He would have expressed his skepticism but they were walking again and, again, they were forced to keep in single file. On the other hand, it was not necessary to express skepticism. Buck knew the trays were not impressive and he enjoyed knowing the slide would be all the more rewarding for Walid if the coming thrill were not obvious. He had not himself been impressed by the potential for tray sliding when he first saw it at the inaugural snowfall in college. It had been a season of firsts, consistently demonstrating that college kids have a million good ideas. He lived in the freshman dorm at the foot of a steep hill, the hill being known only, up until that first day of snow, as the obstruction between breakfast and classes.

Upstate New York is known for "lake-effect' snow. Whereas most places experience snow when a winter storm blows in from the west, north, south or, rarely, east, the Finger Lakes region, from the week before first term exams until mid-term of second semester, requires only that moist air pass over ever-frigid Erie. In Buck's freshman year, he had not yet heard of lake-effect snow and assumed the eight inches that fell overnight on a Tuesday in December was uncommon for the latitude. Classes were held as normal, eight inches not being enough to stop a place accustomed to more. He finished his last class at 4:30 and went to the student union for an early dinner. It was nearly dark by the time he finished eating and headed down the hill. He was stunned by the view from the top of the hill. There were hundreds of fellow students, each blissful even without competing for grades or status or sexual contact.

Buck had considered himself an expert at sledding, but the happy vision of that slope compelled him to accept immediately that there was more than he realized to the experience. While he had not applied himself well to classes, he had learned in his opening term to respect his fellow students' capacity for play. He quickly realized what they were doing and hustled back to the cafeteria for a tray. He bought an apple on a paper plate on a tray and went outside before putting on his coat. Petty theft was already familiar to him. Back at the hill, he first slid face down, the favored position for sledding because it was amenable to a running start. The tray had no runners to keep it square to the route, but it slid easily, using the relentless pull of gravity to keep in a more or less straight path toward the bottom. Without a hint from anyone, he sensed how to keep it square by dragging one foot or the other briefly. And this simple technique allowed him to steer, charging toward slower sliders, but pulling away without hitting them after they saw him coming. After a couple runs in this fashion, he stopped to watch the others more closely and saw the predominant style was to sit upright. He tried that too. It was slower and less controlled. He felt superior for using his style, fast and aggressive and attributed the more common approach to the presence in the crowd of girls, guys with girls, and guys with less guts. But the sitting posture was interesting too because it let the rider see more and, oddly, because it allowed less control. It posed a challenge to his fundamental values, just as college tended to do. Before he could resolve its attraction, someone started a chain, linking several tray riders together by placing each rider's legs around the body of the person in front. This tended to further reduce control and often ended in a pile-up and people struggled to steer by simply shifting their weight. In the dark, no one knew whose legs were around his waist; it might even be a girl's, but regardless of whose legs one was feeling or whose torso one was grasping, the person would be replaced by another in a moment and remain ever a stranger. Buck stayed an hour, maybe a little more, until it was too cold to stay. He had not dressed for frolicking in the frost.   He was not in the least disappointed to quit the hillside and he stood at the bottom for several minutes watching and listening, aware he was building a memory he would want to replay in the years after college, before going in to the cafeteria in his dorm to warm his fingers by wrapping them around a large cup of cocoa.

Buck led the way through the narrow trails where they were available and in the streets when there was no trail, until they came to a park with a long, steep hill. There were some children with sleds at the top of the hill, but they did not slide far in the deep snow. Buck was too excited to climb the hill gracefully and he ran as hard as he could, toward the top. He ran with a stride that threw his feet in circles outside his body and over the top of the snow, plowing as little as possible through the deep powder. Halfway up the hill he was already winded and he fell into a slower version of the dance, pacing himself to reach the top without stopping, working hard, looking only at the space immediately in front of himself. The top came slowly but it arrived before Buck was broken. He fell forward when he reached the highest point and rolled over to await Walid. His panting had ended by the time Walid stood over him. He jumped up and scanned the topology. He felt sad for the urban children at play. They were not getting full advantage of the resources before them.

"Too many clueless parents here, Walid. Walk behind me, but don't step in my exact footprints."

"I've been doing that all day," answered Walid amicably while he added silently to himself, "and I've been doing it since college, except that I can't keep up." Walid was not usually a follower; he had been essentially independent since coming to the United States while still in his late teens. He must have been independent-minded before then since he had sought to make the move overseas and begged his father for two years before finally going off on his own. In a family with eight children, he had never been smothered with attention. And he had no ambition to be like Buck; they had such different origins, it seemed a ridiculous proposition. And yet when they were together, they nearly always followed Buck's agenda. Walid did not mind it. It was comfortable and interesting to let Buck lead.

The two tromped a track that started straight down the hill at its steepest point away from the disturbance of the children at play and then zigged and zagged to the bottom. They walked in small steps back up the track, giving it a relatively firm base and enough width for a tray in most places. Back on the top, Buck screamed as he ran a dozen yards in his deep snow stride and bellyflopped onto his tray. His hips were centered on the tray and he lifted his torso as high as he could. His face rode only 6 inches above the snow while the tray cruised over the tracks without sinking deeply, the way the sleds did with their runners. He leaned his weight to steer since the track was too soft to drag a foot, but the path was so deep already he hardly needed to steer. His first run went three times farther than any of the routes the sleds had managed. He succumbed to a reflex from many years before and looked to the children to see if they acknowledged his superiority. He recognized the motive in his gesture and felt a surge of guilt for his pettiness but quickly forgave himself because no one was looking and so he had done no harm. He had forgotten about Walid. Walid was new to sledding and defeating him in an undefined game was no victory.

Walid watched Buck through the screen of the falling snow and enjoyed the slide along with him. He did not appreciate the accomplishment of going so far, assuming everything was automatic, falling down a hill like falling off a log although he noted that Buck was dragging a foot sometimes to follow the pathway. When he took his first run, he overthought the steering process and made it only 20 yards before he plowed into a drift face first and tumbled off his tray. There he uttered his scream. He was delighted and jumped up right away and ran back to the top of the track. He did not wait for Buck to reach him before he threw himself, more boldly than before, onto his tray. He made it farther and slid faster than on his first try. When he plowed into the edge of the track his momentum carried him off the front of the tray, pushing snow into his face and down his collar. It only felt refreshing in Walid's state of ecstasy and he rolled a half dozen turns down the hill, carrying him well past his initial momentum before sanity returned. His lungs were heaving as he felt the cold turn from pleasure to discomfort. He wanted to take off his coat and shirt to wipe away the water running to his belly, but he knew it was simply the price of the thrill.

Buck stood over him, grinning, "That's what snow means to a child, man. And you're not yet too old to be one.

"Show me how to get to the bottom of the hill!" called Walid as he jumped up and raced to the top of the track, sliding and falling as he went. Buck told him he had no technique to teach; that Walid just had to get the feel of it. Doing was the only way to learn. However, he also promised it would get easier as the track was used, forming walls and firming up the base. They did a few more runs, with Walid getting farther each time while Buck consistently reached the bottom of the run, extending it each time a little more. Eventually the kids of the hill noticed what they were doing and quietly drifted over with their sleds and saucers. Buck and Walid welcomed them but Walid was getting cold, his teeth were chattering, and his naturally brown lips would have showed a blue cast if the light were better. Buck noticed his speech was thick with some loss of lip control.

"How are your fingers? Can you feel your fingertips?" Buck asked

"Not really. Especially on my left hand."

"Pull them inside your gloves, and make a fist. They'll probably warm up on their own. How are your feet?"

"Like blocks of ice!" Walid answered.

"Time for cocoa! Let's see if they sell it in the hospital cafeteria. We can get your frostbite treated at the same time." Buck suggested.

Chapter 4

THE FIRST TELEPHONE CALL

Back in his apartment, Buck shook off the snow from his shoulders and hung his coat on the back of a chair so it would dry overnight. He stripped out of the rest of his wet clothes in the bathroom and left them in the tub to be dealt with later. Then he put on his pajamas, bathrobe, and slippers, ready early for a comfortable, quiet night, tucked away from the storm. He put a pot of water on the stove to boil; he would have macaroni and cheese this night, a child's dinner and completely appropriate this night. He turned on the computer, planning only to read any messages that might say if his office would be open tomorrow. While the machine was getting started, he worried that he had pushed Walid too much. Walid had suffered quietly, but substantially, when his toes began to warm up. Buck had accepted that pain as part of winter when he was a child but realized as an adult that it was dangerous, and real-- permanent damage could occur. He would have felt terrible to have damaged Walid. He resolved to take his responsibilities to others more seriously. Suddenly his computer came on line, but he had one more nagging thought before he could check his e-mail. His gloves were still in his pocket and would be wet with melting snow.

66

He went back to his coat to take out his gloves so they would be dry by morning too. First he took out the glove from his left pocket and all the napkins there, now too damp to use. He was surprised when a napkin fell to the floor from his right pocket. He did not recall using one all afternoon; no tissue was needed when walking outside alone or with Walid. He looked at it to see if it were used or just misplaced. It bore a message: "Please help me. I don't want money. Ms. Karen Dam." And a phone number.

At first, he denied the note existed. He had not run across the Asian woman all day. She could not have snuck up behind him in the hospital or the drug store café, but seconds later he realized it had been in his pocket since the night before. At the least, its existence was impossible to deny for long. She had pushed a note to him on the bar, but was clever enough to put another into his pocket. He was pleased to think she might have anticipated that he would not take the one on the bar. He could not remember the details of the evening to be sure of whether she had a chance to write a second note after he refused the first one. He thought not.

A sentence was heard in his mind as if it had been spoken to him, "No good can come of this." Curiosity was his strongest motivation for calling the number, but he was convinced his intuition, honed by years of exposure to urban scams and needy women, was making a very good point. His pride took the side of making a call, demonstrating he was not afraid of the unknown. But his pride also argued against the call: he was not so desperate for female companionship as to bite on what was clearly a con. He weighed the possibility that she actually was an innocent in need of help. There was no scenario he could formulate in which a legitimate woman of her sexual attractiveness would innocently place her phone number in his pocket. And yet, and yet, there was that sexual attractiveness. If he was very careful, he might see more of her without losing his wallet. What clinched it was the realization of what a fine story it would make to tell Walid.

Having reasoned out that he needed to be especially careful since he was crossing the sort of line he never considered crossing, he applied what he had learned from television and did not call from his own telephone. So far, she only knew he was a guy in Maxie's bar, a far off Maxie's bar. He turned off the stove, dressed back into street clothes, layered against the cold of night with snow still falling on the 18 inches already accumulated. He remembered seeing a phone booth about two blocks away. He trekked the two blocks, conscious of getting snow on another pair of pants to dry in the tub overnight. The phone booth was just where he remembered even though he had not used a phone booth for several years. Unfortunately, there was no telephone in the booth.

He doubted the adventure of, maybe, learning what dodge the Asian woman was using was fading to a simple bad idea. It might be a good tale, if a small one, for Walid. He could facetiously blame the evening's waste of time on Walid: "Oh, the lengths I go to entertain my friends!" But he did not want to tell that tale and he walked on five more blocks to the train station where he was sure to find a working telephone.

The station put out a ghastly greenish shade of light into the storm. Buck blew his nose into a snow bank before he was close enough to the windows of the station to be noticed by anyone who might be looking out. It was too warm inside the train station and he opened his coat and removed his hat as soon as he breathed the tropical atmosphere. There were only three other people in the lobby, if the clerk behind the ticket window could be said to be outside the lobby. Two of them looked like college students, undergraduates by the naiveté in their manner, waiting for a bus that must have been a long way off since at most one other person was ready to join them. However, that other person did not look as if he were really waiting for a bus; he was more likely someone who had no home or no home he wanted to see this night. He could be warm at the train station without anyone asking him to buy another drink. Buck looked at his clothes to guess his station in life. He wore jeans and heavy shoes in good repair, suggesting he might work in construction or some other job where the work was physical. Buck could not tell if his hands were well worn, but his face looked hard used. Not homeless, Buck decided, and not going home tonight either.

Two phone booths were set into the wall between the men's and ladies' rooms. Buck had not taken a train since he was in college but could not even remember exactly when he had last used a payphone. He pushed the middle of the folding door and it opened in the classic phone booth fashion. Inside was the seat curved into a shape intended to ease entry to the booth. It would have been adequate back in the mid-Twentieth Century, but a high proportion of modern Americans were too large to slide comfortably onto the seat and many were too large, to fit inside the booth at all. Buck slid in gracefully, but he had forgotten that pay phones require coins and his pockets were inaccessible under his multiple layers of clothing while seated in the tight space. So he back stepped outside, feeling abashed despite having no audience but himself, and took out a few quarters, pleased that he had some. He put them on the shelf below the telephone. The label on the telephone was torn, but enough remained to show the minimum charge was fifty cents, an amount Buck might have guessed but did not actually know in advance. He picked up one quarter and put it in the slot, listening through the receiver to the clunk it made. Then he picked up the second quarter and did the same. He dialed carefully since he had not used a rotary dial in years and was not sure he still knew the feel of it. Yet it was familiar when he tried it and he soon heard the buzz of a connection on the other end. There were three rings before she picked up.

"Hello. This is the man with the crooked nose."

"It's not very crooked. I did not even notice it until that awful man pointed to it."

"And I did not notice your scar, but that was only because it was on the other side of you. Once I did see it, I liked it. I would hate to analyze why it is so appealing, so I won't, and I can't deny it is a lovely accessory.

"I understand you do not want money, but I do not understand what you would like from me. There is no reason for you to think I can help with anything even if I wanted to. Are you looking for company?"

"No company! I do not need friend. I need help because someone wants to get something from me. I do not understand this country. The people here are same as people in my country, but I cannot tell what people are thinking here."

"You see, I knew I could not help you. I do not know what people are thinking here either." It was a facile, unsympathetic comment which he regretted before the words had entirely left his mouth. He had only said it because it followed in the style he imagined for banter with a woman met in a bar. But she was not a generic woman. He had never met a generic woman. The only generic women were people he had not met. So he pulled back his attitude, just to feel better about himself, not thinking it might affect the woman on the phone.

"I'm sorry. I am not used to being asked by a stranger for help when there is no evidence I can help. If you had a flat tire, I would help."

"I need someone who knows this country better than me."

"But surely you did not go to Maxie's bar with that in mind."

"I just went in there to get away from the men that were following me again."

Buck had no answer for this assertion and the telephone was silent on both ends for an uncomfortable number of seconds.

Buck broke the lull, "I'd like to call you by your name."

"I am Karen."

"Is that what you are called in your country?"

"I am Keahi at home."

"That is your first name? Is it your family name?"

"Keahi Dam."

"Thank you, I am Buckminster. I believe your name is Keahi Dam. I do not believe anyone is following you or that you believe that. Someone may follow you one night, but it is a very odd thing to do outside the movies. You said 'again', even odder. But if someone is following you, I am definitely not the right person to help you. That is outside my experience, capabilities, and interest. If it is true, see the police. This is just the kind of thing they would love to deal with."

"I cannot go to police. I am not legal in this country."

"I am sorry to hear that. It does make your claim a little more plausible, but it does not make me any more useful to you. In fact, I am also useless for that problem. I doubt you would think I could help, so I am still wondering what you would really like from me."

"I ask you because I think you understand Americans. And I think you are good man. You made the men in the bar leave me alone and you only did that because you wanted to help a person you do not know."

Buck saw the truth in her words but still did not believe her motivation. There had to be a better explanation for her seeking him out; something simple and common. He did not see the scam yet, but he was as sure as ever that there was one. Her claim of faith in his character, however well founded it happened to be or he thought it to be or he wanted it to be on a good day, was a classic approach in a con.

"I might be able to find someone to help you. There are organizations to help people in need, including illegal immigrants. Try to tell me your problem and I will see if I can suggest something productive for you." While he thought to himself additionally, "Provided you convince me you really have this need you describe."

"I am scared to talk to you... to talk to anyone about this"

"I am very sorry you are scared. That is no way to be living your life. Is someone angry with you?"

"No, I did not do anything to anybody."

The phone was quiet for a few seconds and Buck gave her time to say more. Finally he answered, "You don't need to do anyone wrong to get them mad at you."

"They are not mad at me." Again she said nothing useful. Buck did not know how to read her. If this were a con, it might proceed exactly like this. A good con is hard to spot and Buck had always avoided cons rather than confront them.

"You said "they'. Who is it that concerns you? Who is scaring you?" He could hear her moving, small rustling sounds, perhaps as she squirmed in her chair, perhaps someone pushing against her cheek to listen in on the call. Maybe they were writing notes to each other about what to say next. Buck was not scared; he had not risked anything so far. He was untraceable by anything less than movie-grade CIA technology. He wondered if he should get off the phone before there was time to trace the call.

"Some men were following me last night. Two men. They have followed me before."

"You mean the men in the bar?" Buck recalled there were three of them.

"No, not them. I just went into that place because it was open and people were inside."

"Did they wait for you to leave?"

"No, I am sure they did not. I was in that place for more than an hour. I was standing by the door and looking out until you came in. I did not see them again. When I went outside there was so much snow..."

"And then you waited for me to come out?"

"Yes, I wanted to see you going home, but I could not talk to you anymore. It was too cold and too dark."

"That does not quite add up, but many true things in life don't add up."

"Thank you for calling me. Does that mean you will help me?"

"Not likely. What do these fellows want, these ones who are following you?"

"I can't know what they want. They did not speak to me. But, yes, I know they have something to do with my work.   Someone wants me to help them with some information. But I do not know if the men who are following me want this information or if they want me to protect the information."

"Information? That is pretty vague. What is this information? Is it from your work or some neighborhood issue? Did you see something that could get someone in trouble?"

"I cannot tell you anything about the information. It does not seem very important, but I cannot talk about it. I just want these men to leave me alone. Can you speak to them? Maybe you can tell them you are police?"

"Oh no, no, no. I cannot do that and I doubt it would help you if someone did. They want something and could always find another way to bother you. Besides, I could not pretend to be police. That would be very dangerous in addition to being illegal." The telephone was silent for a few seconds. "A private detective could do something like that."

"I don't have any money. I could not afford detective."

"I don't know how much they cost. I'll look into it for you." Buck did not think it was feasible and he was not about to subsidize her, but it was all he could think of to do. She did not answer his suggestion. "May I call you at this number in a couple days?"

"You mean you will not do anything today?"

"Well, I was thinking the storm would be keeping people away from their offices. I did not go in today. Did you?" He heard a nondescript sound come through the receiver. "Maybe I could find something on-line."

"I already looked on-line. I use computer very much."

"Keahi, I don't know what to do, but I should convince myself first about the cost. If it is not too much, it will be hard to convince myself I should jump in."

"Good. You are thinking of jumping in. That is good. But please do not take too long. I am scared these men will do something."

"Maybe the storm will keep you safe for another day. Do you need to go anywhere?"

"Maybe to my work."

"I hope your work is nearby. But they will not want to follow you in this weather."

"Yes, that is good."

"You know, I am smart enough in the things I do. But I only do a few things. I stay a long way from crime and violence. I watch movies, but I do not especially like mysteries. I do not do well in figuring them out. I prefer to relax when I watch movies not to think about something serious, you know, or lessons for mankind, maybe. My mother liked mysteries, or claimed to. She watched Perry Mason and said she always knew the ending before it came. Of course she never told us the ending since that would spoil it. I did not think the endings were discernible from the information we were given. Do you know Perry Mason?"

"No, I don't know what you are talking about."

"Sorry, I do not mean to make light of your problem. I just mean this is not something for me."

"I liked when you talked about your mother."

"This was a case, I don't mean a case, I mean an instance when I did not follow her. She read detective stories too. But I was skeptical she liked them. I thought she was just copying her father's taste. He, my grandfather, had stacks of them leaning against the wall in his bedroom. He used to drive out to the Miami airport just to go through the racks of paperbacks."

"You are not interested in this literature?"

"Oh, a smarty-pants!"

"I don't know what that means."

"I recently read 'Murder on the Orient Express', which was a seminal work in a certain strand of that literature. It was just the sort my mother would have claimed to like since it was a direct challenge to the reader to figure out the mystery. It even had a diagram of the train because the clues were so dense, they surpassed the writer's capacity to feed them to the reader in the usual way, that is, with words. I thought the solution was very contrived and that the clues were not complete enough to reveal it. I have not looked at another mystery since.

"But you said you read it recently. So it does not mean much that you have not read any since then."

"Sharp one. You surely don't need my help to figure out your mystery."

"Please, it is not joke."

"It is late. I will look on-line in the morning to convince myself a private eye is not feasible. Then I will call you. May I use this number if you go to work?

"This is my cell. Call me early, please. And please tell me your number. And your last name."

"I still doubt I can do much for you. I will call you early and you think about whether you can tell me a little more about why these guys may be following you. It was still snowing when I started this call. You will not have any place to go in the morning."

"What is your last name, your family name?"

"We have yet to see if there is any reason for you to fill a few cells in your brain with that information. Sleep well. I'll be thinking of you. Good night." Buck hung up as his words ended.

He felt he had talked too long. They had not said much. She did not trust him and he did not trust her. Still he had enjoyed talking to her. How much of that was the image in his mind of her slender figure and exotic face? The conversation itself had not been interesting, skirting substance that might have given some facts to convert the matter from mystery to action. It had not suggested to him that he could help her. He did not know what to do but figured he needed to do something. He was not the kind of guy to just walk away from a difficult spot. She had said she chose him because he seemed like a good person. He believed she was right. Good, perhaps, but not so smart. He would call Walid to talk it through. Walid would not know what to do, and Buck was unlikely to take his advice, but Walid was a good person and was ever and always a good listener. And he was smart, smarter than Buck though, like Keahi, not deeply conversant in American culture. Except, Buck suddenly realized, Walid knew a great deal about immigration. He had immigrated himself, gained U.S. citizenship and participated in various immigration stages with several cousins. Buck could call him for his expertise without sounding like he was merely sharing gossip.

He rolled up his sleeve to check his watch and saw that he had left it back at the apartment. Of course the train station had a conspicuous clock on the wall. Given the retro feel of the room generally, it was odd that the clock was digital. It read 8:14, not too late to call Walid. The call would have to wait until Buck was back in the apartment as he had not brought his cell phone and had only one quarter left for the pay phone and did not know Walid's number from memory.

The cold outside felt wonderful on his face. The Greyhound sign lit the snow falling in large flakes, more vertically than before, signaling to Buck that the wind had declined. He wrapped his scarf over his chin and pulled up his hood, hoping to keep his core warm during the walk back to the apartment. He was comfortable in his first minute outside but knew winter well enough to understand the cold would penetrate any opening he might allow. With the lesser wind, and the late hour, the footprints he made approaching the train station entry remained recognizable although his track was much harder to see where it mingled with the foot traffic along the street. Even so, there were a few places where he thought he remembered stepping beside the main path. He liked making his own print and, besides, the path made by all the people before him was narrow and icy from time to time; it was better to stride through loose snow than to mindlessly go where others had been.

He was back in his apartment early to make a call to Walid although it might be impolitely late for a call to a lesser friend.

"Hello Masha! Have you been enjoying the storm?

...

"Oh, don't you think it is grand to have everything changed all of a sudden?

...

"Yes. I dragged poor Walid into the deepest snow I could find and he, if you must know, loved it terribly too! Will you go out with us tomorrow to see what fun it can be?"

...

"I understand Walid's taste in friends is not quite identical to yours, dearest Marya.

...

"Maybe we could leave Walid at home tomorrow, and you and I could explore the possibilities of deepest winter then?

...

"Well, I suppose I am stuck with second best then. May I speak to him?

...

"Yo Walid. How many toes do you have left?

...

"And how many fingers?

...

"Listen Buddy, I've got some very intriguing news for you. You're going to want to consult on this in the morning. I'll leave the general idea with you tonight. Let's get together for breakfast at the drugstore.

...

"No, not her; the other one. I found a note from her in my coat pocket. She gave me her phone number but I didn't see it until I was cooking dinner tonight. And that reminds me, I still did not get dinner so I need to make this quick; I'll give you just enough to get your help in the morning. I called her. She didn't tell me much but she claims she is in some danger but can't go to the police because she's illegal.

...

"I'm not sure where, maybe Vietnam or someplace like that. They have some gangs in the city, I think. I sure don't want anything to do with them.

...

"I thought you might have some ideas about the INS. Probably the best I can do is advise her on dealing with the immigration thing. If she really is in trouble, all I can do is help her get legal protection.

...

"I don't know... I don't know more about anything. We talked awhile but we danced around the facts. I don't think she's trying to get something from me, just some help with a problem I can't really help... if I knew what it was.

...

"Well yes, that's a factor. But I am not a teenager who wants to sit on the floor and talk to a girl for an hour. It just seemed like it might be worth going one more step... and Walid, maybe I can help her.

...

"It is nice, intoxicating even, to have a woman of her attributes treating me like her savior.

...

"I don't know any more, but I have some questions and would like to have some more to say when I call her next time. I promised to look into how much a private eye would be. One might help her more directly than I could. Let's go over it in the morning. You know me; I need to write down an approach and list all my facts on one page and my next steps on another page.

...

"It's past 9 and I have not cooked dinner yet. Let's get together at, say ten tomorrow. That would give me time to make some notes in the morning.

...

"There is no way you will have any work tomorrow. It's still snowing and snowing hard! Alright, if you are working, we'll talk and set up another time. Thanks, Bud. Let me get something to eat now."

The thought of macaroni and cheese, with the cheese coming in an envelope of orange powder, was very attractive to Buck at this moment. He cooked the whole box, an amount the text claims was sufficient for a family of four. He surmised the dietician who had made that assessment assumed the family was eating some vegetables, or meat or dessert to accompany the starch, something that did not apply to Buck's dinner. Variety came only in meals eaten outside the apartment.

While the water heated back to boiling, he started looking into the cost of private detectives. The simple phrase "private detective" and his city's name came up with nearly 300 listings of licensed investigators and the local chapter of their professional organization. There was also a category of worker called "protective services." The ads did not list prices, but Buck wanted numbers. He looked at job listings in the field. They did not promise much compensation and he noticed the protective services, presumably the more dangerous alternative, was substantially less, $37 grand per year on average compared to $43 grand. Protection might have required less skill. Maybe these levels were not terrible in light of the Department of Labor claim that the median salary for all occupations was $33 grand.

The ads for training as a detective emphasized that no college degree was required. Buck understood many very bright people do not go to college just as many less bright people succeed due to the opportunity to associate with more capable ones, dim bulbs on a majestic chandelier. Cheap labor lacking expensive training in a competitive field would all be consistent with inexpensive services. Without a reliable recommendation, it would be hard to know if the services of a particular firm were worth even a low price. The incentives within the industry, Buck concluded, seemed to favor low intensity of effort.

Although the detective agencies did not post their rates, free services were frequently offered. These were surely consultations to determine how the company might serve the interests of the client. Although several advertised being open 24 hours a day, he did not think it was a good idea to start a consultation at 9:30 in the evening with a pot boiling on the stove. He had seen enough to feel there would be a company willing and able to solve her problem of two men following her, assuming that really was her problem.

With a glass of orange juice and a steaming, fragrant bowl of macaroni and cheese in front of him (Buck was too civilized to eat from the pot most days), Buck began to plot his strategy. He wrote on a yellow, legal-sized pad with a mechanical pencil. First he made a list of topics to consider, like the ones he told Walid he would write out. Then he filled in some thoughts under each topic as they came to him. He washed the dishes at 11:30, having no more ideas bubbling to his hand at that point, but while engaged in the kitchen, away from his pencil, he saw where his thoughts had been taking some poorly devised routes and he rushed to get back to work. He did not make it to bed until 2:30 in the morning, at which time his adrenaline was exhausted and he suddenly felt incompetent to think any further. He set his alarm for 9 am. He knew he would wake before then, but planned to roll over each time he woke until the alarm went off. He knew the storm would keep his office closed another day no matter what public services the mayor claimed to have marshaled.

Chapter 5

SECOND MORNING OF THE STORM

The alarm jolted Buck into a certain degree of consciousness for the first time since his head neared the pillow at 3:30 am. His hand swept onto the shut-off button within a couple seconds. He could not decide whether to be pleased that he had slept well or disappointed that his internal clock had so thoroughly malfunctioned. It seemed important to decide between these alternatives until his feet touched the cold floor and his level of consciousness rose another notch closer to wakefulness. His feet felt the cold linoleum despite the rug next to the bed because he had sat up facing the wall rather than the room. He was not superstitious in a way that would make him worry about the adage of waking on the wrong side of the bed. And when he reminded himself of that, he knew he was coming awake.

His first action under full mental control was to look out the window. For a second morning, he was greeted by falling snow. The clouds were dark but the rate of snow was not heavy. The street had been plowed, but was not clear. The dark asphalt showed through in places. A good driver would get around adequately, and buses would be able to navigate, but the deep snow off the street would ensure a sense that everyone was entitled to another day off. Buck turned on the computer to check for a message from the office and ran water for a warm shower while the computer went through its set up.

His telephone rang when he was stepping into the shower. He did not want anyone to know he was just getting up at something after nine o'clock so he stepped back, dripping and ran into the bedroom to pick up the phone and answered it with a chipper voice.

"Yo!"

...

"Hey Walid. You working today?"

...

"No, not me either. But to be honest, I don't know if the office is closed. I haven't checked in yet. I was up too late for my tender body."

...

"No, not to Maxie's. But I was close to her last night. Like I told you, I talked to her on the phone."

...

"Yeah, it was weird. It's already a long story."

...

"No, I don't know what she wants from me and I don't know what I want from her. But look, this is not a tale for the telephone. Do you want some breakfast?"

...

"Well then, do you want to watch me eat mine?"

...

"Yeah, you should do what that girl wants most of the time. Take care of her, Walid. But tell Masha we can meet up with her after breakfast and take her into the snow."

...

"I know sliding on a stolen tray would not be her style, even if her husband had a good time on one. She'd like a toboggan. It is comforting to ride sitting up in a cluster. Of course I don't know where to steal one of those on short notice. There is more to do in the snow than sled. We'll take her out on an adventure at her scale. I know you want to hear about my call last night and I could us some advice on what to do next."

...

"I can get to the drugstore in twenty minutes. It's not much of a place, but it's probably open and that makes it better than any other place I could name."

Buck scraped off enough body odor in thirty seconds to regard his shower as adequate and then put on most of the same clothes he wore yesterday, to save time in dressing. He glanced quickly at the message from the office and understood it to say he was not to come in due to the continuing snow situation, and then he printed his notes from the previous night. He was out the door twelve minutes after hanging up with Walid. Although he had rushed since the phone call, he had risen late and was surprised at how dark the day was. The snow was not falling hard at that moment, but the heavy clouds remained and the air was well below the freezing point.

He tried to jog to the drugstore but the road was too slushy to run safely. So he slid one foot at a time, like a cross-country skier, in the snowy part of the road close to the edge and maintained a good pace while enjoying himself. He cursed the places where the salt managed to melt all the way to the snow bank, forcing him to take a step or two rather than slide. Once he tried to slide through a slushy patch and his boot caught on the asphalt. He might have stumbled forward, but he allowed himself to roll onto the deep snow. He landed on his back where the hood tied over his face kept his neck warm and dry. He made a quick angel and jumped back up into his stylish trot.

He was warm and panting as he stomped into the drugstore, knocking off snow just inside the door and feeling guilty for making a mess there but relieved no one was paying any attention to him. He pulled back his hood and unzipped his coat as he waked briskly to the café in back. Walid was not there yet.

"She's not here yet," said the waitress as he slid into one of the booths.

"Who's not here?" he asked. Had Keahi tracked him down somehow, bugged his phone, known he was coming to the drugstore, and communicated with the waitress?

"Oh, I thought you two had hit it off. She looks like the type you'd remember."

"Yet? You said 'yet.' She is coming in again?"

"She usually comes in around ten, has coffee and a bagel."

"You are most helpful (turn a little to the left, please)... Sarah." He read the name on her blouse pocket. "Would you believe me if I explained I had no thought of her when I decided to come here? You're just the only place I know that's open today."

"OK, it's just that she never talks to anyone and you two seemed to hit it off."

"Funny, I did not have the same impression. She is out of my league and she knows it. I'm surprised you didn't know it too."

"Guess I wasn't watchin' that close."

"Maybe I'll take another shot if the opportunity comes up and I have any creativity in me."

"You just getting' up for breakfast?"

"You know, Sarah, now that I've found this place, I may come back here when the storm's over. Are you open early?"

"Sure, not the store, just the restaurant."

"Say six am?"

"We open at six."

"All right. I'll start working my way through the menu. Cheese omelet, toast, and coffee?"

"You wanna know her name?"

"I'm just here to get breakfast and sass from the waitress."

"Sure." And Sarah walked away to place his order with the cook.

Walid came in before the eggs were ready. He slid onto the opposite bench seat and lifted his chin in a friendly but silent greeting.

"Too early to vocalize?" asked Buck.

"Too cold," Walid answered.

"Hmm. Cold as a windy dawn on the north shore of Lake Superior in February. Didn't we talk about dressing for the cold? My fault. I should have made a point of it yesterday. It's not bad if you're running up the hill every few minutes, but it's a killer if you're standing around. Layers, you know. More than a big coat, you need to wear layers. Legs and feet too."

"I nearly froze my feet yesterday even with the running. I just didn't notice it right way."

"Ask Sarah for a hot cup of something. Did you already have coffee this morning?"

"Who's Sarah? The waitress? She doesn't look like your type."

"Oh, she's my type of waitress. She was going to fix me up with the redhead from yesterday."

"But she didn't?"

"You know that would not have gone anywhere no matter what leverage Sarah might apply."

"Why not? You liked her."

"She was damn good to look at. I could not imagine her taking me seriously."

"You can be a serious guy."

"But I can't be a match to her."

"I don't know how good looking you are, but I know Julie was damn good to look at and she liked you."

"We're not going to talk about Julie."

The waitress came back with Buck's omelet. "Her name's not Julie."

Walid laughed while Sarah looked Buck in the eye. "Something hot for Walid, please, Sarah. You say you already had your morning coffee, Walid?"

"Of course I did. It's almost ten o'clock. No offense, Ms. Sarah; I doubt your coffee can compare with my wife's but I'd like to try it anyway."

"Cuppa coffee," said Sarah and she glided away.

"How is it you get into conversations with every damn woman that crosses your path? Half the time you don't even want to talk to them," Walid asked rhetorically while he watched the waitress decant his coffee from a stainless steel urn on the counter.

"'Her name's not Julie'," muttered Buck aloud.

"Thought we weren't going to talk about Julie."

"We're not. We're going to talk about Keahi Dam."

"Is that her name?"

"The one from the bar."

"Alright. Let's talk about that one."

"Best not be talking about some other woman when Red comes in. She might not like that," said Sarah the waitress as she sat Walid's coffee in front of him in a thick, plain white mug.

"Red will have to wait her turn. If she does not get here on time, we have to take up other topics," answered Buck.

When Sarah had gone away, Buck continued, "She left me a note in my pocket when I was at the bar, but I didn't notice it. Gee, I could have lost it when we were rolling around in the snow. Anyway, I gave her a call and asked her what she wanted. Seriously, I can't believe she wants to be my buddy. I was thinking it was some scam she pulls on guys all the time. But she would have to be small time to pull it on me, just a quiet guy in a lousy bar. But she did not look like a player and didn't act like one. You see, that's the problem, if she was acting, she was too good to direct it at me; I mean, based on what she could have known about me."

"What do you mean acting? Do you think the city is full of women pretending to be in trouble so they can get you in an alley and have their boyfriend conk you on the head and take your wallet?"

"You're right. I am too suspicious. But it is an odd thing. So she won't really tell me what is going on. Says she is being followed and can't go to the police because she's an illegal. If she's being followed, there has to be a reason. I made some notes last night." Buck reached to the coat hanging on the back of his chair to take out his notebook.

"Of course he did," said Walid to no one in particular.

"She may be mixed up in some personal thing, a boyfriend or a girlfriend who has something to lose or who wants her back. I dismiss those things."

"Why, is she too nice for that?"

"I don't know if she is nice or just seems nice when you see her once in a bar. You know I make my judgments on evidence, not impressions. I have no intuitive capacities. No, she said there were two men following her. If it is personal, two private eyes would be expensive and unnecessary. By the way, did you know there are millions of private eyes in this city? I guess they really are private because I never noticed one. I looked 'em up on the internet last night. They don't seem to make much money.

"So I think it more likely she has information of some value. She says she doesn't know why they are following her, but I don't know if I believe her in this. She might have knowledge about criminal or political people. They're different people, right? Sometimes? She might have seen something around her neighborhood or known something about people back in wherever the heck she's from.

"But why follow her? What can a blackmailer learn by following her? I think it is an attempt to intimidate her. Someone who is reasonably good at following should not be noticed and should not be doing it in pairs anyway. It seems more likely a 'rough shadow', a tail intended to be seen."

"A 'rough shadow'? Walid asked. Where did you ever learn a term like that? Are you secretly a private eye and never told me?"

"Well, it wouldn't be secret if I told you. I don't know where I heard it. Maybe I didn't and it isn't a term of art. Maybe I ran across it in a book or a movie. ...A book, I think it was."

"So it doesn't sound like you learned much. What are you going to do with her? Are you getting together?"

"I have some more ideas in my notes." Buck looked back at his notes and placed a finger to hold his place when he turned back to Walid. "I guess there are two major scenarios: either she is true or she is false. If she is true, she doesn't know why they are following her and that doesn't tally with a rough shadow, unless they, and I don't know what 'they' means here, unless they think she knows what they want or, and this is my favored position, they haven't asked for it yet and are just softening her up. I can see them play it out: 'alright Ms. Dam, do you know Mr. Slim and Mr. Wide standing on the street over there. Yes? I know them too. And they want certain documents from your employer. But I don't want them asking you. They are not the most gentle of men. I thought I might make things easier, smoother you know, be just asking you in a nice way. I can absolutely guarantee they will disappear forever for a few pages in your employers files.' Something like that, maybe. What do you think?"

"Hello, Walid! Having another day off? Nice isn't it?" The redhead spoke to Walid without a glance in Buck's direction and without slowing the pace of her walk to her spot at the counter. She was gone before Buck realized she was there.

“She knew my name!”

“Yes, she seems to be alert.”

“Why didn’t she speak to you?”

“Either she especially dislikes me or she especially likes me. Obviously it is not quite normal to speak to the one you have not met and ignore the one you have.”

“She is one fine looking woman! She took her coat off before coming to the café part of the store just so she could share that stuff with the rest of us, don’t you think? You need to get over there and find out which of those especiallies applies.”

“I know which one applies and I don’t need to have the point reiterated. It is truly a weird day when the option of the cagey Asian woman is the more realistic one.”

“C’mon, that was an invitation. It would be rude if one of us didn’t go over there and I know for certain it won’t be me.”

“Forget her. Listen to my next steps for Keahi. I’ll call her later and try to convince her to hire a private detective. I’ll recommend one or two, based on the internet. That won’t work because I already talked to her about it and she can’t afford it. So then I’ll ask some questions. And if I feel enough truth in her, I’ll ask a few more questions to see if there is anything I can do that really would help. And if I feel I can do something, I’ll ask to meet her again, someplace safe from her boyfriend in the alley.”

“You’re not giving up on her. I knew you wouldn’t. I wish I had the chances you’ve had. I would not have taken all the chances you took, but some, I would have taken some. You've shown me taking a chance can get you somewhere."

Sarah came back. "Would you like some more coffee? I'm sorry I don't have a pot to pour from. The management likes those urns so people can get their own refills. But I don't mind doing it. It's going to be another quiet day. We won't make any money. We oughtta be closed like everyone else. But it's nice when it's quiet for a day or two. Then it gets boring. She asked me if you were gay. What do I tell her?"

"Tell her you're pretty sure I'm gay but not Walid. He's married and committed and really does not need that kind of rumor."

Sarah nooded and then Buck continued, "No, don't tell her I'm gay. Tell her despite that, I am even more stunning when you see me up close and I am ready to walk out of here with her as soon as I finish one more cup of your coffee. Which is not any better than the coffee my wife makes because I don't have a wife."

Sarah took his mug to refill it, and Walid asked in a low tone, "Are you seriously not going to go over there. I thought you were the one who takes all the chances. What can you lose? She's not the one with thugs hiding around the corner."

"Oh, she's trouble you can be sure. God played a big role in making her but he did not put that dress on her this morning or require her to hook her boot on the stool so the shape of her leg would stun anyone passing by."

"I saw that leg too."

"I've been damaged more by a woman teasing some interest in me than by any thugs."

"That's right, you have. Forgive me for forgetting. We're not talking about Julie though, right?"

"Right. And we're not talking about Red either. And I think we're about done talking about Keahi. But I'd like some back-up on her. I'll call her again and probably see her. In case something really outrageous happens, I'll leave you her name and number. That's all I know about her at this point." Buck had already written these on a slip of paper which he handed to Walid, folded in half. "You'll never need to call her, but it is only smart to have a little back-up."

"You are really taking this seriously. It's hard to see if you are willing to take risks or if you have to think everything through so much there is no risk in the end."

Buck waved to Sarah for the check.

"Are we meeting Masha to show her what to do in the snow?"

"She thinks you're crazy. She thinks I'm crazy for playing like a child yesterday. She says she did not like it even when she was a child. Some boy, who probably liked her, pushed snow in her face and she has barely been able to like men after that."

"She grew up in Moscow and did not like snow?"

"She didn't like a lot of things in Moscow. That's why she came to the States when she got her first chance and never went back."

"She should have gone to Georgia and missed the snow."

"That's a good one. Masha in Georgia! She's a city girl."

"Ever hear of Atlanta?"

Sarah arrived with the check.

"You can pay me here," she said dully.

"Sarah, you and Walid here need a thrill. Please go back to the cash register and I'll meet you there so you both can watch my rejection."

Buck put on his coat as he walked toward the cash register, just two stools away from the red haired woman. She did not lift her head from the paperback book she was reading.

He handed his credit card to Sarah and turned to the woman.

"I believe I saw you sitting on that stool yesterday. I wonder what the odds are to come in here twice in a lifetime, both times when it is almost empty, and see the same person on that stool."

"I come here because it is usually a quiet place to read at this time of day."

Buck looked at her book. It was not the standard size for pulp and the paper was yellowed.

"Let's see if we have anything at all in common beyond a two-day run at the drugstore counter. Tell me the author of your book and I'll tell what I have read by him or her."

"You read?"

"If it was written in English, or, if it is available in English translation."

"I didn't mean 'can you read'. I meant 'do you read'."

"I understood your question. I did not presume you would be so rude as to ask if I was able to read."

"E.L. Doctorow." She said without consulting the cover of her book.

"I have never been certain how to pronounce his name. I heard him mentioned on the radio once and doubted the speaker had said it right. I'd have to say I enjoyed *Ragtime* more than most, which is a hard claim to back up since it was so well liked. But, you see, I play a little music and have a great respect for the early figures of jazz and for what they endured. His use of historical figures was playful. I always admired Emma Goldman and his use of her is very unusual in *America.* I read *Billy Bathgate* out of respect for Doctorow and was glad I did. ...Gangster story from a very odd perspective. I have another of his on my shelf of books to be read; I can't now recall the title. I know he wrote *World's Fair* and I liked that title so I'm sure that's not the one I have waiting. Reading a third or fourth novel by one author does not happen very often for me. Of course I have read everything ever written by my favorite authors; Doctorow is not in that rank. What do you have there?"

"Why did you like that title?"

"I have a good answer for that, but it would take more time than I have now. No, I have no reason to lie to you. I won't even see you again. I do have a good answer for that, good from my perspective, but it would take longer to tell than I could possibly hold your attention. I am going out of this encounter very, very pleased to have met you and in no danger of boring you since I am leaving on your question!" Buck smiled with sincere pleasure and performed a bow with a little snap of the head at the end to make it friendly rather than stuffy. He turned his attention to Sarah who handed him the credit card slip to which he affixed a generous tip.

Walid said, "Good-bye, Miss," to which the redhead answered, "Angela. I'm Angela, Walid. Nice to have met you. Did you know you have a strange friend?" And he answered "Strange friend? Me? No. Which one do you mean?" as looked back while walking out beside Buck who did not look back.

When they were outside Buck shuttered in the cold and bundled up his collar, pulled up his hood and put on his gloves. He enjoyed stepping into the cold only when he was mentally prepared. He decided he would take a moment in the future before stepping through the door to consider what he was about to feel, at least in the winter. Maybe he would not have this feeling he would never be warm again. Of course, he never did keep this resolution and he always did feel warm again after each shock of going outside in winter.

They did not go back to pick up Marya to show her the snow because Walid explained that although she trusted Buck's intentions, there was no way to convince her that it was good to go out on a day like this. She claimed she knew snow and all things people do in it for fun, and she had enough of it already to last a lifetime. Walid asked to try some other snow adventure, but Buck had enjoyed walking out on Angela when she wanted to see more of him, and had a similar notion for Walid; by not searching for some snow thing to do, a thing likely to be less exciting than the traying had been, Buck would leave Walid wanting to do it again. Buck would find a day when he had a good idea of a snow thing and call on Walid then.

He was not inspired to play in the snow at this time. He was ready to call Keahi back. And another day out of the office had him worried about Pulter. Keahi's mystery had taken up his unconscious thoughts so his brain was not working on Pulter at any of its levels.

"So Buck, how're you going to see Angela again?"

They walked side by side in the street, bent forward to keep the wind off their faces. Tiny shards of ice were in the wind. Buck could not tell if they came from the thick dark clouds above or the deep white accumulation below, nor could he tell if they were rising or falling; it was more that the wind was composed of solid particles, the better to cut through man's defenses.

"I'm not. That wouldn't go anywhere. If I had answered one more question from her, she would have dropped me like a lead nickel."

"What's a lead nickel? ...Hey, man, I don't believe you don't have a plan for her. She really liked you. I can see it might not turn out perfect but you've got to give it a try. Don't forget, I've seen you make it with beautiful women. I don't know why they go for you, but it has happened before."

"We're not talking about Julie."

"I'm not talking about Julie. You're the one bringing her up. What about that woman you met on the bus a couple years ago? She hung around as long as you let her. And that real skinny one with the 'legs that went on forever', you used to say."

"What about Keahi? Isn't it enough to be chasing her?"

"You shouldn't be chasing her. She's trouble and you know it."

"Angela's trouble too. At least, she'd be trouble if she doesn't just drop me the moment I give her the chance."

"Yeah, yeah, she's trouble the way they're always trouble for you. You're not giving up. You better not give up. I need the thrills. That Keahi is trouble you don't need. She can't be any better than Angela anyway. Imagine lifting up her hair and drawing your tongue along her smooth, pale throat while she moans with her eyes closed and turns her body into you..."

"You're right to build up the fantasy with her eyes closed. I'll keep you in touch with developments on Keahi. Remember, you're my back-up."

"I know why you are stuck on her. She got to you first. She turned up a day before Angela and you're loyal to her already."

They reached the corner where their routes home diverged. Walid did not recognize it dressed in drifts and with his head turned down. He had been following along with Buck and was surprised when they stopped. Buck gave him a soft punch on the chest and pointed to the street sign.

"I'll call you after I talk to Keahi."

"OK."

"Give Marya a kiss for me."

"OK."

Buck watched Walid shuffle off. He did not want to worry Walid by showing how careful he was being with Keahi. When Walid was gone into the distance, Buck walked to the hospital to use a pay phone. Keahi answered on the first ring.

"Good morning Keahi."

...

"I understand you are worried...

...

"Yes, I see; maybe 'frightened' is a better word. You should remember I am not the right person to provide protection. I really am not capable of it. Like I said before, maybe I can advise you...

...

"I looked into the private detective business. I know a tiny bit more than I did yesterday. I don't know what to recommend for you because I don't understand your problem well enough. I don't need to know everything, but if you really feel you want some advice from someone who knows America, part of it anyway, and who is not involved in your problem, we can sit somewhere and go over a few things. I wrote down some issues that might clear up the situation, in my mind at least.

...

"We can meet at some quiet place near Maxie's Bar. Do you know a place near there?

...

"I don't know what's open today. More people are using the streets. Most of the buses are running I think. Probably most places will be open.

   ...

"I don't know the neighborhood. I don't think I was ever there before the night I met you.

   ...

"No, not your place and not my place. How about the library? It's on Wilson Avenue, near Sixth. Do you know it? Past the city park with all the baseball diamonds? Do you know Wilson Avenue? Can you ask someone how to get to the library? Or look it up on the web?

   ...

"And what time can you be there?

   ...

"It will be closed by then. Why so late? If this is a crisis for you, can't you get away?

   ...

"Oh, I'm sorry. I didn't have any work today so it feels like a weekend. What time do you get off?

   ...

"Sure, I guess we all will need to put in some extra time to make up for the snow day. But we need a place to meet. Wait, do you know the Black Fog? It's a club, a bar, I guess. I'm not really sure. I've never been there but my friend goes there with his wife. I've been meaning to see it one of these days. It's on the same side of town as Maxie's. I don't know the address exactly, but you can look it up on the web too. Be there at nine o'clock? Black Fog. 'F-O-G'

See you at nine. I hope you catch up on your work before then, Keahi."

Buck was pleased with the arrangement. He had given away nothing of himself, except that he was not from the area around Maxie's Bar. And he was going to see Keahi again. He had a light step, despite his heavy clothes, as he went back to his apartment to switch his mind over to solving the Pulter issue.

Chapter 6

SOME UNRESOLVED BREAKTHROUGHS

It was still early in the afternoon when Buck checked his e-mail. There were three messages from his boss but they all asked essentially the same thing: was he making progress on Pulter? Buck had no intention of answering until the answer was 'yes'. He saw it was his own fault that Pulter had become a problem. No one else had seen anything worrisome in their records. The auditors gave them a clean review. Buck was not even a real accountant and did not understand much of what the real accountants did. But he had felt something was covered up in the record. His advantage, he thought, was that he did not do what accountants and auditors do, so someone who knows their business might leave signs only Buck would notice.

Trouble was, everything added up just fine. It was only the sense of the numbers that bothered Buck. Numbers were genetically his milieu, not his pleasure or his interest. He had a talent for them. Bodies of data spoke to him in ways they did not speak to others. He found he could make a living out of his talent but he was careful never to describe it that way to others. He preferred people thought he worked hard and had a variety of talents. He tended to couch his discoveries in terms of their implications rather than as anomalies he discovered like a savant.

He attacked the Pulter investigation in his usual way; turning as much as possible of their history into numbers, organized into tables in several dimensions. Then he organized and reorganized the figures. It was a computer game. Buck never played commercial computer games because he knew he was capable of getting lost in them. And this is how he got the numbers in a job like the Pulter investigation to speak. He played with them, looking for something interesting. But to hear them, he needed to sink into their universe. That took time. He had not devoted the time yet. He did not know how much it would take, but he had noticed in his initial compilation enough to convince him something interesting lay within. And he made the error of telling this to his boss. So now his boss wanted to know what was so interesting; only Buck did not know what it was. It was an emotion thus far. He looked forward to finding the song in the data, provided it really was there. His initial sense was not reliable. He might have just had a good night's sleep and a solid breakfast on the day he was finishing the data compilation and his happiness might have been due to no more than that. He should not have said anything to his boss. It was not intended as a finding or as a promise of a finding, but that is how it came out and the longer he delayed resolving the matter, the more his boss expected a dramatic result.

Buck stood at his window, feeling warm again, dressed in a flannel shirt, jeans, and thick socks, as comfortable as it gets for him. He looked at the quiet city street. The lights were on in the apartments he could see despite the early afternoon hour. The day had never gotten bright and he estimated it would be nearly dark as night by five o'clock. Looking at the familiar, boring scene, he managed to get Pulter back in mind. Suddenly he went to his desk and turned on his laptop, called up his Pulter files and started to look for patterns he could bring out. His approach was not purely numerical. He had to know what the numbers represented in order to organize them. He could tell how some vectors ought to relate to others and he would put them side by side to see where the anomalies lay. He created matrices of related variables and inverted them to see how they behaved. And then tried to interpret the new matrix. It was only mildly entertaining to manipulate the data. He needed the payoff of discovering something out of place. Slowly he found himself focusing in on the many new accounts Pulter had opened in the past few years. He could find nothing wrong in them. There were a dozen or more ways to recheck the funds and the transactions and every one yielded the same innocence.

It was past seven when the insight hit him. The oddity was that there were *so many* new internal accounts. Their purposes were not well justified. Someone was doing something. He was sure this was his opening and he did not want to return to the mystery of Keahi, no matter how shapely her torso might be. It occurred to him that he had not had a good look at her body so the image in his mind must have been one he created and he had created it well. But he was not going to deal with her until it was time to go to the Fog. Only it *was* time to go to the Fog. He considered

calling her to reschedule. It might take hours to get the
Pulter insight moving forward again. He reminded himself
the real reason for meeting Keahi was to help her. The
virtue of progressing on his work was outweighed by the
virtue of trying once more to find if he could help a woman
in apparent need.

Buck showered but did not use the body wash that
would leave a scent. He did not want to appear to be trying
to be attractive. He did not shave and had accumulated a few
days' growth. It might help make him seem more capable of
handling danger. He put on a dark shirt and his sport coat.
It made him look more mature than he believed he actually
was. He checked the cash in his wallet: forty-two dollars. He
could afford a drink for each of them. He needed the rest to
get through to payday. His bank account would be no help
and his credit cards had already taught him to ignore their
allure. He sat on the chair by the door to lace up and tie his
heavy boots. He was not going out dancing; he planned to sit
with his feet under the table.

The walk to the Black Fog took twenty minutes. A
few cars, a few taxis, and the normal number of buses passed
him. He stepped well off the street when any of them
appeared. He did not trust their steering where it was icy and
did not want to be splashed where the salt had melted the ice
to slurry. It occurred to him that he could, in theory, be
tracked back to his apartment by the print of his boots where
he stepped into the snow, but he doubted his prints were
legible or that anyone would be patient enough to search
through the countless prints that had accumulated since the

fresh snow had tapered off. In a couple hours the wind would disguise which prints were newest. But the worry had him adjust his route so he approached the club from a direction that did not point toward his apartment.

A faded billboard under glass at street level announced the house quartet was playing six nights a week, starting at nine. Buck was pleased to see that. He had heard Walid mention a band here but had assumed, for no good reason, it only played on Friday and Saturday. But the presence of the band implied a cover charge, ten dollars each. He hoped they stayed long enough to make it worthwhile even with his one drink limit. He went down the steps to the door of the club, under the stairs of an apartment building. There was a short hallway inside, with a bouncer sitting on a stool.

"Nice to get out of that wind!" Buck remarked to the bouncer. "Listen, I'm meeting my girl here and I said I'd meet her outside the door. I know she's gonna be late, but there's a chance she's already here and would not wait in the cold. So how 'bout I pay you for my cover now, and I just check inside to be sure she's not here, then I'll pay you for her cover and wait outside, like we agreed to do."

"She ain't here, man. There's no solo girls inside."

"Oh, I know she's not here. To be here she would have had to come on time and she would never do that! So let me pay both covers now, but I'll just look inside in case she brought her brother along or something."

She was not there, but she was not late either, not yet. Buck had arrived early intentionally, but he did not feel that detail needed to reach the bouncer. Back outside, standing next to the billboard, he looked across the street to where it was darkest. And then he crossed over and placed himself there to await Keahi. He might catch someone following her. He wrapped his scarf over his face. He would not look silly since no one would see him. Even so, the wind cut into his skin and his eyes teared steadily. He blinked to keep his vision clear. The cold kept him alert. He did not mind its effect on his face as much as how it made his legs stiff. One layer of wool pants was sufficient when he was walking but it hardly helped when he just stood in that weather. He wished Keahi would arrive soon.

He backed into a doorway, away from the direct wind. He stamped his feet a little, but did not want to make himself conspicuous. He checked his watch with difficulty, pushing aside his coat, his sport coat and his shirtsleeve with a gloved hand. He had to step into the light to read it: ten past eight. He was glad for that; she was already ten minutes past due and he had not been too impatient. He thought he had come back outside about twenty-five minutes earlier. Only two couples had gone inside in that time; no "solo girls." He moved back to his doorway. Five more minutes went by. He searched for something to count to mark the time or, maybe, just to pass the time. A minute between cars felt like a realistic estimate; a minute or more between pedestrians. The neighborhood was quiet on any night but counting street movement on a cold night at the end of a storm was like waiting for the sun to rise on a lifeboat from the Titanic. He started to think about what hour would be late enough to justify giving up his vigil. He would go inside to hear the band at nine; that would be an hour late. He could call her from inside. Further, he had to consider that there was a possibility something had happened to her.

The wait came to an end of its own accord when a small, huddling, hooded figure came slowly to the billboard. She studied the sign and looked around the street before going downstairs. Buck looked for anyone following her. He saw no one; still he waited. He realized she might pay another cover charge, but figured they could get that back once he went inside. This was a good chance to verify her story and he did not to waste it with impatience. He walked on his side of the street a block in the direction she had come. He crossed the street, still going away from the club, and saw no one. He crossed then to her side and turned toward the club. Before crossing the street to the block with the club, he heard a voice nearby. He waited for the light to change even though there was no traffic. He looked in both directions very carefully and turned his head enough to see two men standing in a doorway. He smiled to imagine the suffering they would experience waiting for Keahi to leave. Ahead he saw Keahi come out of the club. He walked quickly and quietly to her and did not respond when she looked toward him. He passed her without slowing and said "Wait a minute, then come inside. Keahi." He added her name at the end in case she did not recognize him in his heavy clothes.

In the small hallway, Buck took off his coat and scarf. He looked presentable when Keahi came in. He waved to the bouncer and said "It's nice to get out of the wind." The bouncer nodded with a slight smile and Buck took Keahi's arm and guided her inside.

"Is this alright?" Buck asked, indicating a table against the wall. He did not want to sit close to the band in case it was loud once it started and he wanted to face the door. She had not said a word yet and took the seat he indicated without taking off her coat.

"Thank you for coming Keahi. Isn't it hard to go out on a night like this?" She looked at him with an expression he took to be waiting for an answer to her problems. "It's warm in here. You can take off your coat." He stood up and offered to take her coat. She wriggled out of it without standing up all the way. Buck liked the way she moved. He stood to the side to fold her coat and used the moment to see as much of her shape as he could. She was long and slim in the torso, just as he had imagined, or remembered. She wore a sweater buttoned up to the top, much more sensible for the season than the open collar Angela had worn. Keahi did not fill out the sweater as much as Angela had filled hers and would not have revealed as much by leaving a few buttons open and yet Buck wished she had shown her throat, confident he would have enjoyed seeing it. He hung her coat over the chair they were not using. While he was still standing, a waitress came to the table. "I'll have a Wild Turkey, neat," said Buck. The Chevas he ordered at Maxie's had not impressed him positively. He expected nothing better from Wild Turkey, but it made sense to change something in his order. He did not know many brand names and did not want to order a mixed drink as if he knew what it was. Wild Turkey sounded less urbane than Chevas, but it was the next name that came to mind. "What will you have Keahi?"

"Nothing for me," she answered softly.

"Do you drink beer?" Buck asked.

"Yes, sometimes," she answered.

"She'll have a draft," Buck said to the waitress with a glance to the door to be sure no one was coming through. Then he looked around the room to find a back door before he sat down. He would keep an eye on it too.

Buck laced his fingers together and placed them on the table in front of himself and leaned forward onto them with his elbows far apart, also on the table, pushing his face toward Keahi. She could see he was now devoting his full attention to her.

"You asked me for help. I don't know if I can help, but I am sure I can only help if you will be open with me. You have to tell me the situation. You have to answer my questions. If you do not want to be honest with me, that's fine. I am not insisting on anything from you. But I will not help if I feel you are hiding significant things from me. Do you understand me on this point?"

"I know what you are saying, Mr. Buckminster."

"OK, let's see how we can get on what you think is important. How do you think I can help you?"

"Two men are following me. I want you to make them stop."

"Good clear answer." Buck waited to see if she would say something helpful. He was more patient with her now that he had seen the two men were real. He was ninety percent of the way to believing she was in trouble and not targeting him for something other than help. When she gave him no more of her story, he placed another credit on her account. He imagined a grifter would have used the moment to set the hook, that is, a mediocre grafter would have. A good grifter would not have wasted time working on Buck in the first place. She did not speak but she was not staring at the patterns of grain on the Formica table either. She looked him in the eye; almost brazenly, he thought. He liked her look. She was waiting for him and seducing him at the same time.

"Why do you think they are following you?"
"I don't know. You think I know but I don't."
"They know where you live, right?"
"Yes."
"And they know where you work?"
"Yes."
"Do you know anyone dangerous?"
"No, not like that."
"Anyone from your home country? Does your family have any trouble back home? Or any of your close friends?"
"No, we are good family. Never have any trouble."
"What kind of work do you do?"

"I am special assistant to Mr. Campbell. My company is York, Sherman, Harley, and Lynch. It is really part of, a susidery, subsidiary of Ringstare, Incorporated"

"You work in a law firm?"

"Yes. I am not a lawyer. I do skilled work."

"I presume then that you have access to information on the firm and on the firm's clients."

"Yes, I have access."

She worked for a law firm even though she was not in the country legally. That did not add up in Buck's intuition, but he did not know much about law firms. They might be more casual or trusting than Buck expected. He wrote the name of the firm in his moleskin. He had several blank books in a drawer awaiting a use and this was the first entry in this book.

Buck was about to try to tease out of his quiet client whether anyone had asked her for sensitive information when he was distracted by a familiar profile at another table. Sitting alone was a man who looked like Walid. Buck blamed himself for giving in to some racial profiling. Walid was the only Algerian he knew and he always thought of Walid as looking unique, but here was a man who looked very much like Walid. He felt compelled to see the man more closely and knew this was making him lose focus on Keahi. He sipped his drink as if he was thinking deeply.

The band began to come in. They were a simple ensemble: drum, piano, bass, and sax. Mostly the drummer had a kit to set up but the sax player had two saxes and a clarinet to assemble and place on their stands. The pianist plucked out a few brief tunes, as if he needed to warm up his fingers after coming in from the awful weather. Buck figured a pianist would always wear good gloves in winter.

"Keahi, I love the way the pianist can play these things when he is not even thinking about it. See how he is talking to the drummer. I'm sure he is not talking about what he is playing."

Keahi murmured a soft sound in acknowledgement of his comment and changed her seat so she would face the band.

When Buck looked back to her, she was looking at him, not the pianist. He felt embarrassed to be enjoying her nearness and her attention. He looked at her hands; her fingers were so slender, they seemed longer than normal, but he decided they were just slimmer than normal. It occurred to him to see if they said anything about her profession. Charlatans had used the signs in the wear on a hand for centuries to learn about people. In a modern city, in dim light, there is not much evidence to distinguish among the possible jobs a woman might hold. They were not the hands of a laborer. Her skin was smooth and unmarked. He began to think her hands were her best feature.

"Keahi, I need to focus on your problem. You're not helping."

She smiled slightly, understanding his meaning, and looked at the table again. "I am not making you talk about the pianist."

"No, I like the music and I am excited to wait for it. Even in a little place like this. I have heard of this band. A friend of mine comes here."

"I want to answer your questions. You will see you can help me. I can pay you. I can pay you a little, not as much as a professional."

"No, you cannot pay me. I do not need more money. I don't need less money either. Do you need money?"

"Everyone needs money; me too. That is not my problem."

"Do you like your work, Keahi?" Buck did not think this was an important issue. He wanted to get some questions to her that did not tie to the problem so she would not be in a pattern of seeing the connection between his questions and the issues. He just wanted her to answer his questions. This was an interrogation strategy he devised late at night when envisioning this moment.

"Please wait for me a minute. I will come back right away."

She took her pocketbook with her to the ladies room. Buck used the occasion to blow his nose into his napkin. He leafed through his notes. The light was too dim to read them easily, but he could make out the words if he stared at them. At least they were written in his own hand.

Keahi came back soon but Buck was ready at that point and his questions began to flow easily, like the script in an old movie. They were not all good questions but his confident delivery and his occasional notetaking gave Keahi the impression he had become the detective he claimed never to have been. Buck felt out her family situation, past and present boyfriends, and friends without finding any sign of a motive for targeting her. He told her the problem must originate in her workplace and switched over to questions about how she might be useful to someone who might use physical intimidation. Without her pointing to a particular person or case tied to such a person, Buck doubted he could do anything to help her. He was drawn to the possibility that someone wanted her to give information from the records she kept or wanted her to alter something in those records because looking through various company files was a familiar task for him, but the only basis for linking her job to the tail was lack of finding any other basis. Her personal life, as she described it, contained no obvious prospect for criminal intrigue beyond her exposure as an illegal.

Buck twisted in his chair to get better light in his notebook. He went through the issues he planned to consider and then went through the answers she had given. He checked off the ones that might make a difference if she had not been honest with him. He looked up and smiled at her. She sensed his movement and turned her face toward him. In the dim light of the bar, her details were not distinct and his brain put in whatever details it wanted, leaving a most enticing image. He shook his head slightly to wash away the image, knowing it was not entirely true. He looked down at her hands, resting calmly on the table. She should be more agitated, he thought, after going through her vulnerabilities with a stranger in a bar.

"You feeling alright tonight?" he asked.

"I feel good to be trusting you," she answered and she smiled just a little with her real and imagined facial features stabbing Buck deep in the eyes.

This was not what Buck wanted to hear. He was expecting to run through the items he marked to confirm whether she was hiding something, whether purposefully or shyly, and then tell her he was dropping the investigation. He would be gentle, but he would not let her charms affect his decision. He had always been able to separate business from personal pleasure. He tapped the eraser of his pencil on his notebook. He was troubled that he had devoted an unmarked moleskin to the Keahi project and it was closing up with only a dozen pages used. Nonetheless, it might be a pleasant memory to keep even if he found a further use for the remaining pages.

"Keahi..." was all he got out before the drummer beat the familiar taps that set the tempo for the first number. The bass player took the intro alone. Buck stopped talking out of respect for the music. The bass was hard to hear if there was much chatter in the room. The piano came in with a rhythm role, building the pattern under the beat for another eight bars before the tenor brought in the melody. They were doing "Mack the Knife." They ran through the melody straight and then let the bass pump out a couple bars before it took the chords to a new place. It was a heavy and cool use of a tune devised near a hundred years before. There were no vocals but Buck knew the words well and felt their irony just when he was playing on the fringe of the criminal world.

He sat back, comfortable that he was leaving that fringe shortly after the song would end, and uncomfortable that he would also be leaving the woman sitting beside him. He raised a finger to indicate they would wait for the band to play and when she nodded some minimum of understanding and looked to the band, Buck laid his hand on top of hers, grasping a few of her fingers. Sinatra's version had some apt lines:

> But with Quincy's big band, right behind me
> Swinging hard, Jack, I know I can't lose
> When I tell you, all about Mack the Knife, Babe
> It's an offer, you can never refuse.

"I can refuse you, Keani," Buck mentally formed the words. The piano took over, staying closer to Blitzstein's original tune. Buck pulled his hand back. He closed the notebook, marked his page with a ribbon and wrapped the black moleskin band around it. The tenor came back and covered the melody straight. It is a short line, so he played it twice and then did a credenza that harkened back to his solo. They came together for one last minor chord. The small audience applauded appreciatively, led by Buck who transferred the stress of what he was about to say to Keahi into slow, loud claps. Then the bass player introduced the guys in the band. He droned on longer than the minor venue justified. Buck did not listen and he doubted anyone else did either.

"Keahi, I would like to help you. If I could, really, I would. I can't see what I could do to help. If you asked me a specific question about dealing with official America or commercial America, I would be right with you. But the strange part of America with two men following you for no apparent reason leaves me with no ideas. I will find and pay for a private investigator, someone who can deal with this. I don't have a lot of money so I am limited in how much I can pay, but let's try it for a day and see what comes up. That's the best I can do. After that, I am outta this."

"I do not want your money."

"I am not giving you money. I am hiring, for a short time, a better person for the job. I need to stick with what I know; what I can do."

She knew she was being brushed off. "We have a client with accounts in a secret kind of bank on an island. The people from this company seem very dangerous. I think they may be the ones following me."

"Do you mean an island nation? Caymens, maybe? Bermuda? Isle of Man? Cyprus?"

"I don't remember. Are those all islands?"

"Doesn't matter. They're just good places to hide money. Some are British. They're legal but not everyone who uses them is always legal. The people with these accounts, have they asked you for something?"

"No, they have never said anything to me, but they act strange. They want to everyone to think they are dangerous."

"That's not a good way to hide illegal intent."

"They want people like me to be afraid of them but they do not decide to scare me. They always smile at me and then they have a dangerous face right away after they smile."

The combo interrupted him by starting another number. Buck leaned close to Keahi, "I need to explain something, Keahi, I saw the men trailing you tonight."

"You saw them tonight?" she asked with a tilt to her head.

"Yes. Didn't you see them?"

"I don't want to see them. I did not look back."

"Just so you know I believe you."

"I have the records of this company, the trouble one."

Keahi put a flashdrive on the table. Buck pushed it back toward her although it did pique his curiosity. He leaned back.

"Where are you from, Keahi?"

"Pakse," said Keahi and she giggled a little before she added, "Laos."

"Is Pakse a city or a village?"

"It is city; one of the biggest in Laos."

"Do you know other Laotians in America?"

"There are not many in this area. My uncle is here."

This exchange dismissed Buck's idea that she might be feeling pressure from a local Laotian gang, if there existed such a thing anywhere in America. Her theory that the culprit was the shady client was as good as any although it was hard to see what might be gained by following her.

The other people in the bar clapped politely for the short solo by the pianist. Buck looked to the band to see why he would have such attention and saw it was not the same pianist; it was Walid. Apparently, he sat in after the first tune. Maybe he had been introduced when the bass player was talking. Buck wanted to get away before the two of them were linked.

Buck stood up and quickly thrust the moleskin into his pocket. "I will call you to arrange the investigator. Then, remember, I am finished. Sorry I can't do more. Listen... wait here three minutes. Can you tell three minutes on your watch? Then leave. I'll just make sure the street's safe. When you get outside, turn left and walk around the corner on your way back home or wherever you are going. Don't look for me. Three minutes, OK?"

"What is wrong? Why won't you help all of a sudden?" Her voice hinted there were tears slipping from her eyes, but they were not visible in the bar lighting.

"I'm going to see Mutt and Jeff. I will call."

"What? Who? Give me your number, Mr. Buckminster!"

Buck put a ten on the bar on his way out. He would need meals cheaper than macaroni for the rest of the week. He finished buttoning his coat when he was outside. He knew it was as cold as when he went in, probably colder, but he did not wrap his scarf over his face and did not mind the wind, not immediately anyway. He read the billboard again, turned to the right, and went to the end of the block. Across the street he could see the shadow of the tall man in the doorway. He crossed the street and walked purposefully to the shadow. The short man could just barely be seen behind him.

"Cold one, eh, gentlemen?" He spoke distinctly, emphasizing the plural of "gentlemen." "You might be more comfortable inside the Black Fog. I know the name is not especially inviting, but the band is pretty good."

"Wadda you want?" asked the tall man and the short man squeezed into full view. Buck kept an eye on them to be sure their attention was entirely on him.

"What I want at this point is to get into a warm bed and that's what I am about to do. On another night, I might aspire to getting into bed beside a warm woman, but I am too tired to wish for that tonight. Unfortunately, I have a long walk to reach that bed. I fear my feet will be frozen blocks by the time I get there. How is it you are able to keep your feet warm in those thin leather shoes on a night like this?"

The tall man looked down at his feet, surprising Buck with the possibility he might answer the question, but the short man came forward with a portion of the aggression Buck had anticipated from men in their position. "Who the hell are you?" It was not as firm as it might have been. They were either a little worried about him or were not as bad as Buck had imagined.

"I'm nobody, ...as you probably imagined. It's just that I noticed you there when I went into the Fog and I shiver to think what you must feel like to be out here all this time."

"Thanks for your concern. Now fuck off," said the short man, raising his aggression by his degree of profanity.

"Oh, I am on my way to that warm bed. You fellows can ramble along too. Keahi left the club a while ago so there is no point in enduring this post any longer." Without a moment's further hesitation, Buck rotated on the ball of one foot and the heel of the other to face the block at a right angle to the two men and stepped quickly away. He listened intently for the sound of their footsteps, though he worried the snow and ice might mask them. He was confident he could outrun them and was ready to bolt. He imagined the two men looked at each other with surprise and inquiry at his departing shot because there was a gap of two or three seconds before they shouted at Buck. They were both shouting so their words were jumbled when they reached Buck's ears, but he understood they were calling for him to stop and explain who he was. Buck looked over his shoulder, thinking they may be upon him, but they were standing on the street corner where he had left them, just calling out rather than acting. "Good," thought Buck. "Two on one and they still are not inclined to mix it up."

After peeking back, Buck did not speed up his pace. His apparent confidence might hold them back until he had put a safe distance between them. At the end of the block, he turned left, away from the back of the Black Fog. He looked hard toward the men on the corner, without slackening his pace, until his line of sight was cut off. He did not see them clearly, but he was sure they were not racing toward him. They seemed to be talking to each other, maybe even arguing. Buck stopped walking as soon as he was out of sight. He went down on his knees at the edge of the building and looked around the corner. He presumed they would be less likely to notice him looking back if his head was at an unexpected level. He stared for a few seconds and was sure they were not looking his way. They had given up on him and must have been figuring what to do next. Buck hoped they would take his advice and go home. If they ran, they could catch up with Keahi and might confront her since Buck had shifted the game.

Buck jumped up and began jogging. He turned left again at the end of the block and stopped again when he was back to the street where the men had been standing. Without kneeling this time, he peeked around the corner, chest heaving though not heavily, the cold air scorching his throat, and the fog in his face marking the loss of his heat and moisture from his core. He could not see the men at first. And then the light from the Black Fog billboard was blocked for a moment and Buck recognized the silhouette of the short man walking back and forth, maybe waiting, maybe trying to look through the windows.

Buck knew nothing could be seen through the windows; they were covered by cardboard taped on the inside. Buck crossed the street and walked toward the Black Fog along the opposite side. Buck looked for the tall man and did not see him. When he looked back to the Black Fog, the short man had disappeared. Buck stopped in a doorway and slid back into the shadow. He preferred to lose them over running into them in the wrong place. Suddenly the short man appeared again, coming from the stairwell of the Fog. He was running back to the corner where he had been waiting all night. Buck looked back and saw the tall man emerge from the shadows of his doorway again. The two met and had an agitated conversation whose emotional content reached to Buck in sound but not clearly enough for him to understand any words. Buck was smiling broadly as he wrapped his scarf over his face, finally relaxed enough to notice the discomfort of his body. If they did not leave immediately, they would not be able to catch up with Keahi, even if they knew where she was going, but they showed no interest in finding her again this night and continued their argument, for the tone in their words and rapid movements Buck was watching assured him they were arguing. Buck could see the short man was the leader of the two, so he resolved to follow him if the two split. He hoped to follow him to an office or to his home address. Eventually they quieted and stood side by side on the curb, facing the street and stamping their feet slowly to keep up the circulation. Finally a car came and slowed at the club before suddenly bursting forward a block to pick them up. Buck let the car start forward before running across the street, pausing halfway to read the license plate number. He repeated the numbers to himself a few times as he looked for a pattern in them to help his memory. Then he went back in the Black Fog and borrowed a pencil from the bouncer to write them down on the edge of a dollar bill because he forgot he had a moleskin with many empty pages dedicated to the current project. He could not do much with the license number, but he might bring it up if something further happened. He would give it to Walid in a sealed envelope. But first he needed to get home and he kept next to the buildings and out of the lights as much as possible on his roundabout walk back.

Chapter 7

THIRD MORNING OF THE STORM

Buck locked the door to his apartment and leaned back against it to feel the warm, dry air adapt to him and he to it. After a minute, he dropped his hat and scarf and gloves on the floor in front of him as if were easier to undress than to walk another step. He considered sliding down to the floor and sleeping on the spot. He was certain he would fall asleep as soon as the weight of his body was off his muscles, but he did not want to face moving to the bed later and realized it was best to stagger farther inside before quitting the day. But he continued to undress, reasoning it would be easier to stagger if he was not wearing so much and that it would be better to get his wet clothes off before lying on the bed. As the clothes came off, he absorbed some warmth from the room and felt better. He slid to the floor to pull off his socks, just the outer socks, the wet ones, he thought, and then he was asleep.

There was no way for Buck to know how long he slept: a second, an hour, or all night. He woke to the sound of his phone buzzing in the pocket of the coat on the floor beside him. The room lights were on. His legs were stiff when he bent forward to get the phone, making him believe he had been slouched against the door for some time.

"Hello?" he muttered as well as his tired tongue could execute, intoning the word as a question since his eyes were too clouded to read the name of the person calling.

"Buck? Sorry to wake you, man. You OK?"

Buck recognized Walid's voice. His head cleared most of the way as he also recognized an unsettling insecurity in Walid's question.

"Yeah, sure. What time is it?"

"About 3, I'd say. I didn't see you leave the Fog and I wasn't sure where you went. I guessed you were alright. I mean why not? But I got a phone call a couple minutes ago and someone said just one sentence and hung up: 'Mind your own business'. If I'm going to back you up, I may need to know what's what with Keahi."

"Nothing's up. I quit her. That can't be why you got that call. No one knows I said you should back me up. No one, including Keahi, even knows my name."

"Someone knows my name but I did not give it to anyone. Keahi didn't even ask me for it."

"When did you talk to her? After I left the club?"

"No, man. I called her. That's why I went to the Fog. She said she would be meeting you there. I went to back you up."

"You called her? Why didn't you ask me where I was going to meet her?"

"You wouldn't have told me. You would have said to sit back, that you didn't need anything yet."

Buck knew Walid was right and enjoyed that Walid knew him so well.

"Walid, my friend. We don't like to talk about it, but we both know you are smarter than I am. And we know you have faced adversity in your life, more than I have, yet we also both know that I am far better at dealing with slimy characters and slippery situations. Your nature is too open; you haven't the experience of thinking as they do, while I think as they do all the time, though I do not act as they do very often."

"No, you don't think like a criminal. You work in an office, and love art and women and snow. And you are good in the office, and not so good with women but you have never lived on the rough part of life."

"Walid, you know what I would have said if you had asked where to go tonight, but you do not know what is in my head. I am glad I have not revealed too much of it to you. But I am cold sitting on the floor by my door at three am. I am not seeing Ms Dam again. We need to make it clear to whoever cares about it that you will mind your own business too. Did your phone get the number of that caller?"

"What you mean: Ms Dam?"

"Dam, that's Keahi's last name."

"I don't know if the caller ID did work. I don't want to call him back. What happened tonight? Why are you dropping Keahi? Is she in it with them?"

"I don't know what this is about, but I know for sure it is not something I can help. I'm going to pay for a private detective but I am not going to hear what he does. I have more sleaze in me than you know, but not enough to get into this thing. This is not something for you or me, Walid. You called her, right? Keahi, I mean? She can get your number if you called from your phone. She must be working with the troublemakers here. Or maybe she's not; there still isn't anything we can do. Except I'll pay for a little of a detective's time." Buck noticed suddenly that he was standing up and shivering in his skivvies. "What you need to do is call that number and just say 'I will mind my own business.' You can do that, right? Don't you think that makes sense?"

"Are you really dropping this thing?"

"Like a lava rock blown from the mouth of Kilauea!"

"Does Keahi know you are out of it?"

"I'll call her one more time. But give me their phone number just in case there is any more fuss."

"Hold on. I'll check the number." He put Buck on hold and came back a moment later. "The call came from Keahi's phone. You think she's in trouble?"

"I am not going to try to figure out what that woman is doing. Did you get the call a few minutes ago? Call right now and say your sentence. Then hang up and call me back."

Buck went over to the closet to get his bathrobe. He was tying the belt when his phone rang again.

"Hello, Walid. How'd it go?"

"No one answered."

"Did you leave a message?"

"No. Thought I check with you again."

"Let's go to sleep. Forget about it."

"Aren't you worried about her?"

"Yeah, I'm worried, but I'm tired and there's not a thing I can do. Doesn't Masha miss you?"

"I don't know what I'm going to tell her."

"I know. You're a terrible liar. Not enough practice. You should lie once in a while just to learn how in case you need it."

"I'm going to say you called. I'll tell her you're having trouble with a new girlfriend. Say she ran out on you at three am and you wanted to talk it over."

"That's good. She'll believe that. I can play the starring role as a failed lover, having been there before."

"She doesn't know how often, but she knows it's not the first time."

"Glad to be of help in your first excursion into fiction with your wife."

"So do you still want me to leave a message? If Keahi gets it, it will sound rude."

"Yes, leave the message. We're not getting involved with her."

"And what happened tonight that made you decide this?"

"Not so much. I tried to get her to tell me her problem in actionable terms. It was never clear at all except that it is not something I can help. I got in late and I expect to have work tomorrow. Let's get together on the weekend."

"Let's get together for breakfast before work."

"I need to get some sleep, Walid."

"Talk now or later, but the weekend is too far off. I'll make the call, but I gotta hear what happened."

"Can you be at the drugstore by 6:30?"

"Be there, Buck."

Buck stripped off the rest of his clothes since he suspected they were damp. He was so cold, but it was mostly from the slow circulation of sleep. He set the alarm for six and piled his quilt on top of the blanket.

When his alarm jangled less than three hours later, he became alert immediately, without the slow recovery that might reasonably follow several late nights. His thoughts had worked on his problems through his slumber. He did not know what solutions had been proposed during his final two hours, but could sense an excitement betwixt his ears about the chase. He stretched briefly because that was his morning routine, but he was too impatient to take the exercise seriously. As he lathered his chin for the first shave since the snow began, he felt a twinge of guilt that his mental clarity was being expended on Keahi's case rather than on Pulter, despite the kind attitude he held toward his workplace for having given him two days of vacation to play in the snow. Two significant facts from the 3 am call engaged him. The first point was that someone had access to Keahi's phone. It might have been acquired before the appointment at the Fog, but people these days, other than Buck himself, tended to keep their phones close. She might be in physical trouble. Secondly the call to Walid could only be interpreted as a threat, a threat to his best friend. Buck could no longer consider letting the situation go. He was not confident he could do anything to end it well, but he was calculating how he could borrow some money and hire a good detective for the time it took to work things out. He would wait until a decent hour to call Keahi so he did not alarm her more than necessary. Then he would get some details, like her address, and call around the detective agencies. But first, he would see Walid and get him to relax and stay out of the mix. They had always been honest with each other and Buck hated to break that trust, but he could only see Walid as a victim in this caper if things continued in the direction they were taking.

He looked outside to assess what whether the office would be open and what to wear. The clouds were dark but no longer threatening to paralyze the city's transportation systems. Light flurries were falling, the afterthought of a storm now lacking the vigor needed to bury the landscape, relying now for its headlines only on the weapon of cold.

He dressed for the office and pulled on rubbers to protect his good shoes. It was hard to get the rubbers on because he had big feet and the rubbers did not come in large sizes. So he stretched the black fabric, it was unlikely to be actual rubber, and then pushed and twisted it to fit as smoothly as possible. It was not enough protection if he stepped into the deep snow, but he expected to find a relatively clear path all the way to the drugstore. Walking across the wood floor of his apartment, Buck squeaked and felt embarrassed. Rubbers, he thought, were for children and urban executives, but he would have been embarrassed more by carrying his work shoes with him so he could wear boots for walking. The snow, as all weather, was ever and always his ally so he needed an easy relationship with it, respectful of its power in order to embrace it. He wore a tie but not a sport coat. A sweater was formal enough for his workplace. Putting on the clothes reminded him of his usual life in which his job dominated his day, certainly his morning thoughts. It was not doing so this morning. He asked if the days off and the snowy landscape were distracting him from his pattern but he knew the problem, the alertness, the thrill of starting out a new day was tied to Keahi, either to her or her situation.

He was shocked out of his internal reflections by the harsh cold hitting his lungs. He had not prepared himself for the shock although he had promised himself to always do so. He bent forward to shelter his face from the wind and tried to think of Pulter. And within a block, he changed his focus. He has a plan of sorts for Keahi, but he needed a plan for Walid too and that plan would begin implementation at breakfast. He had to get Walid to let it go. It would be hard to fool him. He trudged forward, sliding his rubbers on the icy patches and sloshing through the slush where the salt had done its messy job.

Buck reached the drugstore early. He allowed himself to anticipate the warmth inside. After a quick look behind himself to be sure no one was there, he removed a glove and used a bare finger to hold one nostril shut so he could snort the other one. He brushed his face with his hand to be sure he had not slopped some snot on himself. It was hard to tell with his face being numb. He wryly noted he was ahead of schedule on a day when he should be late, when he should have gotten more sleep and should have taken a few minutes to prepare a presentation to his boss on Pulter.

Maybe he could still do that; sit in the drugstore café with an extra cup of coffee to outline the "ad libs" he would use on the boss to show he was making progress, would deliver what was needed, something valuable, something only he, Buck, could have done. He decided to arrive in the office late. It would be better to be late on the day after the storm than to have no thoughts to share on Pulter. Besides, the weather was still rough and the roads far from clear. Others would be late too.

Inside the drugstore, as he crossed the large open space of the shop, going toward the café, he saw a woman dressed in white sitting at the counter. He imagined it was Angela, an impression aided by her attractive posture. He knew his imagination tended to idealize a distant woman so he was surprised that she looked better and better as he approached. "What," he imagined, "were the odds of meeting two beautiful women in a shabby place as this?" But this paradox was replaced by another when he got close enough that the woman turned to see who had come near her.

"G'morning, Angela" he greeted her. "We're both getting an early start today." Her hair had not looked as red as he thought it would; he had interpreted it as strawberry blond from a distance.

"Umm," was all she answered, but she kept her casual gaze in his direction. Buck kept walking but he kept his head turned toward her too for the next couple steps. Then he turned to look where he was going and stood still to take stock of his situation. He could sit down, get a coffee before

Walid's arrival and adjust his thoughts to Pulter. But he would be interrupted when Walid came in and would have to shift to the task of easing Walid out of the Keahi case. And was he to completely ignore the possibly inviting glance from the possibly not impossible woman? He put his shoulder bag on a table in a booth and stood beside it, building his resolve. A motion behind the counter caught his eye. It was Sarah and he waved to her and mimed drinking coffee and pointed at the table. She nodded almost imperceptibly. Buck wondered if she thought he had indicated coffee or juice, but it did not matter.

He walked over to Angela. "I hope you have a shorter walk to get here than I do. The wind nearly sliced off my nose." He paused. "It would not be as much a loss in my case as it would be in yours." He stood behind the stool next to her. She had a cup of coffee and toast in front of her. She took a piece of the toast and scooped a bit of jam from a small plastic tub onto it and did not respond to Buck's voice. Buck suspected she was comfortable that the world had returned to its familiar pattern with the guy who had not chased her, that is himself, now asking for her attention. But he did not feel ignored. Maybe she was comfortable with his standing there and was merely waiting for something beyond empty opening banter. Or maybe she was as vain and arrogant as her spectacular appearance might justify. Least likely, maybe she was uncomfortable with the presence of a fellow as clever and suave as himself. Whatever her motivation, Buck was not the sort to assume the worst and walk away; having invested himself this far on a day with many stresses, he would need a more overt signal of disinterest.

"It seems oddly unlikely that I would come here two hours earlier than yesterday and find the only other person here is the same one as yesterday."

"Sit, if you like." She again did not turn her head.

He sat on the stool. It would be more relaxed to look in the same general direction as her if she were not going to look his way.

"Walid will be here momentarily. He's very good at keeping appointments on time."

"You always meet for breakfast?"

"Fair question, but no, we hardly ever do. We got together to enjoy the snow when it was fresh. Then yesterday we had some business to do. Now, today, we can finish up that business before getting to our separate offices." He reached forward, grabbed the salt shaker, and rolled it between his hands. It might have been interpreted as a nervous gesture, but it was more calculated than that. While the salt shaker appeared to be his physical focus, he was looking at Angela with as much peripheral vision as he could achieve without turning his head noticeably. From up close, her skin was as clear and soft as imagined. Her eyes were made up with some shadow and liner, but not too much. The long lashes might have been natural. He could not discern any makeup on her cheek, but she was wearing a subtle shade of lipstick. Buck had never considered dating a woman who wore lipstick. She was wearing a string of pearls, which drew his eye to her throat, where it might have gone anyway. Her sweater was thin, showing her curve, but not cut low enough to reveal anything that is not normally seen in public in winter. He thought the sweater was not made for winter; it was made for enticement in the right body.

"Did you go skiing that first day?"

He fumbled the salt shaker enough to justify an adjustment in the angle of his head so he could reassure himself her legs looked as good up close as they did from across the room. That was when he saw the flaw in her appearance. It was so stark, he wondered he had not seen it before. She was wearing thin, wet, fabric shoes, one of which had a small hole worn through the top near her big toe. Instantly, he felt sympathy for her. She was no longer the chosen one; she lacked money, and her attention to other details of dress, now noticeably inexpensive, suggested she was bothered by her shabby shoes, in addition to their discomfort in such weather.

"Skiing?" Buck's mental drift to her shoes and their implications delayed answering her, but the little gap in time came across as cool. "No. We would have needed to leave very early to get somewhere to ski. We went sliding in the park with the children."

"Children? Married?"

"Oh yes, married. No children though. Masha is too focused on her career, I think. She works in a hospital and believes strongly in public service." He waited a couple seconds, imagining Angela was becoming icy. "They have been married for seven or eight years and I've never heard either of them mention an interest in having children." He waited another couple seconds for her to adjust to his joke. "The children in the snow were strangers to us. They were city kids and did not know how to slide very well in deep snow, so we made a runway. Walid had never played in the snow and he had quite a time." Now he waited for her to answer.

But she took a long sip of her coffee. Sarah placed Buck's empty coffee cup in front of him. He would have to fill it himself at the urns on the sideboard. He smiled at her. She offered him a menu. "G'morning, Sarah. Thank you for the coffee cup. I'll order some breakfast as soon as my friend gets here," and he tilted his head to indicate the booth where his briefcase lay. When he looked back toward Angela, she was watching him. He noticed her eyes were amber; more gold than brown. "Have you enjoyed the storm?"

"I never thought cold and wind and two feet of snow would be enjoyable."

"Did you have a couple days off? I enjoyed a break from work. I wonder if we're going to be paid. Guess I would have enjoyed it less if I had asked that question earlier."

"Here is Walid." Buck followed her line of sight and saw Walid taking off his coat at the booth. "You have business to do."

"Reality returns. Yes, I have business to do. More than you know. More than I care to have. But I thank you for taking my mind off it for a few moments." He stood and smiled at her. She answered with a smile of her own.

"Hey Walid! How was the walk over? Did you dress in layers today?"

"Don't let me cut in. If you're in a conversation, I can just eat my bran muffin over here like a stranger. I'll be happy to hear about it all another time."

"Man, you know I could never be with a woman that beautiful."

"No, I don't know that even if it makes sense. I can't say why they go for you."

"Yeah, I have known a few. The ones I liked don't know they were beautiful. Only you and I know."

"Julie-bird had every guy turn his head when she went by."

"She claimed they didn't, but they did."

"Go on back. Talk to her. You need a woman, even a beauty would be good for you."

"I can't try on another one."

"You holding out for Keahi, aren't you?"

"No, Keahi's finished for me. Too much trouble."

"They're all trouble for you."

"Keahi has a whole other kind of trouble."

"Just what you need."

"New topic. I don't have any more answers in this game. You ready for work?"

"Yeah, I'm ready for work, but I'm not ready to talk about it. I came here to hear about the Fog."

"You hit those keys nice. I didn't spot you until you sat in with the band. ...I saw the guys following her. I talked to them. That's how I know her troubles are too much for me. I thought it was something beyond me but then I saw those guys are real and I know for certain it's something I can't handle. What do I know about confrontation on the street? I told her I couldn't help her and did not ask for any more information after a while."

"What do you mean 'after a while?'"

I started asking her questions and she was not very forthcoming and did not have any good leads. And then she suddenly came up with one, a suspicion it had something to do with some company with accounts in an offshore tax haven."

"A tax haven is not for criminal types. Those are legal. They go for secrecy or low accountability."

"Sure, you're right, but she doesn't recognize that distinction. She just thought they were sleazy. She had no evidence even if she did have some file with her."

"When did you see the tail?"

"I saw it before I met her. I talked to them afterwards to distract them so she could go home without them."

"They must know by now where she lives."

"Yeah. She said so too. Maybe they're watching to see who she meets. They tracked her phone calls."

"I heard. So what did they say? What did you say?"

"I didn't say much. I said Keahi's name so they would know I was with her. They could not decide whether to follow me and missed their chance. I was going to follow them but they made a call and someone picked them up. I got the license plate."

"What are you going to do with that? Can you find out who owns the car?"

"I'll give the number to the private eye. I pay for a day or two of his time and then I am out of it."

"No you're not. You could not turn down a game like this. And I'm pretty sure you could not turn down Keahi."

"This is way over my head."

"Prove it. Prove you aren't thinking of using this to get something from Keahi. Go over to that woman (Angela isn't it?) and make a date. Then I'll believe you."

Walid had him. Maybe he knew Buck better than Buck knew himself. Buck did not feel he was after Keahi. He felt he had decided against helping her. Yet he was still in the game because he needed to be sure he had not brought Walid into something dangerous. And there was a relief in hanging onto the Keahi matter. She was needy; she had come to him for help. Buck could imagine she would accept him. He disgusted himself to reduce his need to stand by his friend into a sexual choice based on what woman was easier to get. Everyone deserved better.

"Walid, I'm not playing your game. You may be right. It doesn't matter. I know what I have to do and I don't have to know every beautiful woman who might let me talk to her."

Sarah came by to take their orders. Buck was not hungry anymore and wanted to get into the office where he could bury his energies into Pulter.

"How's it going with Red?" Sarah asked while still writing on her pad.

"Kind of you to ask," Buck answered. "I guess the romance is over already."

"She doesn't talk to anyone. It was odd that she took up with you. She came in early 'cause I told her your friend called this morning to see when we opened and then he said you two would meet here at six thirty. She had called early too."

"Really?" Buck thought and Walid said aloud.

Buck tried not to show any reaction. He had never blushed in his life, as far as he could recall, and he was not blushing now, but he did feel frozen. He twirled his fork a bit and lifted his eyes to Walid, who sensed his friend's paralysis and protected him by speaking up.

"You think she came in early 'cause you told her that?"

"Uh huh," Sarah answered, smiling almost unperceptively.

"She never comes in this early?"

"She's here every day at 10 am. Don't think she'll be back at ten today."

"Don't you think it's terrible that Buckminster here hasn't the nerve to ask her to lunch someday? Or for a walk in the snow?"

"Uh huh." Sarah stayed with Walid and Buck, resting her stack of menus on the table and slouching as if she had been waiting too long for them to make up their minds what to order.

"I happen to know he has no girl friend at the moment. He had one and lost her. That's a long story that he won't talk about. And he thought about getting another one but she's too dangerous for his taste."

"What do you think his problem is?" Sarah asked.

"Dunno."

"Sarah," Buck said softly, "You may be the kindest waitress I'll ever meet. And that woman over there may be the most beautiful. You know what? This problem I am having at work, a problem I have ignored for two days of leisure, has sapped my confidence. I cannot convince myself I have anything to offer my boss or the woman sitting at the counter."

"You're working your way through the menu, right? I'll get you a waffle for today."

"Thank you Sarah."

Buck tried to focus on Walid's life for the rest of his breakfast. He begged Walid to distract him. He spoke of Pulter as a crisis, but the crisis something he had made up, not like the crisis named Keahi. He hid his worries by quizzing his friend about how two days off was likely to affect his job and his wife's job, and whether he was going to teach Mariya to enjoy the snow. Buck's upbeat banter nearly convinced himself that his morning was manageable. He ended breakfast by cursing Angela for turning up on a day when he could not spare the energy to pursue her. The whole breakfast had been torture; deceiving his friend, delaying getting to work on the Pulter file, and, of course, always the question of what to do about Keahi.

The café was getting crowded as Buck was rewinterizing himself with scarf, coat and gloves, but he called across the room: "Ciao, Angela." She raised one hand a few inches in a minimal wave without looking toward the voice. The adrenalin coursing through Buck after his restrained conversation over breakfast drove him toward his office in a trot. He knew of a bus that might have gotten him to work faster, but he needed to run. It drained the excess energy and, more importantly, emptied his mind. He never thought of much when he ran and this morning the challenge of finding safe footing on the icy streets was all his brain could handle. He was glad to have worn his rubbers because he imagined they offered good traction although he felt himself slip from time to time anyway. He had not dressed as heavily as on the previous days; it was not needed for commuting. The exercise of jogging kept his blood running and he felt only the cut of the cold wind on his face where it was a pleasure as one more distraction from his thoughts.

Finally his building was in sight. Before reaching the door, he looked around to see if anyone was near. There were people arriving so he waited before clearing his only functioning nasal passage. Buck stood near the door in the lobby to unwrap and unbutton himself. He took a napkin from his pocket and blew his nose like a normal person. He waved at the guard and walked past the elevators to the stairs. He could not remember having used them before except during the annual fire drill. At the first landing he took his cell phone out of his briefcase and started to dial Keahi's number before remembering he wanted to avoid using a traceable number. This made him feel foolish and bode poorly on his prospects for resolving the various problems he faced. It made him feel better about dropping Angela. He needed the simplification.

He weighed his options: whether to log on to his computer and check his messages quickly, or go back outside to find a pay phone, or just call on his own cellphone. He thought about calling on an office phone that would not link back to himself easily but decided to act smart when he knew the smart thing to do. He bundled himself up again and went outside. He could not think of a pay phone in his area and started to walk toward the bus station. It would be a long walk although there was a prospect of finding a phone along the way. On the first block he saw nothing that might have a public phone. He could feel the sweat from his earlier jog dripping down his back. It felt like a sign of his bad planning that he was back on the cold streets instead of at his desk. He stopped thinking and began to jog to the bus station.

At the bus station there was a wall beside the lockers with two pay phones that worked and three that did not. Two was one more than he needed so he settled in one booth and pulled the door closed. He took the phone number out of his briefcase and waited a moment to think about what he should say. Then he stood up and opened the door so he could take off his coat. He did not want any more discomfort than necessary in the confines of the booth. Finally he dialed. He waited four rings and was preparing to leave a message that he would call back at noon when a male voice answered.

"Hello."

"Hello. I'm trying to reach Keahi Dam. Is this her number?"

"Yeah, who are you?"

"I am Roger Wentworth, assistant store manager at the downtown Walmart. Ms. Dam left her credit card here. Should we mail it to her?"

"Yeah, OK. Mail it."

"I'll need to speak to her to confirm the number. Is she available?"

"No, she's not here now."

"Is there another number where we can reach her or a time you would suggest for me to call back?"

"I don't know when she's coming back."

"May I leave my number for her to call us?"

"Yeah, OK. Wait a minute... OK, I have a pencil now.

"Please have her call Roger Wentworth at 447-2938. If I am not here, she can explain why she is calling to whomever answers the phone." The number was entirely fictitious.

"OK, thanks. She'll call when she gets back."

Buck was impatient for some resolution. If he could not get Keahi on the telephone, he could not discuss a private detective; he did not have a good back-up plan. He was not going to be stopped so easily, so he tried another approach.

"Is this Mutt or Jeff?"

"What?"

"Are you the short one or the tall one?"

"What are you talking about?"

Buck heard the genuine lack of comprehension in the voice, but he noticed the voice did not hang up. There was some curiosity in there. Mainly he wanted to know if the voice belonged to a husband or to a thug.

"If you run into either of the two gentlemen who froze to the sidewalk in front of the Black Fog, tell them to go on inside next time. I'll pay the cover charge."

"Who the hell are you?"

"They don't need to worry about that. I'll be around." Buck almost hung up. He felt safe with only the telephone connection between them.

"Can you get a message to Mutt, Jeff or the people who hired them?"

"I don't know any Mutt or Jeff. Tell me who I'm talking to and maybe we can work something out."

"You want to work something out? I'll be at the fountain on 12th Street and Chestnut at 6 pm tonight. The fountain's dry at this time of year of course. You know the place?"

"I know the place, but I'm not going there to meet you. What do you really want and why do you want to meet anyone?"

"What are you doing with Keahi's phone?" There was no immediate answer and Buck felt he had an advantage. "I'll be there at 6 pm, wearing a watch cap and a blue wool parka. Maybe you can get some answers too."

Buck hung up. The reaction had not been husbandly but he worried he should feel out whether the speaker might have been police or FBI. On the whole, however, he thought the call went as well as it could. He was certainly glad he had been aggressive. He must have put the fellow on the phone off balance.

Chapter 8

IN AND OUT OF THE OFFICE

At his desk by 8:30, not too late, Buck laid out the Pulter documents and transferred his matrices and notes from a thumb-drive to his desktop computer. And then he stared at the numbers, willing them to speak to him. If he could get into a trance, the morning might melt away with the sensation of under an hour and he would have a breakthrough he could convert over the rest of the week with a journeyman's skills into a solid case. The numbers were silent. They demanded more than a willing receptacle; they demanded his full attention and that he could not provide. Keahi preyed on his attention. He could not do anything until the afternoon; he had exhausted his ideas, pending further information. At 9:30 his office mate came in. She wanted to talk about the storm, tell her tale of suffering as if it were unique or, at least interesting, although it was neither. Buck tried to be courteous. He may have to share an office with her for another year or more. Buck worked hard to hide his impatience, but was very poor at controlling body language and the officemate understood Buck's disinterest and went out to talk to someone more sociable.

Buck looked at his watch and read 9:42 on its analog face. He had utterly wasted an hour and twelve minutes of

154

good mental energy unable to focus on his task. It was eighteen minutes until ten o'clock and he could not see why that seemed important. He rechecked his calendar. He had nothing scheduled for ten or any other time for this day here in the office. He had promised himself he would stick to the Pulter account until after lunch, leaving three hours until he could try to contact find Keahi again. It was two and a half hours until he could leave the office for lunch. The idea of walking to a restaurant was attractive. It would burn off some of the energy that added to his distraction. And his hyperactive cerebrum reminded him he did not need to waste an additional few hours to get some exercise. Abandoning his promise, he waved cordially to his office mate as he passed her talking animatedly to a secretary enraptured by her story.

Buck did not feel irresponsible for leaving the office, more like a victim of circumstances; it was beyond his capacity this day to be productive. He needed to get his head in order; that required a change. Going to the café would break the thought pattern that was blocking his progress. He did not want to admit it to himself, but he remembered that Angela's normal visit to the coffee shop was at 10:00.

He had not dressed for a long walk in the cold. If his subconscious was plotting to meet her again, it should have directed him to dress better for the hike of ten blocks. John Coulter had explored Yellowstone in the winter, coming off a trek to the Pacific with Lewis and Clark, clothed in animal skins. Buck was not going to complain about his urban tramp along a roadway that was paved, flat, and lined with warm shops. The wind had picked up and burned his face pleasantly. He was wide awake and thought his brain ought to be as well.

The streets were slushy and very quiet, apart from the rooster tail of cold water the more adventurous cars threw up. His shoes for the office quickly soaked through, making his feet cold. He did not care about the shoes *per se*, but he dreaded having to buy new ones. He suspected that the salt in the slush would damage them more than the water itself. That was a comforting though as he could just admit that the shoes were done and not need to think further about how to salvage them. The sidewalks were nearly empty. He ignored the stoplights and crossed the streets when he judged it safe. His city was bordering on anarchy and Buck could feel it in the air. He was not greatly embarrassed by having reached this point. Anarchy was fun for someone like himself; he had little enough to lose.

The coffee-shop came into view sooner than he expected. He stood behind a parked service van, invisible to anyone in the shop. And there he pressed one finger against one nostril and blew the open nostril clean. It was messier than usual and some snot hung down from his nose. He bent forward to keep it off his coat. It was too thick to fall from its own weight so he brushed it away with a gloved hand. The glove retained some sign of the action, so he bent over and washed it in the snow. He crossed the street feeling refreshed and tried to whistle a slow Ellington tune (Sophisticated Lady) but his lips were too cold to produce music.

The shop was very warm which would feel good for the first minute or two. He looked at the café counter in back and thought he could see Angela there. Having had "Sophisticated Lady" in mind, he acted cool. He did not stare at her to be sure whether she was Angela or not. He was not sure how she should look from the back anyway, having misread her hair color last time. He thought it possible she could see him in one of the mirrored surfaces that made the place look large, or maybe on the shiny toaster across the counter from her. He sat two stools away and did not turn his head toward her.

Buck spoke up loudly enough to be clear he was addressing Angela, and not murmuring to himself or his cell phone. "I do love an orange juice in the morning. I like it on a frigid day, a third frigid day of the greatest blizzard our city has seen in my time here. In fact, despite tradition, I like it any time of day although it feels decadent to have orange juice after noon so I rarely drink it but at breakfast." He rested his elbows on the countertop, but slowly rotated his upper body to face Angela. She did not answer, but turned her head halfway toward him, not enough to see him, but enough to acknowledge she had heard him. The pale color of her face contrasted only slightly with the lightness of her hair but the soft firmness of one was clear relative to the soft looseness of the other.

"And yet I did not come here for the juice. This place is outside the range of my commuting. I only found it because the storm had closed my usual haunts." Angela turned her head halfway again, as if she were looking at the empty stool next to her, with the effect of indicating she was listening. "I came today to see if I might be allowed to buy Angela's breakfast."

She looked him in the eye and he shuddered to see that face directed at him and with an act of self-control requiring a measure of concentration he had prepared for the moment, he did not avert his own. He raised the level of his smile just slightly and did not look at her since that was likely to break his concentration.

"I know Walid's name but not yours."

"I am Buckminster Reese."

"What a mouthful!"

"No one calls me that but me."

Sarah came by and held her pad in businesslike fashion but did not speak. She looked back and forth between them, not sure who was ordering.

Buck spoke up, relieved at having something easy to say. "Good morning, Sarah. I know you have been at work through the storm, but this is my first full day back and yet I am taking a huge coffee break rather than earning my pay. Breaking in gradually, you know."

Sarah held her pencil on her pad. Her head was bowed, matching her posture of waiting to write an order but her eyes were raised toward Buck, peering over the top of her glasses.

"I see you are dressed up for the office."

"I wear a tie, but not a starched white shirt," Buck responded. "Angela, please go ahead."

Angela allowed herself a smile. "Sarah knows what I am having."

"I see. And, Sarah, is Angela having breakfast or just coffee-break fare?"

Sarah looked to Angela, as if for permission to reveal her secrets. Angela nodded innocently.

"She comes for the ritual, not the food."

"Hmmm," answered Buck deliberately. "I was thinking something heavy might be right for my mood, but it looks so disgusting to eat very much by oneself. May I have an orange juice and one pancake?"

"Is there any coffee in your coffee break?" Sarah asked.

"Oh, no, no, Sarah. That is not at all what I need this morning. Make that a large juice, please. And I'll take it at a table." Buck pointed vaguely with his thumb toward the tables without selecting one in particular. "And Sarah, please give me Angela's bill regardless of whether she joins me."

Buck stood up and slowly collected his coat and scarf from the stool beside him. Angela hesitated for an instant and then stood herself. Buck waved with his hand to invite her to choose a table. She looked around and shrugged as she walked toward the table in the corner. Buck stepped quickly to get ahead of her so he could sit facing the room. He also felt more comfortable to be in front where Angela was not imagining his look upon her body as she walked. Buck hung his coat on a hook and then took Angela's and hung it on top of his. He reached in his coat's left pocket for a napkin to blow his nose, just to be sure it was clean. He felt something hard there. Before he had it out he knew what it was, the flashdrive Keahi had offered him at the Black Fog. And yet when he looked at it sitting in the palm of his hand, he could hardly believe it was real. Just when he was prepared to put Keahi aside for a few minutes, here she was, demanding his attention. He could not even be angry since her need seemed both real and pressing. Lying to Walid would be the easiest of the pressing matters for the morning. He put the flash-drive in his pant pocket. When they were both seated, neither spoke immediately.

"Thank you for humoring me, Angela. I am not usually a big talker, but I have a few things on my mind today. I thought I'd try them out on you. Don't know if they might appeal to you. Don't hesitate to say so if they don't."

"That's a lot of 'don'ts'."

"Don't let's dress ourselves in defensive raiment. We have nothing in common but a chance meeting and little chance of knowing each other for long. Little to lose, right? So let's just speak frankly. Not 'frankly' like the diplomatic codeword for 'in disagreement', but 'frankly' as in honestly, just not as corny as 'honesty' between youngish strangers. We'll see how it goes."

"My raiment may be less than fully frank already, but I'll give you a shot. You got a line I never heard before."

"Well, you see there are two main things on my mind: one is a project at work and one is about a certain woman with an odd problem. The project at work would surely bore you or anyone, and, fortunately, I have no interest in explaining that to anyone. The thing with the woman, however, cries out for discussion with someone. Usually I would take such a matter to my friend Walid. In fact, it is because he and I share these kinds of issues that I know discussion with a friend can be very helpful."

"And you have invited me to hear about your girl troubles? What's wrong with Walid? Does he like this girl too? Is she anyone I know?"

"I like to directly answer the questions I am asked, but you are not on the right track here. Let me answer the last one first. The woman at issue in this story is not someone you know. The only women you and I both know is Sarah. She is innocent so far as I know. The reason I thought of speaking to you is largely because you do not know her and cannot be connected with her in any way. I suspect a certain danger in her situation and Walid has gotten too close to the matter. I suspect there is a danger to him so I am trying to keep him from any more contact on it."

"Danger, you say? And Walid does not have his eye on her?"

"Really, he has no interest in her except as she might affect my interests. But, frankly, he is not as suspicious and cautious as I am and may get on the wrong side of the nasty characters I think are involved in this."

"But you think I might have advice to help you with this woman?"

"Advice? I do not seek advice from you. I suppose the best I would hope from you in this is to have some good questions, questions that lead somewhere. Right now I am overwhelmed with questions. I cannot sort them into something I can investigate, you know, into priorities or some kind of hierarchy or decision tree that would move the case along."

"So my role in this is to be interested and engaged so I can help you think through the danger from this woman?"

"That is close to my vision of the forthcoming conversation. But the way you said it sounds just a little off. The danger is more essentially *to* this woman. But I guess I am inviting you to a form of friendship. And this form of friendship carries responsibilities on my part as well. I would expect to be available to hear whatever you have in your life that might benefit from sharing with another human."

Sarah came by with Buck's breakfast and gave Angela a slice of coffeecake and a cup for coffee. She slid two bills onto Buck's side of the table. Buck busied himself with pouring syrup evenly on his pancake. Angela thanked her for the cake and cut off a small piece with her fork. She chewed it gracefully before speaking again.

"And why do you offer this privilege to me?"

"I must admit, you do offer questions in abundance! I wonder if I intuited that tendency from you... Why you? Largely because everyone I know already knows too much about me. This is a matter that needs to be secret, as you will see if we get far enough along as to talk about it. You and Sarah are the most remote acquaintances I have and she is at work. But also, seeing you here alone several times has given me the impression you might have room in your social schedule for another friendship. ...And I must address how much your appearance entered into my approaching you. It is a simple fact that you are amazingly beautiful. I do appreciate that but it does not drive my decisions. I have known beauty. My former girlfriend, who left me not very long ago for her very good reasons, was as beautiful as ever a woman could be. More so than you? That is not possible, but there is no such competition. She was different. And I knew her much more than you, obviously, so it was a smaller percentage of my perception of her. The experience of her taught me, if I needed it, that the greatest part of any woman is outside physical presence."

"Is that why she left you?"

"No, not exactly. Not at all, I think. What I meant is that, well, I admired her for her physical attributes and felt impossibly complemented that she would bother with me and even that she came to love me, but we did so many things together I sometimes ceased to be aware of her physical essence and thought of her for her thoughts, philosophy, experiences, ethics, skills, interests, and dreams. Maybe it was her dreams that I had the most trouble grasping. I failed to see myself properly in her dreams. And maybe that was because it was hard to visualize myself in them. She wanted more of me than I would give. I did understand her at the last, understood enough anyway to be clear with her. She was smart to move on. Her dreams were good and did not need me. I do not replay that relationship into a different path. It was doomed to an ending. It probably should have been earlier. I regret only that she wasted the time and effort on it. But this is absolutely not what I would share with you."

"So am I excessively attractive?"

"You weaken my knees when you look my way, but I won't collapse. Walid encouraged me to ask you out. He has a great wife and wants a woman for me. It seemed an impossibility to build a relationship with you. I have always relied on the circumstances of life to introduce me to new people. I have never initiated meeting a woman. And your lovely face and healthy figure conspired to make any approach on my part appear superficial since I had little else to justify my interest. I told him I hadn't the least criticism of you and that I could overcome my self-doubts, but life was too complicated at the moment to seek a new girlfriend."

"But here you are."

"Here I am but I am not looking for a girlfriend. I am just looking for a friend, a safe friend. Frankly, this conversation has already lasted long enough that I have lost awareness of your looks."

"And you imagine that I could be that friend, despite my vanity? Aren't you trying to do better this time than you did with your girlfriend?"

"You know I did not accuse you of any vanity. I would have no basis for it. I cannot know your view on being so extraordinary in appearance. Being so damn attractive does not mean you believe it is important. I can see you have put some effort into it and it such an obvious fact that it's apparent to people when they first meet you, like myself. I would imagine you long ago found it was vastly insufficient as an identity and tiresome to have people see it as all that is you. That is my guess and if I am wrong and you do think it is important, you would not sit for long at a table with a guy having my crooked nose."

"Let me see that... I had not noticed."

"You can take the rest of your coffee cake back to the counter now."

"It does not look bad."

"But is crooked."

"Yes, it is. You could not have a career modeling eyeglasses."

"And there you go giving advice. Although I am not seeking advice, I firmly resolve to follow your guidance on that point. And since you have not finished your cake, I'll launch into my story."

Buck took a sip of his juice, knowing she would wait for him to do it, and building a degree of tension as well as providing a break from the introductory banter. She was, for now, accepting the role of friend as he had laid it out.

He started by explaining Keahi's situation, as far as he knew it, rather than telling how he met her. He did not hesitate to say he found Keahi attractive and acknowledged that meeting two attractive women within 24 hours was part of the complication that kept him from asking Angela for a date. Angela showed no interest in exploring any competition in his mind between the two women and apparently accepted his assertion that his continued involvement with Keahi was due to his concern first with the risk to Walid and secondly his self-image as a nice guy, a form of vanity, he admitted, that Keahi had learned to tap.

"Angela, thank you for listening. Your quiet attention kept me focused on telling the story as well as I could. I tend to be lazy so it was very useful for you to let me work through it. I got an idea or two as I went through it." Buck had not looked at her during his recitation, although his eyes faced in her direction enough to disguise his efforts to ignore her presence.

"And what did my beauty help you realize?"

Angela spoke softly, almost too softly for Buck to hear her. She was aware of the nearby tables filling with the early lunch crowd.

"Speaking with you made me define my priority interest which is,... what did you hear me say to this point?"

"Walid's safety."

"Damn, toss my heart on the pile of those you have broken already. What a star! Yes! Yes! Walid's safety. What can I do about it? I cannot tell him what to do and would not want to anyway. I ought not to make the mistake I did with Julie, that's my former girlfriend, and fail to appreciate his commitment to me. I must allay his fears for my safety, of course. Talking won't be enough. He knows me too well. I need to set a trap for him to figure out for himself that the danger is past. He would not expect that from me because it is not typical of me. The only reason I have it in mind now is you; you have me thinking differently. And then I need to convince the thugs that Walid is irrelevant to them. I have in mind giving them the impression I pose a greater threat than I do, make them focus on me. I can reach 'em by phone."

"You may have a few details to work out."

"Yeah. Like how this comes to an end. I have to be an immediate threat or they will have time to try going through Walid. I think I get to the end by getting Keahi to give them whatever they want, assuming it is within her power. I mean, I am sure they don't mean to harm to her personally. She must know something or have access to information they want. She should just give it to them. If it has the potential to harm someone, she can reveal to that person that the information is not secure. Sure, sure, there're a few gaps in this plan but it is only a couple minutes old. I'll have to put off the mystery I am working on at the office and fill in the holes in Keahi's plan. What I need is an upsurge in this storm to give me an excuse to stay out of the office for another day."

Buck leaned to the side slightly and looked past Angela to see if he could see through a window. The café was hidden from a view of the door by a rack of greeting cards, and he could not see much through the windows because they were filled with displays of wheelchairs and braces.

"You figure you're smart enough for both jobs?"

"Sitting in my apartment, with a clear head and a leisurely evening before me, I would know better, but on a morning break when I go into a café and break bread with a stunner who is kind enough to accept my queer and sincere offer of friendship, I believe I can change the world, that is to say, the part of the world on the block where I live. You have firmed my resolve to make a difference. I have in my lifetime, in an earlier hard winter storm, found a mythical ice cave and that memory encourages me I might reach beyond my rational limitations."

Buck knew well enough he had not solved any of his problems. He did appreciate the confidence she instilled in him even if it was incomplete. At least he had an overall strategy in mind. He needed to write it down. "Now I do not intend to work this afternoon while I have these questions hanging over me, but I need to be at my desk so I can continue to receive a paycheck."

"Sounds like fraud to me."

"Dead right you are. I care little about fraud if I am not caught... and if I escape the moral implications, in this case, by returning to my boss far more value than my salary. I am secure on the moral issue, not every day, but over the course of a month, any month."

"So you are worth something?"

"I am to my company. Not so much to society at large... Listen, you have been more than great, and I greatly hope, aspire, desire and fervently wish to build a friendship of the sort we discussed but at this minute I've got to get back to the office. May I hear your story someday soon?"

"I have no story. My curse is proven by your finding me in a nondescript café in the morning rather than someplace where I might be productive to a boss or to some portion of humanity."

She would have said more and Buck intuited that he should let her speak since he had dominated the conversation so far, but he did not like the direction of her words.

"Pardon me, please. I'll not have it that way. Your fortunate genes are not in lieu of a story in your history. Maybe they are not even fortunate from your side. One can be sure they have colored the reaction of humanity to you. I may be a friend by hearing your story and getting you to see it. If I might give you an outline for the day you might tell me some part of it... How is it you come to this place? I suspect you like the anonymity of it, which I have destroyed, perhaps. And why the retro look? There is something behind those pearls. The hairstyle is lovely, to be sure, but no one else in this city has worn it for a generation." Here he decided to be bold. He would not win her playing safe. He stood up, took his coat out from under hers and returned hers to the hook. He drew the two bills toward himself and added: "In addition to your feet, there is a story in those shoes, Dear."

Chapter 9

BUCK BECOMES A POET

Back in the office, Buck put some document with the name "Pulter" showing conspicuously on his screen and then started looking into Keahi's flash-drive. He would switch back to the Pulter screen if he heard any approaching footsteps. She had given him an extensive collection of files from the parent company called "Ringstare." There was no introductory message he could find to say why any of it was significant. That was enough news for him at one time. It seemed more dangerous to be dipping into an anonymous company's books than to run around the streets with thugs tracking a stranger. Figuring out the mystery in the files was his singular skill, but Keahi could not have known that. She must have hidden a message for him or she just wanted him to be her safe deposit box. He was a lousy safe deposit box for her since she did not know how to contact him. And now he had lost his ability to contact her. He felt frustrated.

Suddenly he realized he probably could reach her through Ringstare. Maybe that was her place of work. Why had it not been obvious immediately to try that? He was humbled by the weakness of his logical processes. He had harbored an undue arrogance that he could do something significant despite any experience in such work. Now he felt real danger, not just the cartoon danger of theoretical scenarios.

A footstep in the hallway alerted him to click back onto the Pulter file. Someone walked by his door without stopping. He felt guilt and shook nervously. Was it a surge of adrenalin or a state of fear? Was there a difference between them in a world where danger is real? It had always been too easy for him to coast along in a moderate, undemanding lifestyle. Was that why he felt so little ambition at work; just enough to drive him to solve the little puzzles of his job? He refused to ask himself if his languid personality could be repaired or, if it could, would it be possible to get back together with his Julie-bird.

Another footfall came to his ear; he leaned toward his screen. "Buck! You doing anything for lunch?"

He swiveled around. "Hey Bobby. How was your cold vacation? Well, I should hear about that later. I think I am getting close on this one and can't stop. I'll check with you later, OK?"

Bobby did not expect Buck to go to lunch with him. They hardly ever went out together, but this was an odd day already, coming back from an unplanned break.

Buck wondered how the lunch hour had arrived so soon. He should have made some progress on something by mid-day. He turned to the spreadsheet he had begun a week before on Pulter. What was missing? He had put in the figures for all the indicators built into the sheet but he had only a vague hypothesis on what was wrong in it. Entering the figures usually led directly to a few anomalies through a mental process he did not control or fathom. He decided to think again about that idea about too many internal accounts, the only original idea he had so far. He was back on Pulter.

Two hours went by without Buck sensing any passage of time. His boss came in, saying Bobby had told him Buck should be done with Pulter before the end of the workday. "I would always like to keep moving it on, but I am getting some signals that Pulter is in a hurry. They never gave me a deadline, but this guy Harley has been leaving messages all week and called twice already this morning. He's polite, but damned persistent. Now Bobby said you're close. Can we wrap up your position today? You can write it up formally tomorrow." Buck suggested in his mind that Bobby could never have dealt with the Pulter questions himself but was trying to gain some association with their resolution. He pretended to study the screen while he uttered some sounds in his throat to indicate he was about to speak. Several snide put-downs of Bobby came to mind, but there was no reason to say them aloud. "Rich, I am struggling here. It is impossible to put a clock on an open question like this." Rich was not content but he knew there was nothing to be gained by pressing Buck further so he closed with an encouraging remark and went away. Buck thought he would devote all of his late lunch hour to Pulter to see if he could get a better grasp on it.

"OK Pulter, where could the money flow? Money is like water, always tending to escape confinement as if it has intent. I would hate to be a plumber. Knowing there would be a moment of truth coming at the end of my installation when the water is turned on and some leak appears somewhere. Or when I must find a leak that was too small to be noticed until the weakened dining room ceiling collapsed on the Thanksgiving dinner. And then the plumber comes in and must get it all right without introducing any new leaks even though those connections are not as secure in practice as in theory. There is a lot of technique in making connections that will withstand the pressure. And will withstand the pressure for years to come. Why is it I feel so insecure with the Pulter plumbing? It has amateurish, homeowner repairs that do not bear the marks of classical, established technique. But Pulter is an established company, the kind that could bleed a half a percent of profit without noticing it, an amount that would justify an individual's taking a risk. It has professional accountants. Why the slap-dash adjustments?" He made a note of all the oddities he could find. They were legal at first look, but he saw something useful in them; they began suddenly in September two years earlier. He could check the personnel files to see if someone new had joined. That might support the innocence of an over-confident, under-competent amateur. If no one had joined the company then, it might be the date when someone got an idea of how to manipulate something. Buck did not mind being an investigatory accountant. He was like a plumber, called in to find or fix a leak. But the leaks created by plumbers were never intentional. His work had the appeal of hunting a human agent. "And that is why I have this silent arrogance in me. I sometimes catch them but no one ever catches me. They will never catch me because I am not tempted in the least to create any flow of funds into my pockets. I am blessed by low ambitions."

Buck looked into the personnel records at Pulter. No one with access to financial systems joined the firm soon before the September at issue. He thought he was onto something now. If it was an intentional leak, the obvious question became, into what tin pan was the leak dripping? Unfortunately, this question was so obvious the answer was usually actively obscured but that was a contest Buck was ready to engage.

He looked at the clock over the door and was mildly surprised that it read past 3:00. He checked the corner of his computer screen to confirm the time. It felt like 30 minutes had passed though it was three hours in reality. Having put some time in on the Pulter case, he felt he had earned some time for Keahi. He looked up her name on Google. Her two names were common name in Laos, but there was no match for the two of them together. They seemed to mean "black fire." Her company was an established American firm, privately owned, with little information in the web. But the headquarters was in his city and there was address and phone number for it. He had not lost touch with her.

He called out to the secretary as he went out, "I'll be back in a few minutes. Some air will do me good." As he knew it would be, it was frigid air that met him at the door to his building. Three breaths and he was cold in his core. Again he rued having dressed this morning under the assumption he would be commuting in conventional, modern, urban transportation.

The sidewalks in the neighborhood of his office had been shoveled or plowed or blown, but were not bare to the concrete. Much of them was covered in slippery, white, compressed snow. There had been no temporary thaw to melt it and let it then harden into ice, but some places were warm enough for the salt spread here and there to have had effect. Buck looked to the low, heavy sky and felt a few fresh flakes land on his face before it was too numb to notice. He half jogged on the insecure surface toward the bus station, looking at the space where he would place each step to assess whether he might slip. As he neared the station, he came to a place where the traffic threw slush onto the sidewalk. It was too salty to freeze, but it was slippery nonetheless. His foot skipped a few inches forward when he hit the different surface, and he pushed off his back foot a bit harder to compensate. It was not enough to regain his balance and he felt himself falling backwards. He made an unconscious decision of whether to lean toward the snowbank for a landing or to push again with his back foot to lift himself forward for another stride. He was pleased that his back foot got good traction and he was strong enough to stay upright for another step. Again his lead foot slipped, but this time it was not enough to make him fall. He came to a standstill and, without moving, did a quick inventory of his leg and back muscles to see if anything had been twisted or pulled. He felt no pain beyond the increasingly familiar burn of cold air on his face and in his lungs.

He kept to a walk for the last half block. Someone had scraped the entrance to the station and he could look

ahead without fear of falling. There was time to catch his
breath although he had not been running hard enough to
build up much oxygen deficit. He snorted his good nostril to
clear it. No need to waste a napkin when he was outside.
The glass door to the station dragged on the concrete when
he pulled it open. He was blasted with thick warm air,
exactly opposite to the effect of leaving his building. The
cold was the more comfortable option.

He sat on a bench to catch his breath in the unlikely
event that someone was watching for anyone simply using the
pay phone. And the place might be watched if, say, the FBI
were involved which was possible, he imagined, since he had
called from here before. He was in a hurry to get back to the
office, but fought to look relaxed. He opened his coat and
looked around the waiting room. It was a generic bus
terminal, with luggage lockers where a bum could put keep
his stuff cheaply, paying only when he wanted to access it.
There were no bums in the room at the moment. People
were passing through to the magazine kiosk and the mini-
mall. No one was waiting. No one seemed on the look-out
for a person using the phone to hide his identity, unless it was
the guy behind the ticket window.

He looked at his watch and stood in front of the
posted timetable for a few seconds before going to the
phones. He called the Ringstare number and asked for
Keahi Dam. The woman who answered showed no interest
in the caller and told him Keahi had not come in that day.
Buck thought it an odd phrasing. Why not speak
affirmatively, such as "She is out today?" It sounded to Buck

as if Keahi's reason for being out was not known, not by the woman on the phone. Was it an unplanned, unexcused, unexplained absence? It did not sound suspicious enough to believe there was anything in it, but there was room for speculation. He asked when she would be in and was told they expected her on Monday; that the snow had probably kept her away. He smiled that his suspicion had been confirmed that the absence was unexplained. Buck had not planned any response but he quickly improvised that he had repaired Keahi's laptop and had promised to get it back to her before the weekend. This was to justify asking for her home number but it also might productively worry anyone concerned about Keahi sharing files. The woman on the phone showed no further interest in his call and declined to give Keahi's home number. Buck did not want to play too many moves at a time so he thanked her and hung up. It felt like that woman was uninvolved in the case although she might accidently pass along something about his call.

He went back to the posted timetable and looked at it for a moment. As he turned to leave, he surveyed the room and recognized no one from his earlier scan. He stopped to button up his coat before pushing through the door. He heaved a deep breath of the cold and looked to see if the snow was still falling. He noted the irregular white bits floating aimlessly, as if they sublimated out of the air at street level rather than dropped from above. Buck found it comforting that the peculiar atmosphere remained, perhaps reassuring him he had not lost much time against managing the mysteries to which he was committed. He jogged back to the office. It had taken just 30 minutes to make the call.

He went to his desk quietly, not sneaking in exactly, but not disturbing anyone with his noise. His telephone showed a light indicating he had a message. He logged on to the computer and put up an image of a Pulter-relevant item on the screen before checking the telephone. Walid had left a message: "You need to activate the message function on your cell phone, man. Maybe you are not missing anything important, but you got to get with the century you're in. You're like some hundred-year old guy who never got a digital TV and doesn't know how the remote control works. At least your company takes messages. You know how to get them? Call me if you figure out how. I'm wondering about that project you don't want me doing. You can still tell me about it. I know you are working on it. You know my number, but don't forget to put a '9' in front of it if you are calling from your desk. Ciao, homme!"

Buck called him back. "Walid!"

"Hi Buck."

"Were you just checking in or did you have something you wanted to bring up?"

"Just checkin' in. Any news?"

"I have to admit; there is some news. I had brunch with Angela."

"Angela! Wow! How did you set that up?"

"Just stumbled into it. I was getting stressed by a job; I couldn't get a grasp on it; couldn't make any progress... so I was feeling antsy and just went to the drugstore. Really, I just wanted to get away for a few minutes and there she was."

"And did this accident happen at just about ten o'clock in the morning?"

"Yeah, it was then. I might have hoped to run into her, but not really. I could not imagine ever getting to know her, just based on meeting her at a restaurant."

"But you figured it was worth a try."

"I wasn't thinking that way. She is such a sight, I have to appreciate her, but I don't like pale eyed redheads wearing rings and pearls."

"You like that one."

"It won't last. If I do like her after I get to know her, she will be dumping me soon enough. I'm good for some things, not great... good. And she is not one of those things."

"Did you talk to her?"

"We talked. Mostly I talked. She sat at the table with me. I left on a good basis. Of course I made it easy for her. I told her I was not out for her. And that is the truth, you know. Rings and pearls, and too much of that flawless skin."

"Did she believe you? You can be a mean talker but that is a hard package to sell."

"It is not hard to sell at all. Just talk about another woman. It doesn't even matter if you talk well about the other woman. If you say bad things about the other woman, the one in front of you distrusts you and rejects you. If you speak well of the other woman, the one in front of you thinks you're sincere. I talked about Keahi."

"You said good things, I'm sure."

"I said I liked Keahi, not that I was in love with her or likely to see her again."

"I need to write this kinda stuff down in case I'm ever single again."

"No, no man, it was not a scam to get Angela to relax or divert her attention. That would be creepy. I wanted, at that moment, to talk about Keahi's case. I had given up on the idea of getting close to Angela. She'd be nice to see once in a while. It would help my ego."

"What about Keahi? Did something happen?"

"You know, man, I would rather not get you into it. It may be dangerous and I am keeping a lot of distance between me and whoever is bothering her. I am thinking the FBI could be in it and I would rather not become a subject of their investigation. I have not been in touch with her."

"It would be good if the FBI was on it, right?"

"I don't know. Good for whom? It may not be good for Keahi. She might not have crossed some line they care about but she would certainly be vulnerable to deportation if they looked her very closely. At least that's what she thought. It would just be a nuisance for me if they thought I was involved."

"That's what you said to Angela?"

"Not really. It came out differently with her."

"I bet... Are you going to call Keahi again?"

"Are you going to stay out of it?"

"Whatever you say, man."

"I'm still thinking of what to do. It is hard to just let it go. It could be interesting. I saw too many cowboy movies when I was little to let a cry from a vulnerable damsel go unanswered. I don't wear the black hat. But in the real world, I don't have a pair of six shooters that never miss."

"I didn't watch cowboy movies and I don't know exactly what you said."

"You know enough, Walid. Keahi is out there somewhere and I haven't forgotten her."

"Yes, I know enough for now. Better get back to work. I guess I need to admit why I called. Masha told me to invite you over for dinner. She has a woman for you."

"Masha _is_ the woman for me, except that she has a husband somewhere already. I'll always come over to spend the evening with her."

"Saturday OK?"

"I'll bring the wine."

"You don't know anything about wine."

"I'll ask around."

"Not the internet, right!"

"Masha is not the only sophisticated friend I know. I'll find something appropriate."

Rich appeared in the doorway and waved in a manner to say, "Let me know when you are available." Buck called to him without covering the phone, "Come in, Rich. Now is a good time." Then he turned to the phone and said, "Walid, I'll see you Saturday."

"Rich, are you catching up after our sudden vacation?"

"No, not at all, but our clients really don't care about the snow in our fair city. They want what they want, and they want it when they want it."

Buck knew Rich was dying to hear his clearance to partner with Pulter and he knew Rich understood that Buck would let him know as soon as he was ready to clear that action. He looked at Rich's stiff white shirt, as always, worn with the sleeves rolled up. He also always wore nondescript dark pants that fit a suit whose jacket he never donned once he was inside the building; it was only for wearing under his overcoat during his commute. Buck looked at Rich's tie. He had never noticed any of them and he could tell he would not remember seeing this one of a dark, blue-green background hue and various brown and blue diagonal bands. Maybe it was a pattern associated with his college or some club. More likely, he had others of the same general ilk and none of them meant anything.

Rich was not an awkward person, but he did not sit in the spare chair in Buck's office and could not find a posture to make himself appear relaxed. Buck sympathized with his dilemma, that he was depending on an analysis from Buck and had no sign of how the analysis was going or when it would be complete. Buck was pleased that Rich really did want the analysis; it was not a legal requirement, only a prudent step, given what Buck had turned up on other potential partners in the past. Rich half sat on the windowsill as if pressing his bottom heavily enough to take most of his weight off his feet would make him seem comfortable and casual, and like part of the furnishing of the office. Rich, like most people, wanted to be successful, but he seemed to prefer being indistinguishable from his environment if not exactly undistinguished.

"It's taking longer than usual for you to get through the Pulter file, and I see that as a good thing. I like your work because you do not compromise on quality; you will stay on a lead until it ends or it gets somewhere. If it is taking longer that is because you are following a lead, just like you should. Well, I came in to ask if there is somehow I could help. I'll clear away any other demands in the office. We can get someone else or let them slide. How can I help?"

Buck froze his face with a smile on it and his gaze directed into Rich's eyes. Then, very self-consciously, turned his eyes down to the desk and nodded slowly. He knew he was a poor actor and often revealed far more in his body language than he intended. He was holding back a snicker at the offer of help from Rich. Rich did not deserve a snicker or any other sign of disrespect, and Buck did not hold him any disrespect, but his body might have said otherwise if he let it relax. Rich could not help with the Pulter case. He had no idea what issues to study and would not understand much of whatever issues Buck put into his final report. Rich could only comprehend the "go" or "no go" signal Buck was preparing and it was Buck's great advantage that Rich would have complete faith in his signal. Buck was not sure he had projected his respect for Rich's offer.

"Do you have a few minutes now, Rich? We could go over the analysis and you might help me find a soft spot in it."

Rich looked pleased to be asked. Buck thought it ironic that Rich was impatient about Buck's making progress, but had enough free time himself to listen to a presentation they both knew was unlikely to be productive.

"Here's a summary of the issue that is troubling me, Rich. Here pull your chair up. Can you see the screen? You don't need to read the figures, just see the arrangement. I organized the sales by the sales representative and looked for any pattern in where the funds were placed when the payments came in. You see that two sales reps account for all the funds that went into these three accounts. The individual sales are not among the largest, but they have added up because no funds have ever been taken out of those accounts."

"How much is in the odd accounts now?"

"It's accumulated up to a little under two million dollars."

"Whew, a tidy sum to have hidden away!"

"Oh, it's not hidden. It's all open and legal. It's just odd. And I would not say it is even a large amount. That's part of the oddity. Why have three accounts with, together, less than three percent of your sales? I don't even know if the sales reps know about this. They do not normally have any connection to accounts receivable and would not influence or know about where payments against their sales are placing internally."

"So this is not a problem?" Rich asked, irritated that Buck had elicited a supportive exclamation from him and then shot him down for misunderstanding the point.

"Don't know. That's why you don't have a report on it from me yet. Remember, I am not reporting my results at this moment... Only telling you my troubles. I would not support partnering with these guys if I cannot get this oddity explained and I cannot argue against them either."

"It does not sound that odd to me. A relatively small amount of money, you say, that has remained properly on the books. You don't know lots of things about this company. There might be many explanations for this. I bet I could make up a few. Have you found anything that would block our deal?"

"Yes, Rich, I have and it is this. Am I paranoid? Am I searching for an excuse to say 'no' for the glory of finding something? Am I too obsessive about my numbers to accept there is anything I cannot understand?"

"I did not mean anything like that Buck. I just..."

"I am used to seeing things I do not understand. I hate obsession. Maybe that's because I have some in me, but though I do have some, I do not give in to it often or for long. I am not doing science here, or accounting. I am looking into the minds of our potential partners. My boss, a man named 'Rich', has given me license and a mandate, to find and track down what is suspicious. And this item is the most suspicious I can find. It, this item, lives at the margin of what I need to understand. If I did not take my boss's interests to heart, I might consider moving on in my analysis, but something you said suggested to me that there is something in it."

"What did I say? I do not even really know what this little thing, or big thing, is."

"You said you were being pressed by Mr. Harley to wrap up our analysis. Since I am looking for a suspect to go with my suspicions, I looked him up. Mr. Harley is not the right level person to be pushing you. Mr. Harley is too low in the hierarchy. If Pulter is so interested in getting this settled, why send a minor figure into the negotiations? I called over there and asked for his boss and for his boss's boss. I did not talk to either of them. I am not the right person to negotiate. But I can confirm they were both in the office today. Mr. Harley, is the clerk in accounts receivable. He is the one who allocates the sales income to various accounts, such as the three odd ones that have been bothering me."

"Very dramatic, Buck."

"Which brings us to my question for you. Do you know Mr. Harley?   Is there any previous contact that accounts for his being the one to call you? Did anyone at Pulter offer him as a point of contact? Did he say why he was representing Pulter?"

"You are a sly one, Buck. No, I never heard of Harley before. You do what you need to do. What should I say to Harley when he calls? Maybe I should ask for someone else over at Pulter."

"You're the boss around here and I am glad for it. You know my concerns, but my drama might, as you said before, be explicable. I would advise that you not upset anyone. ...Until they give you a deadline, they can't be too serious about rushing us."

Rich slapped Buck on the back of his head as he pushed his chair back. "OK, I'll be cool. Take the time you need. We are paying you to make the company's future safe, not to be fast."

Buck's eyes pushed on Rich's back as he passed through the door and then they turned above the door to the clock. It was a little after four, plenty of time for another call to Ringstare, although he did not want to use the bus station again. He thought of asking to borrow a cell phone from someone. He asked himself which of his friends he could use, maybe someone would enjoy being told the call was especially secret and might generate a return query. Whom could he trust to be uncooperative? It was a stupid idea all around and he regretted having wasted a minute searching through it. He thought of criminals in the movies; they might buy a cheap phone for a single call. He could afford to buy a phone to use as long as Keahi's case took, but he had an inherent frugalness that rebelled against that solution. He reflected that bad ideas can spawn new thinking. He had taken a class once in creative thinking and it emphasized there was a phase early in problem solving when brainstorming might be encouraged and no idea should be dismissed immediately. Using someone else's phone could be done anonymously. He would go to someplace that sells phones and ask to try one out. This could be done once for every store he could find. In another minute, he located a phone store within a few blocks. Having already stroked Rich enough for the day and having made real progress on Pulter, he felt safe in going out to make the call.

It was darker outside than during his last foray. Buck studied the clouds. He could discern no shapes, just a low-hanging greyness, and he decided they were not any thicker than before; the darkness was because the sun was lower. With the memory of his slip in the slush in mind, he began walking briskly rather than running. The wind was still blowing, not strong, but enough to scape one side of his face. Maybe it was only the darkness, but he felt colder than before, and he began a slow jog, to keep warm and to shorten the trip.

The cell phone store was a small place, looking out of place in its glass and plastic brightness sandwiched between taller, drab stone buildings. But that local environment made its bright lights and modernity more attractive. Buck had no trouble acting the part of consumer. He asked questions he really had about cell phones, but stopped short of asking how to activate the message function. He did not want to lose the excuse of ignorance when Walid next asked why he could not leave a message.

He worked his way around to asking if he could try it out on a local call; presumably to see how the person on the other end heard him. He dialed Ringstare. The same voice as before answered. He kept a smile on his face and looked at the salesman as he asked for Keahi Dam. She hesitated and then said "Keahi what? Keahi who? We don't have anyone like that here." Buck repeated the full name carefully. The voice repeated that she never heard of such a person and then hung up. Buck wondered if she had not been trying to make him understand the falseness of her position by the exaggerated way she disowned Keahi, whom she had immediately recognized a few hours earlier. He thought it odd that she struggled to understand the sound "Dam" but pronounced very well the more difficult sounds of "Keahi." Buck spoke into the empty phone for a few sentences to provide a show for the salesman and then reported that the sound had come through very clearly. He said he liked the model in his hand and would send his wife to look at it soon. Then he confided to the salesman that she always went along with his recommendation on electronics, but liked to go through the motions of being part of the decisions.

Outside the shop, he calculated how far it would be to the Ringstare location he had found on the internet. It was too far to walk, especially if he wanted to be there before everyone went home for the evening, so he stood at the curb and waved for a cab.

Denying Keahi worked there was to be expected from an employer that knew she was an undocumented immigrant, yet it was very uncomfortable that the response had changed in a few hours' time. Had the person on the phone never before today taken a call for an illegal? Was there any reason she had mentioned his call to anyone? The first call had been so routine. Or had she mentioned it to Keahi and Keahi said to deny her presence? She would not have known it was his call.

The cab dropped him two blocks from the address. He pulled up his collar, but could not make himself warm in the dark, windy street. He was in a neighborhood of low buildings, duplexes mixed alongside small commercial outlets. There was a bold sign proclaiming Ringstare's location. It was lit by a row of upturned bulbs. He looked at the sign as he passed by on foot, and saw the bulbs were protected from the snowflakes by a panel of glass. He would have liked to warm himself on the glass, for surely there was heat rising from it. The yellow brick building was newer than its neighbors, in an industrial Deco style that might have been briefly popular among aspiring businessmen in the 1960s. The lights were on inside Ringstare. He decided not to go inside. It would have exposed him too directly, if that mattered. He thought he would see if someone looking important came out. Maybe he could follow the boss home. He decided to call for a cab to meet him one block away. He would have it wait until he was ready. At least there was no parking under the building so he should be able to see everyone come out. Nonetheless, it would be very awkward to identify someone worth following and then run to the cab in time to follow someone. It was a bad plan, but not an impossible one. Before calling the cab, he walked to the back of the building along an unplowed passage beside the yellow brick structure.

He hoped the snow had hardened by water dripping off the roof or by slush from the street, but his first step into the deep snow showed it was as soft as the first day's fluff. It packed inside his pantleg and squeezed into his shoes. Buck did not care much, Coulter the explorer of Yellowstone and all. He dragged through the knee-deep powder for a half block. The building appeared to consist of offices; there would have been a half dozen from front to back. He stamped his feet to drive the snow out of his clothes when he got to the other side. There was a moderate-sized parking lot, so it was good that he had looked here. The important people from Ringstare would probably come out on this side. He could get a cab to sit near the exit of the lot and start a tail very efficiently. At least that is how Buck's willful imagination saw it.

Two people came out. As they passed under the street lamp near the door, he could see they were young, Caucasian, dressed in winter coats that obscured their class, their importance to his case. They left in the same car. Another came out alone, and then another who met someone waiting, probably his wife. Buck doubted he could tell whom to follow even if he had a cab waiting. He watched a few more. The exiting employees did not appear likely to be illegals; not the ones at this hour, he added mentally.

A short woman in a long cloth coat and knit cap came out between two tallish men in dark overcoats. The group seemed slightly odd because they were not interacting socially, but stood very close together, awkwardly, like two dogs and a cat. Buck was surprised that he looked at them for a dozen steps before he realized the woman might be Keahi. Standing in the cold, he had lost his focus and was occupying his mind only to endure the time until something came along to release him. But here was his release. He quickly raced to the row of cars parallel to the one where they were walking. They stopped to get in a car and Buck stepped between the cars, looking down as if he had not noticed them. They might have shifted backward or just slowed their pace but one of the men preferred to step forward and obstruct Buck, claiming the space for himself. Buck stepped back and made a small apologetic sound. He leaned to one side to murmur a further apology to the lady who slid into the front passenger seat. It was Keahi, her face lit by the light inside the car. He caught her eye and nodded. It was too dark to communicate anything by his expression, but Buck was sure she recognized him, maybe she even smiled a little. At the least she turned her head to follow him as he passed on. He looked for the make of car for it was as undistinguished as the men themselves. Crown Victoria, car of tasteless old white men. Maybe of G-men, too. The car backed up from its space and skidded when the driver braked. It drove more carefully as it crunched through the crusty patchwork of ice and refrozen snow in the parking lot, and turned left, away from the central city, and disappeared.

As it was pulling away from him, Buck stared at the license plate to memorize its number until he could write it down. He did not trust his short term memory. Lacking pencil and paper, he wrote the number in a snowbank with his glove. He stepped back and looked at the shadows the lamp made of his numerals. He could read them. They would last only slightly longer than his memory.

More people came out of the Ringstare building. Someone might see the numbers and wonder what he was doing. He felt his pockets to be sure he had no pen and then cursed himself for playing at a detective without carrying even such a simple tool.

Buck went to the Ringstare door and found it locked. So he waited a few moments until someone else came out and grabbed the door before it shut. Inside was a long hallway with offices on either side. He went down the hall and saw the entrance to a large room with equipment, maybe printers or some other light production machinery. He continued to the end of the hall and tried the door. It opened to a small reception room. There was a woman sitting at a desk, a woman he suspected of being the one who answered the telephone. She was older than Buck by ten years, dressed conservatively, soft in the belly and arms. She looked like a working woman.

"Excuse me, Madame," he opened as humbly as possible. "I am a poet, passing your building, and I've had an idea but I've no pencil to save my idea before it is lost. Might I borrow a pencil and a scrap of paper for, oh, even less than a minute?"

"A poet? I never met a poet."

"Anthony Cucelli, at your service," Buck claimed as he bowed ostentatiously. He did not know how that name had come to his lips. It sounded vaguely like a local politician.

She rummaged in her desk drawer. "Will a pen do?"

"Certainly. The tool does not matter."

She offered a pen but when Buck reached for it she drew back. "May I see your poem?"

"Certainly, again. You realize I have only an idea of a poem here, but I will share what I have." She gave him the pen and slid a pad of paper toward him. He tore off a page.

"Soft and harsh, soft and sharp..." he quoted thoughtfully. "I need to feel the cold... Less than a minute, start to finish... I feel like the White Rabbit." Buck spun toward the door and left before she knew he was going. He walked briskly to the exit and put his hat in the door frame so he would not be locked out.

He went over to the entry in the snow. Between the shadows and his remnant memory, he was sure he had the number right. He ran back to the door. No one had come out in the few seconds it took to record the number so he retrieved his hat and went back to the receptionist.
"See. Less than a minute I was, I am sure. I have the idea back. It was not too late. Let me finish the thought." Standing before her, he wrote on the side of the page without the number:

> Soft as the belly fur of wolverines,
> The drifted snow caresses its guest.
> Sharp as the claws of the beast,
> The cold scratches out intruder's screams,
> Dripping cold, white blood under his vest
> 'Til the warm life of humanity comes to rest.

He placed the paper in front of the receptionist and put the pen beside it. "What do *you* think of the extended storm that has fallen upon us this week?" pronouncing an emphasis on the word "you" as if the poem were his view of the storm.

She read without touching the page. Either she read slowly or she read it more than once. Finally she looked up. "I don't read poetry, but I am very impressed. You just made that up?"

"Yes, but do not be impressed. It is only a start of an idea. The winter has a dual nature, you see... no, I should not try to explain a poem I have not even fully written. I hate to explain the ones that are finished. But at this stage, I am stilling planning what it will say. That is the hard part for me, not the actual saying. Even the rhyme scheme may change but at the moment, I like this one. Did you see A-B-B-A-C-C?"

"I think it will be frightening."

"I do not want it to be that, but nature deserves respect... My minute is long gone. I thank you for your assistance." Buck bowed again. The receptionist stood up to shake his hand. She felt the odd incident deserved some ceremony.

Buck shook her hand and, with one hand on the door knob, turned back to her and asked, "Do you have a number for Keahi?"

The receptionist stood without answering. Slowly, her eyes drifted down until she was looking at the blank pad of paper. Softly, she said "I do not know that name and I do not know her number." Still moving slowly, like a deep sea diver, she turned to a filing cabinet. She took out a piece of paper near the front of the cabinet and scanned down the page. She returned the paper and turned back to her desk. Without sitting down, she picked up the pen in a deliberate movement and wrote something. She folded the page and held it toward Buck, still without looking up.

Buck let go of the knob and walked very slowly back to her. He took the page and said "I would like to give back her laptop, you know. ...Before my appointment at six tonight." She nodded slowly, left to right and back, without looking up, and Buck walked out quickly, with the thought that there might be a camera monitoring the room.

Outside, he opened the paper. It held an address, not a phone number. He thrust it into his coat pocket, along with the poem. Then he did the top button on his coat, recalling he was poorly dressed, and jogged back to his office, going the wrong way for a block before passing through a restaurant and out the back door, just to feel safe.

Chapter 10

WALID DEMANDS HIS PLACE

It was past 5:30 when Buck sat at his desk again. He hoped he was early enough that Rich would see him before leaving for the day. Rich did not usually leave before six. It would be too bad if this was a day when Rich had something to do before six and left thinking Buck was already gone. Some days that was alright, but this week had been unproductive for everyone and for Buck in particular.

Oh, he wanted to go over the file Keahi had given him. Things would be different if he could sit down with her after this whole thing was finished and finished because he had been smart enough and courageous enough to fix it. She would not owe him anything; he would make that clear. But she would have to think well of him. Emotionally, she could not fail to feel something positive. It would be a fine foundation from which to be modest. He could relax, not needing to prove anything to her. He could be the negative finding in her biopsy report, the last day of school, the tax refund she had not expected, and if all went very well, he could be the early arrival of spring after a season of violent blizzards lasting a full week and piling drifts deep enough to cover the first floor windows. Buck realized he was staring out the window and he stood up abruptly to break the pattern of his thought. "Pulter, Pulter, Pulter," he chanted to himself as he put the Pulter file back on his computer screen.

His notes from the afternoon reminded him to play out further the implications of Rich's mentioning how he was being pressured. He put the Pulter files back on his screen and tried to concentrate on them. If a mid-level person is pressing for signing the partnership, what does it mean? Are they not serious? Why not just say so? Is he not representing Pulter officially? Buck devised seven possible reasons, including the strawman that there is nothing wrong with it; just Buck's paranoia. He was satisfied that he had a concrete finding; an accomplishment or a real step toward an accomplishment anyway.

At 6:30, Buck went out to the cell phone store again. He told them his wife wanted to hear how the phone sounded when he called her at their land line at home. By 6:45 he accepted it was time to call Keahi's number. There should have been enough time since his six o'clock appointment for whoever was on the other end of that line to stew and reach some conclusion about whoever was on Buck's end.

"Hello. May I speak with Keahi?"

...

"Sorry to hear that. Is there any other way I can reach her?'

...

Sorry to hear that too. Say, were you one of the ones at the fountain at 12th and Chestnut? It's not so beautiful when it is turned off for the winter, is it?"

...

Well there were a couple mugs standing nearby and they looked cold to me."

...

"Personally I like the cold but, of course, not standing around in it, so I didn't hang around for long; just walked by. Took a photo; couple of 'em. I just wanted to see who would show up. I'm working an angle that needed that information. So thanks to you and your pal. That's all for now."

And then he rushed back to the office, hoping Rich had not left yet. He settled in front of a computer screen with the Pulter data. The sound of approaching footsteps was not loud but caught Buck's attention. He did not stir but rolled his eyes up slightly to the mirror affixed to the top of his computer. He saw a shape go by the door. It passed quickly, but Buck recognized the color of Rich's suit and the sweep of his overcoat. The footsteps held his attention even after the sound faded into the silence of the late hour in the office. The door clicked open and banged shut. Buck wondered if Rich noticed the light in his office or his own shape bent over the desk. It mattered just a little, not to gain points toward promotion or some mild blessing, but to reassure Rich that the office remained important to someone other than Rich himself.

Buck rolled his eyes to the bottom right corner of the screen and read 7:05 pm. He was more relaxed with Rich away; now he was not there to show anyone anything, just to do his work. He could focus in completely.

He pressed the key to generate a regression on the data he had marked. The computer hesitated and Buck looked up at the clock on the wall while he waited the few seconds the computer required. His urge to look away from the screen was generated by his need to keep moving mentally. It hurt to look at the computer delay. The time on the clock did not register with him immediately because he was still considering what the regression result would tell him. The regression came out and he studied it for a few seconds, enough to tell it was indeterminate. He tried another ploy and another until he suddenly he realized it was past 8:00. He sat back in his chair and relaxed his shoulders. He was not going to reach a conclusion on Pulter tonight. He might as well go home. He felt charged with the intensity of his engagement with the data, but he figured he was mentally exhausted and was not likely to get a breakthrough until he had slept. He had used all his evening time on Pulter and ignored the data from Keahi. He wanted to see her although it was not professionally responsible to go to a client without having something to report. Of course, he realized there was no professional relationship between them despite his pretense. He logged off and then did a quick inventory of his bodily needs, concluding that he ought to eat before stopping at Keahi's apartment although he had no food with him and was worried he might arrive so late she would distrust his sobriety. He looked in the office coat closet, hoping someone had left a sweater or scarf behind, but there was nothing extra there. He would have to endure the cold again without proper clothes. He would take a cab to minimize his exposure. The cost of it would irritate him further.

Outside he walked to the corner where he might be able to hail a cab. He felt foolish for not calling for a taxi before he left the office. He stamped his feet on the sidewalk, imagining that might warm him, while he looked up the street for a taxi. Suddenly he felt a hand on his shoulder. With an unnatural level of self-control, he turned casually, without appearing startled.

"What the hell are you doing here, Walid?"

"Waiting for you."

"What for? Why didn't you call?"

"I thought you might find a way to ditch me if you knew I was out here."

"How long have you been here? Have you noticed it is cold tonight? Ditch you? Why would I do that?"

"An experienced Northerner once told me to dress in many layers when it is cold so I am comfortable enough. On the other question, I figured you might see Keahi after work and I thought I would tag long."

Buck could not decide if he was more surprised that Walid would want to go along or that Walid was exactly right that he was going to see Keahi. Walid sensed Buck's surprise and muttered softly while looking along the street, understanding they were awaiting a taxi, "I don't need to be close enough for her to see me."

"Walid, I still don't get it."

"I know you are still mixed up with her and it is not good. I might help. You don't want me to help, but I am not asking for your permission."

"Why do you think I am in touch with her?"

"I know you. Don't you realize that?"

"You sound pretty sure of yourself."

"I'm not sure you are going there now, but I am sure you are trying to keep me away because you think she is dangerous. You would not mind telling me more about her if she was just an interesting woman."

"Walid, look over my shoulder!"

"What? I don't see anything."

"Don't look down now. There are sneakers on your feet!"

"I know that. I know how you are always running places so I wore them. It's all right. I'm wearing three pairs of socks too. See how the laces are open real wide?"

Buck did not mean any disrespect in thinking Walid was not the right person for the situation. It was not that he was not smart enough and surely he was more experienced than Buck in many ways, but he was just too nice, too generous, to deal with characters Buck suspected were involved. Yet Walid had made his way through the unsympathetic pathways of immigration to become a success by any standard of measure: more successful than Buck professionally, making more money, married to a great woman, living in a better place. Buck could find no objective basis for his reluctance to accept Walid's help. He would have insisted on helping if the circumstances were reversed.

Walid had been through far more in life, having been born moderately poor in a very poor part of a marginally poor country, and went through whatever unlikely path to establish himself in America. He was not secretive about how he had managed this, but he never volunteered any details. He did not act proud of his accomplishments. He was content to leave the past where it lay. Yet Buck was right to doubt Walid was an apt collaborator in the task at hand. He lacked the requisite deviousness. He had seen evil, but never practiced it. It might have been that the stresses of his life had been so direct, he had not needed to contend with the underhanded techniques of the brutes who bother to seek the impression of respectability. This gap in his capabilities was so pronounced, it seemed inherent in him, fundamental, genetic in origin. Nature or nuture? Is it possible to have the habit of believing well of people in contradiction to all evidence, due to some quirk in the brain? Was there within some group of our early ancestors a period of tens of thousands of years in which this was an attribute favoring survival?

Buck, on the other hand, had no fundamental need to struggle except as it is part of the human condition. He did not feel born to privilege, but he was born to a complete and stable family in a rich and stable country; born with physical health and vigor, and provided, without his asking, with comfort and education and security. Despite this relative ease, and like many an over-confident American male of his class and ethnicity, he regarded himself as a dangerous customer should there be need to act as one. And Buck was not far off in his unpracticed confidence. He knew how to be devious and had not learned fear. He had learned and practiced deviousness during the difficult period in which he forged his own identity, independent of the well-meaning guidance of parents and pastor. The package of values and skills and security he had been handed at birth inhibited his finding a personality he could respect in himself. He was smart enough to see that his apparent successes were not due to him as much as to the gifts he had been granted.

The first skill he discovered in himself that was not consistent with the aspirations imposed upon him was in grappling for dominance with the boys his age. He was quicker and stronger than he looked. He lost only once at the slapping game. In the best known form, each player holds his hands horizontally in front of himself, palm-to-palm with his opponent. The one on the bottom tries to hit the top of the other's hand in one motion. A miss or a false start means the positions must be reversed. A flinch means a free slap. The game is mostly about who is quicker but the winner is also determined by who hits harder and who can play through the pain of the slaps. He sometimes won in a single slap. There were a few, but only a few times, when he was not the quicker player and he won on being willing to take the hits. The time he lost was the last time he played. He was twenty, out of his teens, but not yet a man. He was playing with a football player at his college, unquestionably bigger and stronger than Buck. Buck looked forward to embarrassing him in front of the guys in the dorm. The football player had played the game many times, and expected to win on his talents. The first blow from each cracked loudly but neither showed any sign of pain. They were evenly matched at first, scoring two or three hits before a miss. Five minutes into the contest, both of them were shaking from the elbows down and still both were expressionless, looking straight into the eyes of their opponents. Eventually Buck began to dominate the hits. He made ten or fifteen hits before a miss and then escaped on the first try by his opponent. The palms of his hands became red and sore. He began to do fancy slaps, crossing his arms, doing both hands, hitting the same hand twice in a try. It was clear he could hit at will and still the football player held on without a word. When Buck's palms became sore, the back of his opponent's hands began to shed skin. They became bloody. The veins stood out. The hands shook so much Buck could have called flinch at any time and taken a free slap. The blood splattered onto their bare chests. Finally, after twenty minutes, with half the dorm looking on, Buck spoke for the first time. He reached out, grabbed the wrist of his opponent, raised his arm up and said, "You win."

Buck was an ordinary boy in most ways but quick and strong and competitive enough to become a sometime bully although he rejected the role when he noticed it in himself. He felt he had a power and that he had a responsibility to use it well. As he got bigger, the boys his age were closer to men and the ones still working through their self-image by physical contest were more capable of harm. Buck figured out he could be hurt in the petty contests for group rank, but his ego would not let him give up the contest with anyone who claimed to be above him. He had tactics for escalating faster than his opponent and for breaking off when necessary. Being able to run well was a nice tool. Most important, for all mammalian males, was to avoid harm by projecting confidence. It is hard to fake when the testing begins. With experience, the bluff of words and looks and flexing and boasting had no effect on Buck. But the first pushes and punches and grasps reveal quickly who has the superior native talents. If those tests did not bode well, Buck had to decide between ending it somehow or raising the stakes faster than his opponent could or would. That was based on an assessment of mental state and capacity. It had never been an emotional contest for Buck. When things were most heated, he watched the affair from somewhere outside the fray.

"Walid, my man, I would keep you out of it if I thought it were dangerous. And, well, I think it might be a little bit dangerous. It is not about a woman I want to have. I would want you to be part of that story. This is because I got started and I don't want to stop too fast. I am just playing a few cards and if there are no winners, I am out. Mainly, I am making it easy to get out. I need to keep it simple, man."

"You're saying I'm out?"

"Don't be insulted. I'll tell you if anything comes up. The cards I have are not likely to turn up anything."

"Will I have to follow you in a separate cab then?"

"C'mon, man. Go home to dinner with Masha."

"There's no dinner there. Masha is not expecting me until late." Walid continued to speak quietly and to watch the traffic for a taxi with an "on duty" light.

Buck put a hand on Walid's shoulder, standing behind him, shaking his head as if talking to himself. "I don't know exactly where Keahi is and I know she has no dinner waiting for me. Do you mind a quick stop for fried chicken? I have a lead on her whereabouts. We can try it afterwards."

"Is there someplace near here?"

"Two blocks," answered Buck and led off. They did not speak along the way. It was not necessary. The fast food palace was garishly lit on an otherwise dim street. One step inside the door and Buck had the sensory transition of a tropical vacation: the humid heat covered his face, the spicy odors filled his nostrils, and the multi-glot conversations of people poorer than himself wafted through his ears. The clerks were polite, efficient; the chicken and sides were quick and utterly predictable in quality. Buck reveled in the easy satisfaction it all brought to his appetite, aware that the memory of his greasy fingers and tongue would disgust him for a month or so before he could enjoy another visit.

Buck sketched in his general plan. He would hope to catch Keahi at home and try to get her to explain herself better. She could at least explain the connection between the data she had given him and her dilemma. But they would have to be careful to leave no track from her to their lives, a track that might bring nuisance from thugs or FBI.

Walid objected to Buck's way of framing the issue as a professional undertaking, as if from a movie rather than as a personal favor to a woman in need, but he kept his reservations to himself, still doubting there was any real danger. Maybe he had faced so many threats far more direct than what he had heard in Keahi's case, it seemed to him Buck was romanticizing the encounter. Buck always thought the woman he was currently seeing was the most extraordinary woman in the world. Why not turn an odd encounter with a foreign woman into a spyful intrigue?

This time Buck thought ahead and asked Walid to call for a taxi. They exited three blocks from the apartment and not on the same street. Buck did not mean to play a movie role, but he had seen enough in the movies to understand taxi records can be subpoenaed. Both Buck and Walid were soon cold again; Buck because he was underdressed and Walid because he was not used to cold and had not taken off enough layers during the heat of their dinner.

They walked past the apartment twice to see if anyone was loitering nearby. Buck noted that someone could be monitoring from a window, but there was no way to be completely safe. Having access to another apartment was more likely, he guessed, from police or other government people if they, rather than thugs, were pressuring her. The good thing to remember, he told Walid, is that they had not done anything at all illegal. Walid found a dark corner in view of the door and agreed to watch from there.

They had seen no one go in or out of Keahi's building, so Buck doubted he could get inside by catching the door when someone left it ajar in passing. He took the obvious next step and looked for Keahi's name at the entry. It was not there. He rang the apartment with the number written on his paper. A woman's voice asked who was there. He said "It's me" slowly, hoping Keahi would recognize his voice. The door buzzed open without another word from the speaker. There was an elevator but he walked up the two flights. The door had a small card affixed to it with a person's name, but it was not Keahi. He knocked and the receptionist from Ringstare answered him with a smile. It occurred to Buck that she might have trapped him for some personal reason or as part of the plot against Keahi. He did not go inside immediately and smiled as broadly as he could without looking false.

The room smelled of cooking, but more of baking than frying; not a bad odor. Buck could feel the dust that probably was not present, it looked very tidy, but it was covered everywhere in thick fabrics, carpeting, slip covers over soft upholstery, pillows, an afghan, tablecloth, and drapes. Every fabric had its own pattern, most of which were not prints, but woven. It was dark and the heavy curtains suggested it would be dark at any time day or in any season. There was too much furniture, leaving no floor space except to maneuver carefully from sitting place to sitting place. It was a single woman's apartment, one who had been there a long time.

"I am looking for Ms. Dam, to return her laptop."

"Come inside, please. I do not want to disturb the neighbors."

"Is she here? I cannot leave the laptop with anyone but her."

"Please come inside." She held the door open but stepped aside to give him room to pass. She was not attractive enough or trying to be attractive enough to imagine he could be seduced.

"May I get you something to drink?"

He would have liked something hot, but did not want to stay any longer than necessary.

"I thought you looked up Ms. Dam's address."

"I looked for it but her file was missing. No one had signed it out. People often forget to sign out files but something very strange is going on with Keahi and I want it to stop. She is not happy and I cannot get her to tell me anything."

"You are Margaret Perkins, the name on the door? I am Marty Morgan." He shook her hand. "Are you friends? Have you tried to understand her present situation?"

"We're not close, but, sure, I know her. She has always been good. Would you like coffee or tea or something stronger?"

"I do not even have time to sit down, thank you. But why did you give me your address?"

"I know where she lives. Not the address, but I have been there and I can find it again."

"Will you show me?"

"Why do you want her? Are you a friend?"

"I am sure I know her less than you do. She asked for my help. There is not much I can do, but I will not abandon her if I can help."

"So you know what they are doing."

"Not everything. Can you tell me what you know?"

"I don't know anything. I am not even sure what work *she* does. She has been with us over a year and works in the room full of cubicles. She was always very courteous, and talked to me about things, little things like the weather or the news. She goes to some of the big company meetings but I am never there. A few weeks ago, she became very serious and I see two men are always with her coming and going. She has no time to chat with me. Like I said, she does not seem happy."

"Are you going to show me her place? We can see her together so you are sure I am not part of the problem."

"I don't want to get involved, not real close anyway. Something is not right. I can help you but I don't want my company to think I did anything. I like my job; like it enough, I guess. It's hard to find work. Maybe there is nothing fishy and I will be making enemies of my bosses for nothing."

"So you can point me to her place?"

"I'd like to help, but I don't know you either. You're not a poet from the street."

"You didn't like my poem? I told you, it was only a first draft."

"Maybe you are a poet, but that does not mean you are good for Keahi or safe for me."

"When you're right, you're right. What do you propose? You were willing to let me get this far."

"I don't know. I was only thinking one step ahead. I did want to help her if I could.

"So I need to convince you? I know a few things about Keahi's case. I have been in touch with some unsavory people in it. She came to me and asked for help... Er, I am very careful to avoid causing her any more trouble. I saw her at your workplace, but she was with some quiet men and I did not speak to her. She saw me, I think, and did not speak to me. How much do you want to know? Knowing less might be a good thing for you."

"You saw her at Ringstare?"

"I saw her leaving. Some men drove away with her."

"She is a nice lady, you know."

"I can see you are as well."

"I don't know what they are doing to her and I don't know why they are doing it. We never had anything like this before."

"How long have you worked at Ringstare?"

"Almost eight years now. Keahi came recently, long after I did."

"Your website is not too clear about what the company does. What is it you do?"

"Well, I manage the reception, keep appointments, make sure the executives know what is coming up. Nothing that gets me into the business itself."

"But what would you say is the business? Ringstare does not make anything, I know. What is the service it provides?"

"Mostly it helps companies that want to get a start in the city, companies from all over America. We find real estate and make contacts with suppliers and transportation... Things like that."

"Getting permits and tax breaks sometimes?"

"Permits, yes. Maybe tax issues. I don't know about that that. Our people do know the political people here."

"I can see lots of room for danger in these arrangements. I doubt Keahi would understand much about local personality types."

"Yeah, she was not an innocent babe, but I suppose our culture is all pretty strange to her. Poor girl...Just a minute while I get my coat."

Buck had not taken off his coat so he waited by the door while Margaret Perkins dug a long cloth coat out of the closet, slowly buttoned herself in and tied a scarf carefully around her neck. She was not a hasty woman. Her delay gave Buck a highly productive minute to connect her description of the company to the data from Keahi. The file linked clients to payments that should have been kept invisible. If so, the file would have been given special attention in the office. If Keahi noticed that, she might have targeted it for use some way, maybe she would become a hero by finding it when the bosses panicked or she could find a way to sell it back to them or she could use it as security against being turned in to immigration or... he did not know why she would steal a file. There was no legitimate justification and yet she had done it and now he had it. She was no saint and Buck had no idea how to undo the theft.

Margaret locked the door as they left and then put on her gloves and hat as she went down the stairs. By the time they reached the building door, both she and Buck were unrecognizable bundles of winter cloth. As soon as they stepped outside, Buck let Margaret go a step ahead of him and he cleared out one nostril onto the snowbank. This gesture was to ensure Walid recognized him. He looked around the nearby buildings but did not see Walid, which he took as a good sign that Walid was being careful. Of course it might also mean that Walid had gotten cold and gone inside or left. Or it could mean that nefarious men had taken him away to torture him for information. Buck hoped he would not hold out to the point where he was harmed; better to give up Buck's name and let Buck deal with the consequences.

Margaret turned back to Buck, wondering why he was not walking beside her and he moved forward. He coughed to disguise the sound be had made when clearing his nose, as if that had been a cough too. He was surprised that she remarked on how it must have gotten colder since she had gotten home. He was himself too tense to notice the temperature but it was unlikely it had changed anyway, having been so cold all day. Her comment was just something to say to be polite, but he looked at the weather since she brought it up. Snow was falling lightly again, just enough to show fresh footprints any place that had been cleared to the pavement or the sidewalk.   There were no prints outside Margaret's building, not even Buck's from when he had gone in, so the snow had returned in just the last ten minutes. A stiff breeze was arising, blowing from the east, the direction Margaret was taking. Buck muttered something sarcastic about how much they needed some more snow, but Margaret could not hear him well with the hat pulled over her ears so they fell into a silent trek, each leaning forward and looking down to keep the snow and frigid air off the face as much as possible.

As they waited for a stoplight to turn green at a corner with no moving cars in sight, Margaret pulled Buck's face close so she could say she thought Keahi's apartment was in the next block. Buck gave a firm grunt to make clear he understood her. As soon as they crossed that street, Buck saw what he had been looking to see, a parked car with its engine running. It was out of the light so he could not see how many heads were inside but the cold air made a conspicuous cloud of the exhaust fumes. He put an arm around Margaret and stopped her. Holding her close, almost intimately, he asked her to count the front doors along the block so he would know which one was Keahi's. He did not want her to go any closer. She wanted to take him the rest of the way, and he did not want to worry her more so he laughed that he was always much too cautious and that he did not want to keep her away from her warm rooms any longer than necessary. And then he added that he would not tell Keahi how he had found her place. Margaret could say whatever she wanted of this evening, take credit for helping or stay out of it entirely.

Margaret looked over his shoulder while he held her close and counted out the doorways. "She's in the sixth one. On the right, the same side as we're on. Her apartment is on the third floor. There's only one apartment on each floor in her building."

"Is the door to the building locked or will I need to ring her?"

"You have to call her. Should I call the police or something?"

"No, I don't expect any problem. I'll have a talk with Keahi and make sure she's alright."

"But I am worried someone will do something to you."

"That is sweet of you. I am not a very threatening guy. I'll just leave before there is any real trouble. I'll call you at work tomorrow and tell you how it went, OK?"

Margaret answered in a low voice that his suggestions were acceptable, but she did not pull away from him and return home. She was sheltered from the cold breeze by his body and sensed no harm would come to either of them as long as they stood right where they were on the dark, quiet street, though they were so near the uncertainty of whatever was so odd about Keahi.

Buck had grasped Margaret's arm to hold her attention back when she answered his question about whether the building entrance would be locked. Now he broke loose of her and stepped back. "You were a good friend tonight. You can go home without worries. Good night, Margaret Perkins." Buck smiled. Margaret could not see it, but it came across in his voice and she slowly turned around and began to walk back. With the wind behind her, walking was easier than it had been when she was going directly into her worries. Buck looked in her direction as she crossed the street but his attention was reaching farther along the street, searching, unsuccessfully, for a sign of Walid.

He faced back into the wind and counted six doorways. It occurred to him he could easily go back home then. He might be able to put in some time on the Pulter files. He could not be traced by Keahi or Ringstare. If he spoke no more of it, Walid might enjoy the mystery and keep his silence, assuming he was sure Buck was not going forward without him.

The parked car was near the sixth door. They were not trying to hide from Keahi; she would know they were there. At least it indicated they were not inside her apartment. Buck stopped ten or fifteen yards from the parked car, standing under the closest streetlight. He took out his pad and paper, glad that he had remembered to equip himself this time, and wrote down their license number. He could not see it perfectly, but made a guess on a couple digits, and added some notes on the make and color of the car. He waited to catch the attention of the men inside. Just as he was starting to think they were going to ignore his act, they emerged, each from his own side of the car, chattering a continuation of the conversation they had begun inside the car; it sounded contentious. Buck imagined neither of them wanted to be bothered to go into the cold air to deal with the stranger under the lamppost.

"Is there a problem?" the shorter man asked as he approached Buck.

"Not for me," answered Buck.

"It's that asshole from the other night, back at the Fog," the taller man noted for his partner.

"That right? We see you before? Back at the Black Fog?" asked the shorter one.

"I believe I might have seen you then."

"And you ran off like a pussy?"

"You left before I did. Somebody in a long, dark American car picked you up. I got the number, but it's not with me right now."

"What'r you hangin' around for? Whadda you want?" the shorter one asked.

"What would I like? I'd like you to leave Keahi alone, but I doubt you will leave just because I want it."

"You trying to protect her? She hire you for that?"

"No, not really. She's just a friend. Doesn't deserve the intimidation."

"Intimidation? We haven't done anything like that. We're just sitting in a car."

"Sure. Enjoy yourselves," and Buck touched his forehead with a finger as a departure signal; he turned toward Keahi's door. The shorter man grabbed his arm at the elbow.

"I wasn't done with you yet."

"Is there something I can do for you?"

"You're askin' what I want? Well, I want you to mind your own business. I want it that I never see you again.

Keahi's not your type. Just bug out. And I plan to make what I want come true. I don't give shit whether you like it or not."

The short man stepped close to Buck and Buck stepped backwards. They did this twice until Buck bumped his back against the railing beside the steps going into Keahi's building.

"Is what you want to stand close to me?" asked Buck. "Don't make like it's the playground. Say what you have to say. You don't need to get intimate; I'm listening."

"I already said it. You just didn't listen."

"I heard you. It's not hard to see you want me to forget my friend. And I figure you heard me well enough that I want you to forget her, though I doubt you are her friend. So we understand each other. Good night." Buck slipped sideways to get past the short man. The taller one moved to block Buck from leaving the space beside the railing.

"I can't abandon her if you make me stand beside her stoop."

"You getting smart and getting ready to leave?"

"Yeah, I don't need any trouble. I don't know her that well anyway. I'll just go home now. It's too damn cold to be out here at night. When is it ever going to stop snowing anyway?"

The short man stepped back just enough for Buck to get past him, pressed against both men. Buck looked at the ground and shook his head while he took a few steps away from them. Standing at the foot of the stairs, he cupped his hands to form a megaphone and shouted back in the direction he had come from, "Hey man, call 911! Don't send 'em here yet, but get 'em on the line."

"What an idiot. You think we're that dumb?" laughed the short man. "Stop shouting or we'll drop you right here."

"Just one more moment," Buck answered. "You'll want to hear this one." He turned slightly so he could run if they came forward and cupped his hands again. "Give me a shout when you have 'em on the line!"

"You want to get hurt. We can arrange that," said the short man and he took one step forward before he heard Walid shout, "They're waiting! Should I give 'em the address?"

The two men looked around. Walid could not be seen.

"I lied about abandoning my friend," said Buck and he went up the stairs. Before going inside, he cupped his hands again and shouted up the street, "Hang up for now!"

Walid's voice called back slowly, "All right. I am hanging up... for now!"

Chapter 11

KEAHI'S PLACE

As Margaret Perkins had instructed him, Buck walked up to the third floor and knocked on the door. He heard a scraping sound inside so he stepped back and looked at the faint light coming from under the door in one place where the weather-stripping was missing. The spot went dark, but no one answered the door. He stood close to the door and spoke firmly. "Keahi, this is your friend from the Black Fog. I am sorry to come at this late hour. May we talk a minute?"

The latch clicked and the door opened an inch. An eye saw what it could through the gap and the door opened a little more. Keahi had recognized Buck but was trying to see if he was alone.

"Come in quick," Keahi breathed softly, holding the door open just enough for him to squeeze past. She immediately closed it again and pushed the bureau against it. She had removed one of the drawers and fitted it against the hallway wall to lock the bureau in place. Buck was impressed by her effective stratagem. He waited silently nearby while she barricaded them in. She then turned to him and grabbed at his scarf to unwrap it. Her hands passed over his chest a little more than strictly necessary.

He smiled and asked "How are you, Keahi? Surprised to see me here, I bet."

"Oh. Mr. Buckminster, I am so scared! They will not let me alone! Yes, how did you find me?" She acted frantic, moving in too many, too quick gestures. Her eyes darted around the room as if someone else were there. Her nervousness was reasonable but infectious nonetheless, and Buck looked around again, half expecting to see someone he missed in his first glance. It was a cheap living room with relatively new, matching furniture like that newlyweds who have enough money to get themselves started might have purchased after long, pleasant debates between themselves. More personally, there was a set of calendar photos pinned neatly on the wall, depicting Asian, maybe Laotian, scenery. The kitchenette was separated from the room by a short counter on which a single dinner setting was neatly laid out. A small television was on with the sound turned down low, but maybe still loud enough to hear if you sat close. He saw no newspapers or magazines. A few books sat on a shelf. They looked like reference books mostly. The book on the end, however, was a best seller in hardcover with a plastic dust jacket, like libraries use.

"Doesn't matter. Have things changed? I cannot get you by telephone anymore. Are you alone here?"

"Yes, I am alone inside. They took my phone. They won't let me speak to anyone. How did you get in here? Aren't they waiting outside?"

"Do you know what they want from you? I mean specifically what they are waiting for?"

"Yes, I know now. At least I know in a sort of a way.
I can get you something? Would you like some tea?"

Keahi placed his coat on a hanger and hung it on a
hook on the wall. She came back to him and passed her
hands over his chest and then dropped them to one of his
hands, holding it firmly with both of hers. This posture of
familiarity felt good to Buck. Her breath was slowing to a
more normal pace.

"I see you have a place set. Did you have dinner
yet?"

"That's for tomorrow. I live alone so I get the next
dinner ready when I wash the dishes." She laid her head on
his shoulder.   Buck shivered as if he has just come out of a
cold bath. This was not the time to enjoy Keahi.

"Is there any other way out of here, other than that
door?" and Buck pointed at the barricade.

Keahi sat up straight and answered simply, "No."

Buck touched her face, caressed it really, if only
briefly. Then he went to the window, looking through the
slats of the Venetian blinds. "Any fire escape?"

Again, just a "No."

"Do you have a trash chute?"

"What's that?"

"Never mind; just a bad idea." Buck could see Mutt
and Jeff in their car. That was good since it meant they were
not looking for Walid. "Tell me what they want; keep
talking." Buck went into the bedroom while Keahi stayed on
the couch.

"I think they want you. They changed from asking me things I don't know about the business and now they ask me about you: who are you; what do you know; what do you want, who do you know. They call you the 'detective lover'. I tell them you are not my lover."

"Not yet," Buck thought to himself but he would not be distracted by thinking about it while barricaded against Mutt and Jeff. "Do they know you gave me a thumbdrive?"

"Yes. I had to tell them. I'm sorry to make so much trouble for you."

"You had faith in me, Keahi. There was not much reason for it, but you had faith. I appreciate that. I should have such faith in myself."

There was a polite knock at the door.

Keahi stared at Buck.

"Say you are coming," he suggested and she did so but he held out a hand to indicate she should stay seated. He came close to her ear and whispered, while smelling her most pleasant aroma. "When they are inside, go ahead and tell them whatever you know about me. I don't think you know very much beyond what a nice guy I am."

A more insistent knock rang out.

Buck grabbed his coat and ran into the bathroom. He opened the window and looked down past two stories into an alley. "Can you get me a few sheets?"

Keahi jumped up and quickly found for him a few pages of letter paper. "No, I mean bedsheets," Buck explained as he went back to the front window to check on

Mutt and Jeff. Only Jeff was there, standing beside a long, black caddie, talking to someone inside.

A firm voice came through all the doors to Buck's ear. "Miss Dam, I know you don't want any police involved here, right?"

"I am coming! Just a moment!" Keahi called out. She pointed to the closet in the bedroom.

"Let them come, but slow them down a little, please. It's good they are after me. You'll be OK... Wait, what's the name of the biggest boss at Ringstare?"

"That's Mr. Tarwicks."

Buck found sheets in the bedroom closet and took three of them with him into the bathroom and locked the door behind himself. He tied one sheet to the radiator before he heard the sound of the bureau being dragged away from the apartment door. They were inside the apartment before he had the second sheet tied to the first and he heard them pounding on the bathroom door a few seconds later. He could hear Keahi screaming "There is no one here." He hoped the noise did not inspire a neighbor to call 911. The door frame splintered on the first good try. Probably a real brute had slammed against it. The third sheet was only tied loosely when Buck threw his makeshift rope out the window and clambered behind it. The bathroom door flew open before his head was below the window and he peeked inside at the brute falling onto the floor.

The sheets were an easy climb down. Buck was glad he did not need to go upwards to escape. Together, they were not long enough to get him to the ground, but they reached far enough. He rolled into the snow and lay still for a moment, looking up at the bathroom window where someone was yelling at him. "Come on down yourself!" he called back and jogged out to the street. The man he called Jeff was leaning against the Caddie but he jumped forward when Buck came out of the alley. Buck ran along the street as if to go past him, and turned as they came even and lowered his shoulder into the heavy man. Then he was running down the street again. He turned to look back when he reached the end of the block. No one was following him yet. He waved his hand for Walid to join him.

He heard Walid call out "Should I call 911 again?"

"No man. Where are you?" Walid stepped onto the street and ran over to Buck.

"Good man, Walid. We're done here. I think it went well. Let's see if we can get away now. You lead!" They jogged along the street to their right for a block and turned again, still running for another block and turned again. Finally Buck called to Walid, "Pull over!" and they hid in a shadowed doorway for a few minutes, panting for breath. Although neither could see the other's face in the dark, they were both wearing broad smiles.

The night was not quite over. On his way home, Walid's phone rang. He thought it would be Masha checking to see when he would be back but it was a rude man who answered Walid's neutral "hello" with a question that sounded like an accusation, "Who are you?"

"Who are you calling?" Walid asked in return as he looked for the return number, trying to recall the number he called for Keahi.

"You called here before. You wanted a certain Asian lady."

"You mean Ms. Dam? But I was told she was not at this number anymore."

Walid could hear someone arguing on the other end. He thought he heard them say he was not the one. Walid did not understand what they meant. He did not realize the person who called him had spoken to Buck several times and knew he had a different voice or, at least, a different accent. Finally the man came back to Walid. "What did you want from her?"

"Pardon me," answered Walid. "I will have to speak to her about it."

"Where were you tonight?"

Walid tried to imagine how he would respond if he had nothing to do with the caper. "Excuse me, I need to get to bed." He hung up and waited for a call back. None came and he made his way back to his innocent wife.

Chapter 12

FOURTH MORNING OF THE STORM

Buck sat up in bed suddenly. He must have had an exciting dream, but he could not remember anything of it. It was dark except for the dull red glow of his digital clock. Five antemeridian; an hour before the right time to be getting up; right as defined by the patterns he had intentionally ground into his biology prior to the snowfall. He had much too little sleep on this particular night to be starting out a new day early, despite the energy he felt upon waking. He bounded up from the bed and went straight to his desk to make some notes to capture whatever brilliance might be real in the euphoria of the moment. The ideas flowed in a torrent and took shape, reaping the careful work his brain had accomplished while he slept.

From his seat at the desk, he could look through the partly open blinds. There was not enough light to see through to the neighboring buildings or the street, but he could see the passage of snowflakes near his window, lit by the light from his room. He watched them, wondering how it could still be snowing and suspecting he might be dreaming. To test himself, he daydreamed a memory of his mother reading to him when he was too young to read himself. Somehow he knew it was impossible to night dream and daydream at the same time.

228

It was the story of The Snow Queen and the first metaphor he ever heard. Two children heated coins on the stove so they could thaw a spot of the ice on the window and peek out on a winter day, a day like the one Buck awoke to find every day this week. Their grandmother explained they were seeing the white bees swarming. The story must have been written in an era when children knew enough of nature to know that bees swarm. He could see the bees in the snowflakes, just as he had when his mother read the story to him. But he did not stare outside for long, as his urge to make notes was more compelling.

His notes began sketchy; they were intended to get all the ideas down in a form that would help him retrieve them and expand upon them within a day. They made sense to his waking mind and grew quickly to more substantive form. The data had told its part of the story and now he knew how to write the new chapter. It would all be resolved this day, the fifth day of the storm.

By seven o'clock, he was spending more time watching snowflakes in the dawning light than he was in making notes. His inspiration had run dry yet he was satisfied that it had been enough. He phoned Walid. Marya answered the call.

"Hello," she said in a friendly tone that quickly changed when she realized who had called.

"Oh hi, Marya. Is Walid..."

"What in the world are you doing? Walid won't tell me a thing. I know he is not misbehaving and that only can mean that *you* are. You tell me what is going on."

"Marya! You are exactly right of course. I am misbehaving in my way. Believe me, you do not want to know the details."

"I can't have you doing this to Walid, Buck. I don't need to know *your* business, but I won't let Walid get himself in a place he can't get out of. I know he will go wherever you tell him to go and that is not always to a good place. I told him it's great to have friends; I tell him you are a great friend to have, and he still has to take responsibility for his actions. He has to put his own welfare first but you know full well he won't do that."

"And Marya, you know that I will put Walid's welfare before my own, don't you? You know that Walid will always put your welfare first? We are not the little boys we seem to be. We are responsible and we know it. Even me."

"Bullshit! You are exactly the little boy you seem to be. You live for the adventure of the moment! Don't make Walid be so simple!"

"Marya... You have a good man there. Respect your man. Put him on the phone."

There was a delay and Walid came to the phone.

"Hello, Buck."

"You all right?"

"Yeah, sure. How 'bout you?"

"Slept well, thanks."

"Buck, they called me last night."

"What'd they say?"

"Nothin'. Seemed grouchy. I think they might have been looking for you."

"What'd you say?"

"Nothin., I was polite."

"Of course you were. Can you meet at the café at eight o'clock?"

"I'll be there."

"Give my love to Marya."

"I'll do you a favor and not mention your name to her for a while."

"Better yet."

Next Buck called the café. The phone rang eight times before a male voice answered.

"All-Wright Drug."

"Good morning. May I speak with Ms. Sarah?"

"Sorry, I don't know anyone with that name. This is the All-Write Drug store.

"Yes, I know. She works in the café. She should be there by now."

"The café? Maybe. She's at work then. You'll have to call back later when her shift is over."

"This is not a personal call. I am a customer. She agreed to prepare a breakfast to fit my religious requirements if I called this number. Can't you get her to the phone?"

"Religious? Oh, let me see if she's here."

Buck was surprised that he was not put on hold. He waited several minutes with the drugstore end of the conversation sitting open until he heard footsteps approaching and a voice: "Hello?"

"Hello Sarah. Nice to hear you. I am sorry to take you away from the café at opening hour."

"Who is this? I don't remember any religious issue."

"Never mind the religion thing. This is your friend Buck. Look, I need to find an ice cave that may or may not exist in this endless storm and your help is essential."

"You make me sound very important, Mr. Buck."

"The time is now, Ms. Sarah. I must make my move this morning. Eight o'clock, to be specific. Can you contact Angela? I don't need to speak to her; only to invite her to the crucial meeting at eight o'clock."

"I do not know how to reach her. She just comes in. She is usually here at ten."

"Ten, yes, I know. But ten will be too late. I have to move before then. I will move without her if I must. She is the ice cave. She is the impossible, the unreal. You know what I mean? But she is in your café every day at ten o'clock. I leave it to you. I will be there at eight."

"Does two hours matter in the big picture."

"The big picture is the problem. I must act early today. I cannot wait for the impossible to occur."

""What religion is this that is troubling you, Mr. Buck?"

"Tell Angela there is a right moment and that is eight o'clock or never. She may choose 'never', but it must be her choice."

Buck was at the café ten minutes early. He stood outside and waited for the right moment, trying not to think of the meeting he was about to hold with whomever was there. His ideas were ready; he wanted to keep them fresh. He blew his left nostril open at thirty seconds before the hour and went inside a few seconds early. Walid was standing just inside with his coat still on.

"Close the door, man. You may think it is normal out there but for the rest of us it's too damn cold!"

"'Morning, Walid. Marya all right?"

"She's not happy, I guess. She'll be at work in a few minutes and forget all about this little meeting. At least until she gets home tonight."

"Maybe by then we'll have something good to tell her. C'mon, let's sit down. You can take off your coat now."

"I don't believe you think you have this thing worked out after the best we could do last night was run down dark alleys until we couldn't run anymore."

"I don't have it worked out. That's why you're here now. But I feel like I can see all the pieces. It's making sense in a way. Oh hello, Sarah. Nice to see you again. Nice weather again today, don't you think?"

"No, the weather is terrible again today. I won't say otherwise. I just want it to stop snowing so we can get to the part where everything is wet and cold and filthy instead of this crazy falling skies. All night it snows. What is it in the night? What is going on with this weather?"

"It's just winter, Sarah. The spring will follow."

"There's a booth for you in the corner, you know, in case you want some privacy."

"Uh huh. Do you think there will be three for breakfast?"

"Can't say. Maybe. I did what I could."

"You're a champion, Sarah! I'll tell you the whole story if there is ever a story to tell."

"Thanks. Just what I need to hear-- how someone else made it."

"But Sarah! You sell me short. The story would not be about that. There is so much more to it! We'll have to go to dinner at a dinner restaurant when the streets are cleared."

"Meanwhile, what're you having?"

"I'll have two eggs, over easy, with toast, juice, and coffee."

"Orange juice?"

"Yeah, yeah, orange."

"And you?" Sarah asked of Walid.

"My wife sent me out without any breakfast today. Do you have cereal?"

"Hot or cold?"

"I guess hot makes more sense today."

"It made more sense all week."

"Coffee?"

"Yes, coffee and water, please. Oatmeal is it then? And some toast too. Do you have bagels?"

"We have 'em but there're not very good ones."

"Toast then. With jelly, right?"

"Sure, toast with jelly."

Finally, the two men settled into the booth. Buck took out his notebook and reviewed the sparse comments he had put down that morning.

"Are you going to brief me now that you got me out of the house and out of the office?"

"I was hoping that Angela would be here."

"What does she have to do with last night?"

"Good question! That makes a starting point. She can come in later. It won't be bad if she misses this part. Last night was a bit tense, obviously, but there was also a very nice sexual component to it. Probably Keahi was just nervous and she got touchy. Anyway, she was grabbing my hand and caressing me while she was talking about the situation, not talking about us. It was weird."

"Weird? Yes, but it sounds like you liked it an awful lot. Is that the biggest thing you learned last night?"

"No, not at all. Yeah, sure, I liked it, but that's wasn't any news. What I learned was that it wasn't what I wanted. I was thinking about Angela when I felt those fingers on my chest."

"You're crazy!"

"We're all crazy. I have been thinking about Keahi's situation and I have been thinking at some deeper level about how nice it would be if she wanted me, but then I found out there was a deeper level in me; the one that wanted Angela."

"Like I said, you're crazy. I see you were dreaming about Angela but that's not what you need right now or what you needed last night. I know you didn't jump out the window 'cause you decided you wanted Angela more than Keahi."

"True. But that's why I invited Angela to this discussion."

"What discussion? Are going to wait until ten o'clock for her? Am I here to prepare the way for that?"

"No. We're going to help Keahi. But it'll be the coolest thing I ever did and I want to show it to Angela."

"So why do we have to be here so early? And do you really think we can help Keahi somehow? You didn't look like you were in charge last night."

Sadie came by with Buck's orange juice and reminded them to get their coffee themselves from the urns on the end of the counter. She lingered a moment longer than necessary so Buck explained to her that his friend Walid wanted to hear more about what was unfolding in the storm but he, Buck, wanted to share the story more widely. "Telling Walid about it makes it more real, you know, but having another pair of ears would make it into a global show." And he asked if Sarah could take off for fifteen or twenty minutes, she being in the story herself, although he was not serious that she would have been an adequate audience. He just thought it polite to include her as a central character. She had been exceptionally nice to him even if she had not managed to produce Angela. "You, Ms. Sarah, are an essential part of the whole story. I'll have to fill you in on how it turns out eventually."

"Oh, don't worry about explaining to me. I'll see how it turns out on my own."

"Ahh, dear Sarah, you have no idea how intricate is this mystery."

"And you, Mister whatever-your-name-is, have no idea how much I need to keep my job."

"I can imagine. But that does not mean you are not part of it. We do not control entirely whom we affect and what intricate plots we alter by our actions, innocent or no."

"Did I have any effect on you beyond breakfast? Maybe... by delivering Red to you. She could have effects beyond your plans. Most likely, she will mess up your plans, I think. That sort makes men wish for more than they ever get."

"More than that I think. Although I think your best efforts have not delivered the lovely Angela."

"We'll see. I think that is her taking off her coat in the door."

Walid stood up like a gentleman. He watched Angela while Buck gave her only a glance and then turned back to the menu, waiting until she was near before rising. He was very pleased that she had come but did not want to appear desperate for her.

"You want to join this adventure? I need some back-up, someone they do not know. They know Walid. Damn, it is a bad business with nothing to recommend doing it. But you are an adult. Make your own choices. I made mine and Walid made his. Neither one of us was smart but I think we would do it again if the same situation came up. Thank God it never will."

"I'm in," Angela said and she stared into Buck's face.

"Damn, you are an absolutely fantastic woman! I hate to put you at risk, but I hate even worse to patronize you.

"Here's what's you can do. Take these envelopes. I am giving you two copies of each letter; four different letters. Put each set of four letters into a separate safe place. I am not giving any to Walid. It is better for him this way. He may be a target already. The letters describe portions of Ringstare's corrupt deals. Drop one letter in the mail if you do not hear from me once a week."

Walid started to say something, to object to being excluded, as he felt was occurring. He had in mind that he had already demonstrated it would be hard to leave him out, but the exact words to express this did not come to his lips immediately and he simply uttered some grunts that somehow revealed his point. Buck quieted him without even looking his way by reaching across the table quickly and grasping his hand. He held to it as he continued talking to Angela.

"That's all?" Angela asked.

"That's quite a lot, Angela. A lot of risk. I am not Humphrey Bogart. I don't actually know how much risk. If you ever feel uncomfortable with it, just let me know. I will not try to talk you out of quitting."

"I'll do it."

"You are wonderful. I'll need your e-mail or phone number. Here, I'll write out mine for you. You can just send me a message when you get a chance." Buck wrote in large letter and numbers in ink on an All-Wright napkin. While he wrote, Angela smiled at Walid as if Buck were not there. When Buck gave her the note, she read it to be sure it was legible and then tucked it into her purse.

"And now, here is something to listen to. Walid, they have your number already. May I use your phone?" Buck took out his phone and dialed a number he had written in his small notebook. "Hello. I would like to make an appointment to meet Mr. Tarwicks. I would like to see him thirty minutes from now." He recognized Margaret Perkins but did not show it.

...

"Of course he is busy. Life has demands. Tell him I obtained some documents from Ms. Dam and that I fully understand their meaning and their value. And tell him life has its demands on me so I strongly prefer to see him this morning if he is in the city today. Thank you, I'll wait."

Buck pretended to conduct music while he waited, showing Walid and Angela he was listening to elevator music and that he was lighthearted about it all. Neither of them was amused, but they did not interrupt. Buck's pantomime lasted less than a minute. "Hello, Mr. Tarwicks. Thank you for taking my call.

...

"I would rather not go into anything further on the telephone. If you will see me, you will understand. Please be assured, you will be pleased with our meeting.

...

"It will take me few minutes to get there. You are at the office on Bailey Street? May we say 10:00? Thank you. See you soon."

He returned the phone to Walid. "Mr. Tarwicks was in a bad mood, but he took my meeting."

Chapter 13

THE KEAHI STRATEGY

Buck phoned for a taxi and intended to leave the café alone but Angela walked to the door with him, carrying her coat over her arm. He walked a route across the room that passed close to Sarah and touched her elbow with his fingers as he went by. She was occupied by taking a late breakfast order from an elderly couple. Walid stayed at his table, pretending to nurse his coffee although he was antsy about getting to work late; he just wanted to leave some space for Buck.

Outside the café, Buck turned back to look at Angela. The day was dark with thick clouds obscuring the weak sun. A light, frozen rain was falling with a hiss coming from across the cityscape where the hard pellets beat a note across the crusted snow. He took the coat off her arm and placed it over her shoulders. She leaned into him as he did it. It felt right to kiss her on the cheek to complete the action, but he backed off this gesture, preferring to remain in a relatively real world. "It'll be all right," Angela said. Buck looked to the drugstore sign and back to Angela. He grinned broadly. "No, Angela, I think it will be much better than 'all right. There is a big upside to this risk." She looked into the street; tiny drops of ice bounced off her rusty locks and accumulated on her shoulders like sparkling dandruff. Self-

240

consciously, Buck brushed off his own shoulders. When the cab came, Buck and Angela parted with mutual waves that expressed familiarity rather than awkwardness.

The sidewalk from the street to Ringstare's front door had been cleared but the rain had been water for a few minutes in that part of the city and glazed the surface. It needed a sprinkling of sand or salt. Buck pushed on the door but it was locked. He looked for the security camera, faced it directly and rang the bell. A buzz indicated the lock had been released. There was a small hallway to the reception room where Margaret Perkins regarded him with more curiosity than recognition.

She stood up and asked: "May I help you?"

"I have an appointment with Mr. Tarwicks at 10:00. I am a little early. I'll wait until he is available."

"Who should I say is here?" she asked.

"Margaret, I am Keahi's friend. Have you seen her today?"

Her face went pale and she grimaced involuntarily. She put her hand before her face as if to protect herself. "You're here again," she uttered in a whisper mostly to herself.

"Did she come in?"

"She's here," Margaret finally acknowledged as she composed herself. "She was worried about you... Really worried."

"I'm fine. Maybe you can tell her. I have an appointment now with Mr. Tarwicks. Just say his ten o'clock is here. He will not expect any more than that. But before

241

you speak with him, may I see someone who is responsible for security here? Do you have a guard nearby?" Buck did not wink at her but his friendly expression was intended to remind her they knew each other and that he could be trusted.

Margaret made a quiet call from her desk and a thick man in tie and sport coat came in immediately. She pointed at Buck.

"What's the problem?" the security man asked Buck.

"No problem at all, but I am about to meet with Mr. Tarwicks and would like you to search me first. I will loosen my shirt. You should be sure I don't have a wire."

"Why would you want me to do that?"

"I wouldn't but Mr. Tarwicks needs to be sure. Do you have any way to do an electronic scan?"

The door behind Margaret opened and Tarwicks came out. He had the hirsute and lantern-jawed head of a 1950's leading man, like James Garner or Fred MacMurray or Gregory Peck or Mark Trail. It made him seem more formidable than his slight body would have managed on its own, but his eyes burned confidently forward projecting the personality capable of building the dodgy empire Buck had found in Keahi's data.

"This guy wants me to pat him down. Make sure he's not wearing a wire," the security man said to Tarwicks.

"Why would you want that?" Tarwicks asked Buck.

"It would just make our meeting smoother," answered Buck.

"Do it," said Tarwicks. "Send him in when you're through," Tarwick said to Margaret and he turned around and went back into his office. Shortly thereafter, Buck and the security man followed him. Tarwicks was seated behind a desk. He motioned to the security man to leave.

"Good morning Mr. Tarwicks. Thank you for agreeing to see me on such short notice."

Tarwicks rose from his seat and reached out a hand. When Buck grasped it, he was surprised at its meatiness. As they shook, Tarwicks asked "And you are...?"

"No one around here has quite figured that out yet, I believe. We may be able to clarify it today if we stay on good terms. For the present you may call me 'Buck'."

"And you may call me 'Sticky', as long as we are on good terms."

"It's 'Sticky' then." Buck let go of Tarwicks' hand and sat down. Tarwicks sat behind his desk.

"Yes. It comes from the boys in high school who thought my surname sounded like 'tar' and 'wax'. I don't mind it. Everyone remembers my name."

"People tend to sneer at my name. It is pretentious, I suppose, but there are reasons for it. In most situations it's better than my real name."

"What can I do for you today?"

"Apparently you know already that I am a friend of Keahi's. My reason, my only reason, for coming here is to make her life more secure."

"And who is Keahi?"

"Sticky, you are seeing me because you know who she is. We are speaking frankly aren't we? She has given me some information, some confidential information about your firm. I understand information of this sort very well. In fact, I understand it much better than Keahi does."

"We are speaking frankly so you should call it 'blackmail' if that is what you have in mind."

"No, I do not think my offer contains any blackmail. That is not the right word for it. All I want is her security. What I mean is I want her to feel safe. I am not entirely sure of your concerns about her. If it is just the information she has passed on, then we can make a deal that everyone would like, that is, everyone in this room."

"I do not know what information she has given you that you are attempting to bargain with here. These are company trade secrets?"

"I made a list of some choice items and who might be interested in knowing about them. I have not discussed this with Keahi or given her a copy of the list, but I have, of course, placed detailed instructions for the release of this information in the event I am unable to continue suppressing it." Buck slid a page across the table. "You might note that I have been succinct in this report. There are other points I could make."

Tarwicks affected a casual interest when he picked up the paper and intended to glance it only enough to get a general impression. He did not want to acknowledge that there was any leverage in it, but his glance picked up the listing of key partners and informants. He was drawn into the report, enjoying the breadth of his operation although he felt naked to have it all laid out succinctly, as Buck had called it. He was surprised that so much could have been in the documents Keahi stole and he knew he needed to improve his security, not just to limit access of people like Keahi, but to avoid making it possible to get so much in one place. He thought about one item and then another, looking for how he might defend the assertion contained in Buck's notes. It had all been set up to allow plausible deniability or to apply counter-pressure if anyone wanted to reveal too much yet he could see how his operation could be destroyed by clever use of the information already in Buck's control. He wondered if he might hire Buck to improve his records system. Buck kept his head down while Tarwicks studied the paper to give a sense of privacy to the reading but he lifted his eyes from time to time to see the intensity of Tarwicks' attention and he tried very hard to keep any smile from showing.

"I cannot confirm that any of this is accurate, but it does show a very professional approach to blackmail. How did she ever find you?"

"That is immaterial, but you should keep in mind that she doesn't know what she gave me. She just gave me everything and I figured out what it is. She likes her job here and would probably be willing to go on with it, despite the unfortunate stresses she has endured. Of course that is only her naiveté.

"Obviously, I won't walk into a police station and hand over a flash drive. In this town, with all the connections represented in this information, that would have a greater chance of landing me in the river than of getting Keahi out of hock. Giving it to a journalist is just a movie plot line. No, I would not hand it all over to anyone, not the DA the press or some kind of competitor. If I had to push back, I would release one thing just to remind you that I could. More than that, it would be to show whomever in your firm deals with that one thing that it is not productive to trouble me. I plan to live another day."

"Smart guy."

"Please. I am not boasting. It is not that hard to do. I am just pointing out that Keahi is not really a threat to you. I would also point out that I am not either as long as she is secure."

"I guess she needs a hefty raise for being so uninformed."

"I am not concerned with what you pay her. I presume she is underpaid since she is undocumented, but she has not complained about her pay to me. No, money is not at issue. Just treat her decently, will you? I would think the best thing is to find her a job somewhere outside Ringstare. I would say far outside Ringstare but what I really think would be best would be a job you could continue to ensure is secure for her."

"Why should I treat a blackmailer decently?"

"I am not clever with words, Sticky. I speak best in numbers. Looking at the items on that page, I think the small blackmail of a job for a junior employee is not much to ask. I know numbers well enough to know you are getting a very good deal."

"I don't trust such a good deal walking in the door. I can imagine what you are getting from Keahi. That's not a bad thing. But if you are smart enough to write this paper, you are going to think you will get something more from me, maybe not today, but someday."

"For the record, I am not getting anything like you are thinking from Keahi. I do not expect to see her again after today, assuming you and she stay on good terms. I am not a blackmailer in temperament. I live a small life with small ambitions. It would be a great success for me to have no further dealings with her or Ringstare."

"How 'bout a few grand for the holidays? No? How 'bout for your favorite charity? I can find some cash right now in the office. Just to seal the deal."

"You're too kind, Sticky. But that is not who I am."

"The thing is, Buck, the thing about blackmailers is that they tend to come back again. You don't have any insurance for me."

"Sure I do. If I break the deal, you get Keahi deported."

Tarwicks shook his head slowly from side to side. The deal was not safe. He would have walked over to the window and looked at the cityscape except that his office had no window and there would be only a view outside of a sprawling, barren one-story urban neighborhood of small manufacturing shops and some aged residential duplexes. His urge to think drove him away from his desk, just to make some motion. He went to the filing cabinet as if to take out something, but he knew there was nothing in there to help.

He went past the files to his glass-fronted shelves. There were no books in them, but there was a gag book his daughter-in-law gave him for Father's Day. Inside was a flask. She had given it to him filled with Scotch which he presumed was still there and as palatable as ever. He tried to continue his motion, opening the glass door smoothly, as if the flask had been in his mind when he left the desk, but his hesitation halfway across the room had been noticed by Buck. Buck realized the deal he was offering was too sweet if you subtract out his personal reliability. He let Tarwicks have a minute to consider his proposal. Tarwicks busied himself with finding the flask, took a draught and offered it to Buck. Buck turned him down with a smile. "I'll join you when we reach our agreement."

With the distraction of the flask played out, Tarwicks was out of ideas.

Buck took up the initiative. "We're still speaking frankly, right? I want to get my pull on that flask today. You don't know me and really can't appreciate my lack of ambition to exploit this information further someday. You might have had the idea of setting me up with a significant, steady income, not too big, at least until you can get more information on me and improve your leverage."

"Nah, I want to get this done today too. I just need some insurance."

"I see that. Very reasonable. Like I said before, I can give you my name and address today, if we have a deal we both believe in. The thing is, there is not that much I can give you for leverage on me. I don't amount to much. Lack of ambition is a powerful form of protection. I do have a few more cards since I could let out the information in bits, each of which would hurt. There is a long list on that paper. I guess your insurance is having violence on your side. I have friends and family you could harm, doing damage in bits, matching whatever threat I pose. Sounds like a very risky business for both of us.”

“If you know this, why did you come to me without a better plan? Aren’t you a smart guy?”

“Oh whoa, I’m no smart guy! Getting myself into this proves it.   The whole thing started out just for fun. Something I couldn’t turn down. Let’s just give it a try. I am not asking much from you. Just let Keahi do a job like a regular person. Get her paid what you feel she deserves for the work you find for her. Ignore me. Then if I try to make more of this, I understand we will have to renegotiate. Why not let it run awhile?   See how it goes.”

“Maybe someone is doing some kind of investigation; maybe time will make the case against us stronger.”

“It does not need to be any stronger. I have all anyone needs to put away the folks on that paper. Look, your clients are not a nice bunch of guys. I don’t want to rile them against me any more than I want to see Mutt and Jeff again.”

“Who’s Mutt and Jeff? Oh, you mean the, um, escorts for Keahi.”

“Right... So, you see, you have the upper hand here. It won’t cost you anything. Just the nuisance of helping

Keahi. This is easier than squeezing her to give you back the information she stole."

"Maybe you can be controlled. But Keahi has already sold us out to you. What if she tries it again?"

"She's not very good at it. She doesn't know your weaknesses. Doesn't know where to take it. Doesn't know how to protect herself. She was lucky to find me; pardon my vanity. I am not good for much but this I can do better than most. I don't know how to manage this from her side and I sure won't try to explain it to her. But if she tries something, let me know. Maybe I can get her back in line."

Tarwicks sat back in his chair. He sat the flask on the desk in front of him and folded his hands. He nodded up and down unconsciously. Buck waited until Tarwicks pushed the flask toward him.

"Good," Buck responded. "I am glad you are satisfied with this *interim* arrangement. I am content with this package. All it lacks is my name and address to make it ready for us each to take a snort."

"Right. You want to go first?"

"Well first, I have another request. Something outside the deal. Maybe you'd be able to help me on something, on a question I have been grappling with, something that just feels like it's up your alley."

"Yeah? This oughtta be good."

"I see a brief mention in your documents, in the ones I have seen, to a company named 'Pulter'. I know something of this firm from other sources. I would be interested if you could say something more about them."

"Pulter? I don't recognize the name. Really, I don't. That where you work?"

"Nope."

"So why do you care?"

"It has nothing to do with Ringstare. It's not part of our deal. Just a question... Maybe not an innocent one..."

Tarwicks held up his hands to form a megaphone; it was a warning he was about to shout. "Maggie!" Margaret came in quickly, carrying a pad of steno paper. "Maggie, see if Roger is around, will you? Send him in." She did not answer except by departing. She had not looked in Buck's direction.

"Thanks for checking," said Buck. "If we have a minute for her to check on that, we can celebrate our deal now. This will in fact be much better for you than the situation on your side as of this morning, no?"

They each took a drink. Buck did his best to look as if he liked it. He held the flask to his lips as if he took in two swallows but he really only had a sip. They did not speak until the door opened a couple minutes later.

"Roger!"

"Yes, Boss. What's up?"

"Do we have a client named Pulter?"

"Yeah, I think so. I can't recall much about it off the top of my head. Do you want me to go look it up?"

"Here use my desk." Tarwicks stood up to give Roger access to his computer. Roger banged along for a couple minutes while Buck and Tarwicks sat silently. Finally, Roger made a sign to Tarwicks to look at the screen. Tarwicks sat at his desk and studied the computer screen briefly and then asked Buck what exactly he wanted to know.

"There are some unnecessary accounts within their accounting structure. I can't see that there is any abuse of them but I need to know why they were set up."

"Another cheap blackmail?"

"I'm not a blackmailer," Buck asserted again.

"No, of course not," Tarwicks growled. "Whatta you think, Roger? Any thoughts on odd accounts over there?"

Roger began slowly. "We don't work with them much. As far as I know, everything they do is legit."

Tarwicks interrupted. "Roger, give it to us straight. Bucky here is having a frank and friendly drink. Whatta we know?"

Roger looked into Tarwicks face. "Straight? Everything?"

"Everything," Tarwicks confirmed.

"Pulter is clean as clean. That's what Jackie R's boys liked about them. About a year ago they got a guy on the inside. They're setting up a laundry. Jackie needs to clean six figures of cash per month. I don't know how he's gonna do it. We aren't part of it. Um, you want to know everything, boss?"

"Yeah, what else."

"Not much. They came to us for advice. We gave 'em Pulter. That's all we did. We kinda keep an eye on things in case there's something to know in the future."

"That what you needed to hear?" Tarwicks asked Buck.

Buck allowed himself a grin. "Thanks Roger. I already know Jackie R's guy. What happens if I get him fired? Clean up the place?"

Tarwicks grimaced. "Jackie wants a clean place. If his guy is caught, it falls on him; don't cha think, Roger?"

"That's the risk of going into a clean place. Maybe it wants to stay that way. We told him it's better to work through an established channel. Maybe it would work out good for us. Our advice would be backed up and we could run him through one of our... I mean point him to an established channel."

"I can be pretty sure Buck would not ever connect it to us," Tarwicks noted, looking at Buck.

Buck did not answer, right away. "Got any more in that flask?"

Tarwicks slide the flask across the desk. Buck raised it to his lips and took a full swallow. "While you and, maybe, Roger finish that off, I'll give you my particulars. I'll tell,,," Buck was not sure if Roger needed to know about the rest of the deal. "I'll tell her to relax. She should be in a position she likes very soon, don't you think?"

Tarwicks drank the rest of the scotch. Roger stood silently to the side while Buck wrote out his name and address. "Roger, go get Maggie." Tarwicks turned to Buck. "Shouldn't be too hard to find that Keahi a spot. Not here though. You want her at Pulter? I hear it's clean."

"Too clean to take her on the terms attached to her."

"Low ambitions, huh?" Tarwicks looked at the new page Buck handed him. "Just give Maggie your data." He put the paper on the desk face up and read the name. "I'd like to watch what Buckminster does with Pulter." Tarwicks spoke aloud but he was only talking to himself. Buck had left the room.

Margaret met Buck outside the door to Tarwick's office. "It's all to the good," he said while trying to smile. He held Margaret by the elbow. He was not sure why it was an effort to act upbeat. It really was all to the good. Making a deal with the likes of Tarwicks was like signing your name on fly paper. It was hard to be sure the deal was what he understood it to be or that it would remain for long whatever it was today. He had played his cards. It was not so much to show his hand; Tarbucks could have caught up with him eventually. It was important to give it up when it still had value. It was risky too, he knew, to place much faith in Keahi. She was still a stranger to him and had deceived him several times already. There was nothing to gain from regretting the steps already taken. The past could not be changed. There was basis enough for quiet celebration. It would be sweet to do it with that enticing woman who started him on this road. "Can I see Keahi?"

"Is it really all good? It can't be. What happened? She took documents and they will never let her get away with that."

"Mr. Tarwicks is safe. Keahi is no longer any threat to him. Let me tell her how it goes."

"I have to see Mr. Tarwicks!"

"Okay, Margaret. Do what you have to do." Buck let go of her elbow and smiled as realistically as he could. She took a step toward Tarwicks and put her hand on the doorknob before she looked back to Buck. "Down that hallway; third door on the left. I told her you're here," and she smiled in her nervous way.

Through the third door on the left was a large room with cubicles. Obviously Keahi did not hold a prestigious position in the firm. He walked down one aisle and back through the other, glancing into each at the back of someone's head without finding her. They were all organized so a person going past could see what was on the computer screens. Then he saw her in an isolated corner at the copy machine. She did not notice Buck until he was nearly beside her. He put some effort into a smile to reassure her before she uttered a scream.

"It's all taken care of, now, Keahi. Let me explain it to you. Is there somewhere we can sit down?"

Keahi looked around. No one was in view; they were all inside their cubicles. She grabbed his hand with one of hers and put her other hand on his chest. "What did you do? How can you be here?"

"Let's go somewhere to talk a bit."

"Yes, to my apartment. We can talk there."

Her aggressive touch might have been nervousness or friendliness, as expressed in a different culture than Buck's, or it might have been active enticement. It felt good to Buck and the slender woman staring into his eyes with her invitation was looking very good. He squeezed her hand in return.

"Not today. I need to get to my work. I am behind."
They had spoken softly, but now Buck leaned forward, enjoying her closeness, and whispered, "I met with Tarwicks. He agreed to find you a good job outside Ringstare. You can't stay here. I'll give you my name and phone number so you can tell me if you do not like the new job or the new company. You can't keep any files on Ringstare. Let me know if you have any problems. I can't help with some things, of course, but I think we can get you a good job, a safe job." Buck leaned forward the remaining couple inches and kissed her beside the ear.

It was drizzling when Buck stepped outside Pulter's front door. He stepped carefully onto the wet asphalt walkway to the street in case the rain made the ice even more treacherous. The thin layer of ice was gone and his shoes clung to the asphalt with a friction he had not felt all week.

Chapter 14

RED IS REVEALED

Angela watched Buck get in the cab and waved to him when he looked back at her. After it drove away, she noticed the hiss of the frozen rain for the first time. She listened to it for a few moments, turning her head from side to side to observe how it came from everywhere: sound of space itself, she imagined. And then she remembered she had allowed herself to become a target of criminals and focused her senses back onto sight, searching for anyone lurking in the shadows or, maybe, taking photographs with a long lens. There were no shadows in the dim light except that everything was in the shadow of the clouds. She tried to look casually into the windows facing the street, looking for a shape or a glint or a movement of a curtain. There was only the hiss. Another sense pushed itself to her attention and she felt cold so she pulled her coat around herself and went back into the drugstore.

She saw Walid still sitting in the booth in back, sipping coffee. She kept her coat on while she walked to the café and shook it off before hanging it on a hook beside the booth. "I'll have another cup with you if you have the time. I have a question for you."

Walid looked surprised but he answered calmly, "That would be nice." He did not have time to relax, but there was time to make Angela feel comfortable. She was now part of the plot.

Angela carried her cup to the urns and prepared a fresh cupful, measuring her usual formula for milk and sugar, but taking the almond roast blend just to vary the routine. Walid watched her do this. He watched for the sexual satisfaction of seeing the languid movement of her body against the fortunate fabrics that wrapped her. He was inconspicuous, lifting his cup to his lips and turning his head without revising his attention. No harm in looking, but he turned his eyes down guiltily when she was walking in his direction.

"You believe in him, don't you?" asked Angela as soon as she had slid into her place across from Walid.

"He is very careful. He will be as careful with you as he can be, even though he does not know you very well. But that does not mean this is a safe situation."

"You feel safe enough then?"

"Not really. Sometimes you have to back up your friends."

"Sometimes? When do you do that? Whenever he asks?"

"Whenever he needs it. He doesn't need it often, but he may not know when he needs it."

"Good friend."

"Yes, but you aren't, not yet anyway. Why would you ever get yourself into this odd thing?"

"Buck and Walid. Seems like fun."

"You may be the most insightful person ever. We are fun most of the time. You would be right, but you haven't seen us at it."

"I'm a big optimist."

Walid took the last swallow of his coffee. It felt like the right moment to leave except that there was still no explanation for why Angela had come back to the table to sit with him. He waited for her to say something. She was not drinking her java, just sitting, so Walid spoke again.

"Where are you from, Angela?"

"Here. This city. Not the best part of it. I was born and raised, not poor, not privileged, in this throwback café or some other just like it. All I had, and therefore all I ever truly needed, is in this drugstore, or some other much like it. I have been nowhere else yet, no place worth mentioning. ...I think I will go someplace someday, that I am fated to do so, and am on the path to someplace already although I have not taken a stride beyond the stool where I am sitting at this hour."

"I've been places. Buck has not been very far. I don't think he's looking to go anywhere else. I'm not going back where I came from."

"That's not quite true; what I said, not what you said. Angela was born here, but there is an earlier person inside this shell."

"Sounds like a story coming on," and Walid worried why he was being favored with this confession. He did not want to get mixed up with the woman or any other woman. When she did not continue immediately, he wondered if his own attractive face was influencing Angela. She seemed committed to going further and expected him to be with her for this intimate moment. Her expectation that he would stay with her and hear her felt like the confidence her own experience had drawn from men who were under the influence of her attractive face and other bodily parts. The subject had drifted in his mind far from the meeting's origins in the Keahi case.

Angela, for her part, was scarcely thinking of Walid at all. The morning had put her in a peculiar mood and made her wonder why she had gone along with and so enjoyed the strange little adventure with Buck.

"A story? Yes... I remember when I was very young, spending too much time in the yard; a small brick house baking through a dry August in the reliable Carolina heat of the summer one decade before the new millennium. From dawn to dusk, no shadow offered me any illusion of protection even though skinny pines surrounded our sandy lawn a hundred yards away from the house on three sides. A county road on the fourth side roared steadily from seven am to seven pm on weekdays, connecting the nearby town of Dark Possum to the local metropolis of Peach Pit, fifteen miles northwest. When night approached and the traffic died down, the whine and prick of mosquitos prevented any sensation of relief that might have come from the slow cooling of the still, humid and heavy atmosphere.

"If our house had ever been someone's dream, it was a person with no concern for style. It was the embodiment of a child architect's drawing of a house; two windows on each side of a doorway unadorned by a stoop or a lamp, though it lacked a chimney with a curl of smoke rising to a huge yellow sun. Between the bricks and the asphalt shingle roof, and around the windows, thick white paint peeled and chipped off the simple wood trim revealing how little maintenance the house had seen in recent years, that is, during my lifetime as of then, but from a distance, the home looked strong at least. Maybe the maintenance was a reflection of my father's being missing. My brothers remembered him a little but I did not. It was better for me since I did not miss him. Our mother was proud we had a television since it is more than she had as a girl. But everyone was getting televisions by then. Really nothing in this for a child to laud or to disparage. Not in my earliest days."

"Can't you say you turned out alright? Something to laud in what you are now?"

"I hoped I have not 'turned out' yet, 'cause this is nothing to be so pleased about."

"I won't try to tell you how wonderful you are although I can see some very positive attributes."

"Thank you for not guessing at what they may be. This conversation is not my fishing for reassurance."

"Of course not."

"I am introducing myself for your judgment."

"I am not going to judge you, Angela."

"You may not tell me your conclusions; you may not reach firm conclusions, but you cannot help but judge me.

"I was saying where I began. Soon after my beginnings, I took the form of the only model in front of me:

261

my brothers. It was great to be a tomboy. We were barefoot and all over the place. Climbed trees. Got wet when it rained. I was a teenager before I knew it was possible to get your toenails as clean as your fingernails.

"I wasn't much of a student. My teachers were nice to me anyway. I wanted to be an artist. Didn't care what kind: painting, singing, writing, acting. Don't know if I had any talent for one or the other. We barely touched on art in school. You needed to take some kind of classes on your own for those things. Unless you were a genius, but I'm not one of those. None of us are; no one I ever met is any kind of genius. We never had money for those things. We weren't poor. I saw poor in others. We just didn't have any extra.

That was long ago; not so long that it doesn't still matter though." She stopped as if the story was over although it had not reached any substantive conclusion. Maybe she was enjoying her remembrances in this way. She continued before Walid interrupted, her English and her accent gradually accepting a more colloquial twang.. "My mother was loving. Isn't that the most important thing in a mother? She loved us all. It wasn't enough for my brothers. They turned out bad early on. So when my first brother, the one who taught me to shoot hoops, and start a campfire, bait a fishhook... when that brother followed my father and went off to jail instead of finishing high school, I got real close to my loving mother and spent the rest of my time in the back of the café where she worked, a place on Main Street with six tables for two each and a counter, but hardly anyone ever sat at the counter 'cause it was always full of stuff. They put displays of candy there, boxes of napkins, and such. Even stacks of clean plates instead of hiding 'em underneath or something. I used to look at the operation and see ways it could be done better. I never gave my mother any advice and my mother never gave the owner any either. I sat on a stool. It helped my posture. Haven't you noticed how straight I hold my back?'

"Your back is beautifully straight. I think you know that most guys notice that about you."

"Oh sure. I like being looked at but I tell myself I don't. This look I wear, still like the diner I lived in, 'retro' Buckminster says, but not in a sophisticated way; it's my disguise; where I hide. It's not me. Maybe it's my mother or was my mother. Men can look at this and I take no offense since they can't see me. I don't get lustful stares; I get bemusement. They think I meet the minimum requirements for their leering, but they imagine they are seeing a bumpkin who probably married a close relative when she was 14. And I do not look back so they figure I'm stupid too."

"Buck said you were smart."

"He doesn't know how smart I am. Hell, I don't know how smart I am. He probably said that because my sass exceeded his expectations. I never had any college. Not yet. I'd like to do that. I like to read. I like to learn. I would like to work someplace more interesting and challenging than my mother's café. But guess what? I'm not smart enough to figure out how to do college. And soon I'll be too old. The clock is ticking. It's already too late to get that beautiful college experience with all the young people on their own for the first time in life and figuring out where they are going and how to get there. I imagine they talk about it into the night and help each other think it though even if none of them actually knows how to do it. It is too late for me to experience these. It's not too late to learn a skill, to learn to appreciate civilization. I am not worried about passing barren through my child-bearing years but about passing uneducated through my learning years."

Walid thought of asking her a few questions, like why she was telling him this; why she cared about his judgment. He was interested; she was interesting, but he was also late for work. He did not want to show his impatience and he did not want to be, or even appear to be, one of those men who try to get inappropriately close to her. Silence came between them again. Walid expected her to move and that her move would be to the door, but eventually she went on with her story.

"There weren't other kids living nearby. Well, the closest neighbor had a boy my age. Between our house and their trailer was their watermelon field. One day the father came by and said we could have a watermelon and he said he had a tyke could be a playmate for me. My mother went with me to their place. The boy was running around their sandy front yard in his underwear pants and acting all wild-like. He was a white boy, brown as a berry. I asked him his name. He screamed something back at me such as I couldn't understand him. He was like a dog that's never been inside the house. My mother didn't let me stay. I realized she was protecting me in some way, something I hardly ever noticed from her.

"That little boy wasn't so very different from my own brothers when we were just children. They wore pants sure enough, when they went outside, but they were in the same clothes every day in a season and in summer they were as dark as soul brothers. They were wild too, in a good way. We ran everywhere when there weren't any adults around; no lollygagging. There weren't adults around much. I had one brother older'n me and one younger'n. I wanted to be like the older one and I wanted the younger one to be like me. I sure didn't want to be like my mother; even she didn't want to be like she was, either working or sitting on the couch doing nothing on her best days or drinking on her worst.

"My mother had her opinions on me. Can't say they were always the best. I remember one Christmas was supposed to be a big one. Mother kept sayin' how she did herself up good. My big brother got a baseball glove with too much padding and too little web. My little brother got a bat that was too small even for him. We were using regular hardballs by then and that little bat was like swingin' a sawed off broomstick. The biggest thing was she got me a pjnk princess phone, the kind that's real compact for those days. I didn't like the pink and I didn't have anybody to call but I liked it for a night light. She didn't pay the phone bill and it didn't work for more'n a few months, not for making calls anyway. It was pretty good as a night light."

"I hear your words getting more Carolina as you keep talking," Walid teased her to show he was listening.

"That's not Angela speaking. That's the girl that came before me. My mother ... her mother, um, passed, I mean died, when I, she, the girl before me, was just finishing high school. Car crash. She was drunk; I'm sure of that. She wasn't driving. The guy she was with was probably high on something, but I don't know. Doesn't matter why it happened. Both brothers were in jail by then so that made it easier, I guess. Didn't have their mouths to feed.

I got offered my mother's job at the café. That scared me a lot. I hadn't planned much about what to do in life except that I wasn't going to work in a café. The state messed around with me for a few months until I was 18. It wasn't any help but then I was not in a mood to accept help back then.

"I looked for my father as much as I could. Asked around. Filed a missing persons report. Looked on-line. I worked for a maid service, cleaning houses, you know, once a week for people who could afford it. After a year my big brother got out of jail. He came by the house for a few days. Saw it wasn't much and took off again. Never heard from him again. I hope he's alright wherever he is now."

Sarah looked up from wiping an orange juice ring a patron had left on the counter and wondered about the conversation at Angela's table. She had enjoyed playing matchmaker between her most regular customer and the clever one, Buck. She feared she was watching a betrayal and wondered if she should intervene. Angela should not get involved with someone who would do this to his friend. If she did not like Buck, she should have to go back to waiting for the right guy. Sarah's orientation was toward Angela's welfare. Angela was the quiet, confident princess Sarah had been in her teenage dreams. She noticed that Walid was the prototypical dark, gentle masculine ideal she might have paired herself with in those dreams if she had the confidence to even imagine it. Together they were not some dream, perverse or otherwise, and she felt some responsibility for helping bring about today's obviously critical meeting with its change of relationships. She had never hoped to actually meet a clever or a beautiful boy herself but in this case Buck was there first and that was more important than their relative attributes. It disturbed her that things were not turning out as she wanted, just like a dream that goes awry, but she could not wake up from this one. The stunning woman with the red hair ought to be with the clever man, not the pretty one, if for no other reason than that that is the arrangement she intended when she dug out Angela's charge slips and looked her up and phoned her this morning and talked her into coming in for the mysterious meeting.

But Sarah was wrong. She was not watching Angela shift her attention because she found Walid attractive. She hardly looked at a man's appearance, having learned (and then actively ensured) that her own appearance was not representative of who she was. She had come to regard appearance as nearly irrelevant, at least that aspect of appearance that is inborn and the matinee idol face on Walid and his athletic figure did not tell much about him, not of the things worth knowing.

"When my younger brother got out, he called me up a couple times. We talked a lot. I tried to keep in touch when he was in, you know, but then we couldn't talk for long. I couldn't get him to come see me or to give me a number or address for him. Said he didn't look good. After a few months he stopped calling. I don't think anything really bad happened to him; just nothing good. He had a lot of pride, not too much smarts. That made for two strikes against him and our big brother was the third strike.

"The state dropped me when I turned 18 an then they took the house away from me when I was 19. I could live in a tent under a bridge or I could accept one of those offers of shelter that came easily to a 19-year-old girl in our small town. I went for a permanent thing; not a few nights or a few months here and there. But I never found anything to last. There were some nice fellows in those years, some not so nice but I was mostly with nice ones. I've been on my own for a few years now. Still looking for a chance to go to college. I could be a teacher. ...high school, I think. I'd like to get them excited about learning. Art, maybe, if I could do that. History or English if I didn't have the talent for art. It would be good to make it important to them.

"I had to get away from everything. I got mixed in with one guy who was far from nice and I especially had to get away from him. He had way too much pride and thought he owned me. Really, he accepted, conveniently, those parts of the Southern history and the Christian tradition that allow a man to own a women, to tell her what to do and think and to exploit it and to be jealous of any independence of thought or action. More than anything to be jealous of any other potential owner. I was pretty good at keeping him happy with me, not because I wanted to make him happy but because I was afraid of him and was looking for a way out. And then he got the idea that I was seeing someone else. I wasn't, but he didn't care about the facts. He liked the idea of being a jealous man; it was heroic. He would hint to me about some time when my whereabouts were not certain to him and then he would try out names or descriptions of suspects. I didn't want to play along with his paranoia but I wasn't very good at calming him down. I suppose I tended to pretend to love him just to change the subject and that probably reinforced him. I'm pretty sure he killed one guy; a guy I hardly knew. And then he focused in on another guy that I didn't know at all. He starting talking about him and seeing mirages of evidence and getting mad at me. So I came up north. I switched cities a couple times, changed my name. He's not smart enough to find me anymore; not rich enough to hire someone to do it for him. But I lost all my reserves and a year of my time getting away from him.

"I'm not really on track to get back into school. I can't get a scholarship and I can't save much money to pay my own way. I'm not asking any man to pay my way either. Uh-uh. But it would be nice to have a male friend. I need to grow up; get my adult life going. I see the world is wonderful, with beautiful, exciting things to see and do, and people to know. And I'm just in this waiting pattern, like something is ever going to pick me up and carry me into a better place. At least I got myself out of Carolina.

"My first move was as far as I could get with a bus pass for twelve dollars. I just about starved to death. I was skinny when I left and lost twenty-five more pounds in six months. Good thing was I stayed in the South that first time. I stayed 'cause I couldn't think of bein' up North but it worked out good 'cause I didn't freeze to death. Came close to it, though.

"I stole some clothes and got a job as a cashier in a dollar store and then stole everything in the cash register first chance I got. I couldn't stay. They woulda figured out I lied to them when they tried to send me a pay check. It wasn't much money but it got me out of town a little smarter than the last time I moved.

She stopped speaking and Walid waited for her to resume, then, when she did not, he asked if she were working now. He was not sure what she wanted from him and the question was generated by his sense of duty to ask something pertinent. His actual curiosity was tempered by the stress of feeling the need to get to his own workplace. There must have been some disingenuity in his voice because she did not answer. She just looked at the paper napkin she had been shredding as she spoke. Walid was content to let her ruminate; he had done his part.

Finally she said, "I guess I can fall back into being that little country girl pretty easy when I let down my guard. It wasn't so bad but I'm moving on to something else. I've got to. Walid, I'm not trying for your sympathy. I'm just telling you who I am so maybe you can say if Buck is right for me and I would be good for him. Not say exactly; you can't know that, but what do you think? Should I try for him? Not go after him in a strategic plot kind of way, but just see if we might fit together? I mean, I will keep my promise about the stuff on Ringstare either way. But should I see if there's a future for us?"

Walid felt something was wrong about the role he was being asked to play. He shared Buck's troubles with women but he did not want to participate in them. He had jumped into the problem with Keahi for Buck's safety, not his libido.

Chapter 15

THE PULTER PLAN

J ust before noon Buck got to his office. He had six phone messages from Rich at that point. They made no threats but showed his desperation and his waning patience. He said he was going forward with the purchase of Pulter, Inc. He did not have to say it was a major move and that it would be terrible if Buck had anything to contribute but did not give it up in time.

Buck had sent one text message at 11:40 to say he had been working the project all morning and had a rock solid recommendation for him; that he had evidence no one else could ever have found, but he could say no more in his text since it was the kind of recommendation that needs to be given orally. The text was written when he was in a cab on the way to the office. Though not yet noon when he climbed into the cab, a thick cloud cover made the time seem late. The cabbie complained throughout the drive about the streets. It made sense to him that the plows and salt trucks should have adjusted to the weather over the course of the week and new snow should not have been allowed to remain. He suggested that the fire trucks should hose down the main streets; that the water in the hydrants was clearly warmer than freezing so it would melt the snow while pushing it out of the way. Buck mildly praised the cabbie's creativity and did not tell him what he really thought of the idea. It was not Buck's way to argue with cabbies or to rant about the city's incompetence. He was not prone to disappointment over the city's handling of the blizzard since it was such an unusual event. If he were in charge, he too would not have been well prepared for the hundred-year storm. His goal would have been to preserve health and safety, not to keep businesses going. More than this, he felt at some level of consciousness that he was in charge. It was a democracy. He had given little effort to the city administration and must accept the result.

The cabbie was still whining when Buck got out. Buck thought he ought to appreciate getting a fare on a day when people were again staying home. On the basis of the streets, the city had nearly given up hope. He went straight to Rich's office and noted the time on his watch before he knocked on the doorframe. The door was open but Rich sat with his back to the door so Buck always knocked before stepping inside. He pointed to his watch to indicate he was not very late.

"Whatta ya got?" asked Rich, still holding back his anxiety.

"The full story, Rich," Buck claimed, "but I can't tell it all to you right off. Bottom line: we should buy it. The price is good. But we need to revise the contract just a little. One thing. And we need to do it carefully. Let me work with legal this afternoon. We can get it out today."

"Out all week and late as this today, and you want your unexplained version of a decision to go to the contracts office directly?"

"You're right Rich. I am just excited to have reached the nub of this conundrum. You see, I was troubled by a certain awkwardness in their systems but everything was formally perfect so it did not seem like mere incompetence. So I looked very carefully into potential graft. And I found it. It was so damn hard to find because it is not operational yet; just a criminal enterprise being set up. It is a money laundering thing.   It was set up from outside. The company doesn't know about it, just the one guy hired to do it. Name is 'Harley', Lawrence Harley. Maybe that's a pseudonym, but it's the one he uses at Pulter. We don't need to go after him. Just say his position is redundant with something we already have on our staff. A simple, if personal, contingency. Mr. Harley won't make a fuss. The good part is I have a good basis for liking the rest of the company. The scum behind the scam chose Pulter because it was strong otherwise. I can't say they care about the same things as us, but they determined it was an honest shop to be running their cover. That's good for us."

Rich scraped the floor loudly pulling up the chair beside his desk for Buck to sit down. The noise allowed him to sit for an extra moment without speaking, as if he had said something that was merely unintelligible.

"You have proof of all this?"

"Hell no, I don't. And we are delving into territory where you don't want to know how I know." Buck saw that his recommendation was not going to be taken on simple faith. He should have anticipated that. He had been focused on getting the right recommendation, but when illicit operations are at play, he now realized, recommendations take on an additional layer of complexity. But he thought he held an adequate reserve of trust with Rich to bluff his way through.

"I can show you how the scam was going to work and the architecture that was set up to make it possible." Buck actually had not seen how the laundering was to work but now that he knew the purpose of the odd structures, he might be able to figure it out. He did not want to try; it wasn't necessary for the decisions at hand. "I know you could see it but you might be bored to tears. Let me show it all to Oscar. He has an accounting background and he's loyal to the company."

"Oscar? He's loyal, I suppose, but he is wants to know every detail. If he sees something illegal, he may feel it is a requirement to take it to the Supreme Court. I like your plan to keep it simple, just what affects us. Can you give me a sketch?"

"Sure, but in the short run, I'd like to write a report that the lawyers can use for the contract contingencies. I can get with Oscar to remove the awkward architecture. He'll see it was not used for anything inappropriate so far."

"So how did you figure it out? Did you get this Pulter plant, this Harley, drunk enough to boast of his cunning or his mob connections?"

"The true tale revolves around an Oriental enchantress whose offer to have a drink in her apartment I may yet accept."

"Does Julie know this mysterious woman?"

"Ouch! Worse than that. Julie does not care anymore. Not about whom I see or anything else Buck-related. No, the lovely lady is mine to know better at least until she realizes I am a number cruncher on a mediocre salary living in a studio apartment and balding in the back."

"Now you"re angling for a raise?"

"I'm just saying my prospects with this fine women I met in the storm would be enhanced if I could take her to a better class of club."

"You can paint speckles on a catfish so it shimmers like a trout but it will still feed off the bottom."

"If you know me so well, Rich, you know I am right about Pulter."

"Get with the lawyers today, OK?"

"It won't be a hard fix for them."

Chapter 11

COMPLICATIONS AND DECISIONS

Buck was almost giddy as he put on his coat to leave for the day. It had been an historic day for the Empire of Buckminster, one to remember forever. It could have gone so wrong but it had not. They had sent the offer to Pulter by four o'clock.

His telephone rang. The screen said it was Rich calling. Buck hesitated to answer; he was anxious to get back to Angela and another round of congratulations was not necessary, but he thought it best to maintain the momentum of his day rather than leave Rich disappointed that he had left too early.

Rich asked Buck to come to his office. Buck was surprised by the subdued tone in Rich's request.

There was a man in a blue suit standing in Rich's office along with the company lawyer. Rich introduced him as a Treasury agent. "He's asking why we asked to exclude that position from our merger with Pulter. I wasn't too clear on that particular detail. Could you help with the explanation?"

"Sure can," answered Buck cheerily. He was very impressed that Treasury had seen the offer sheet so quickly, probably minutes after it was sent. They must have had a man inside Pulter watching for the laundering operation.

Ringstare did not know about him. They would not have wanted the merger to fail, not with Buck's leverage. It did seem too fast to be confronting Rich about it.

"It was mainly my recommendation. Rich, there are some competitive issues here. Do we need to limit the discussion to the issues that have no commercial value?"

Rich asked the company lawyer his opinion on that question and the lawyer said Buck should be completely open; that there was no reason for anything in this discussion to get out to potential competitors. Buck did not agree with that assessment at all and he did not respect the lawyer's knowledge of the issues to make such a judgment. Their lawyer was always overly cautious, although in this case it seemed his over-caution to serve the agent was under-caution to protect the company. Rich, on the other hand, was nervous for another reason. He knew there was something fishy at Pulter and wanted nothing to do with legal risks. He was probably already regretting that he had taken Buck's recommendation on the whole deal.

Buck knew there was no getting out of this. He would have to take the lead. He shook the agent's hand and asked to see his credential. He looked closely and tried to memorize the badge number. He could remember the name, but the number was too long to learn without time to study. "I am very sorry to take up your time, Mr. Robbins. I am not used to interviews like this. Just give me a moment to make a note here." No one spoke as Buck wrote the number on the pad he had brought in with him, but Buck could feel the potential for outrage. Rich was giving responsibility for the issue to Buck so he had to give Buck some leeway in how he handled it. The lawyer had made his recommendation and it had been accepted. He could hardly object to formalizing the relationship.

When they are sat down, Buck continued, "Perhaps Rich has explained my role. I look into the financial fit of companies we are considering as partners. I mean, that's not a full time job for me. We don't take on new partners all that often, but when we do, it fits into my portfolio. And what I do is immerse myself in their public information: annual reports, licenses, court records, stuff like that. This Pulter case was not especially difficult from my perspective. Rich had identified it as a good merger candidate based on the compatibility of our product lines and their generally good record over the long run. They had a tough couple years due to what we feel are temporary market circumstances and it left them cash-poor and therefore relatively easy to buy out."

Agent Robbins interrupted impatiently. "I am not interested in why your company wanted this merger. I want to know why you identified an individual to be left out of the new company, this, let me look again, this Harley."

"Sure. I do not know recall the name of the individual we identified as redundant. It was a pretty routine outcome of the analysis. I line up our assets and their assets and look for complementarities, conflicts, and redundancies. There are always some conflicts and redundancies, ways in which the partnership is imperfect. I look at those to see what we can fix and whether the balance is in our favor. This particular person represented a redundancy that was very easy to resolve-- just don't bring him along."

"That's a little harsh, don't you think?" asked the agent.

"Harsh? No, business is business. We did not need him. He would have been a waste of resources. I am sure he would not want to be in a company without work for him to do."

"And you could not find something else for him?"

"Is Treasury interested in labor management issues?" asked Buck. It was, in fact, not his company's role to retrain or reassign the employee. The offer had merely excluded his position. Of course, it had been worded in a way that left no room for a reassignment, but that was not personal.

"I am not at liberty to discuss with you any details of our case. If you do not wish to respond fully now, we can have you testify more formally. I can say this Harley was a person of interest in an investigation of organized crime. Did you have any information relating to that?"

"Ooh-ee," uttered Buck to project as much sincerity as he could. "I don't know anything about him as an individual. I just look into the public record. Look, let me show you just how his position came out and how it fit into the analysis. Hang on a moment while I get the file off my desk."

Without waiting for permission or making eye contact with anyone, Buck was gone. Back in his own office he opened a file drawer and put his hand inside so it would seem he was looking through it if anyone came by while he thought. It was not his way to go too far without a plan and he preferred to formulate a plan after gathering as much background as possible, even seemingly irrelevant background. The agent had said he could not give any details of his investigation, a reasonable statement, and then said rather much about it in a manner that seemed intended to bully them into saying more without going to a Treasury office. Buck looked up the Treasury Department on-line and dialed the number. He said he had a tip relating to organized crime in this city and was reporting it as requested by Agent Robbins, Badge # 7441-090-288. The clerk on the phone tried a few things and asked for his information about a crime but Buck said he would only speak to that agent.

It would be enough for the present to leave his return number for a call back if they could confirm Agent Robbins was legit. Eventually the clerk acknowledged they had no agent by that name or badge number. Buck said he might have copied it wrong from the card the agent left and he would call back after he checked the card. Then he wrote down the name of the agent he was told to call if he could not find the card, the agent who dealt with matters like this around here.

"Very curious," Buck thought. "At least I have bought myself some time." He called Rich's secretary and asked her to get Rich on the line without saying why. Then he told Rich he had checked and Agent Robbins was not known at Treasury. He had one more idea and said just to stall for a minute more.

If this guy represented the people who were planning to launder money through Pulter, they should be happy to have their plan end with no more repercussions than this. If this guy was from that faction, he did not seem to know Ringstare had turned him in. Buck called Pulter. Fortunately, someone was still there this late in the day. Maybe this was a good company for a partner.

"Hello, this is West Cross Hospital emergency room. We have an auto accident victim here with damaged identification. We think he will recover well but need to notify his next of kin. Do you have an employee named Harley, six foot tall, sandy hair, 220 pounds, Caucasian?"

...

"Yes, I am very sorry. Can you give me a number for his family?"

...

"That is unfortunate! Can you give me his supervisor's number?"

...

"Thank you for your help. We will have to ask him for a family contact when he gets out of his initial treatment. We'll contact his supervisor only if we need to. He is fully conscious but I was hoping to get this started before the doctors were finished patching him up. Please do not worry too much. He looks like he will be all right, but I am not sure he will be out of the hospital tonight."

Buck typed up a short note and put it in with some tables he had thrown into the recycling bin. Back in Rich's office, he apologized for taking so long. Agent Robbins was standing by the door, and was angry but not out of control. He relaxed slightly when Buck returned. Buck handed his the papers. "Notice page three in particular," he suggested. That is where Buck had placed his typed page with the name and phone number of Harley's supervisor and the name and phone number of the real Treasury Agent. He referred to the supervisor as "your boss at Pulter, Mr. Harley."

"Now you really should confirm the accuracy of those figures, but I think you can see even in a cursory review that I have done my homework and we are justified in the position we took."

"Robbins" looked paler to Buck. He avoided looking directly at Robbins/Harley. He was trying to reduce the stress in the room. He chattered on as he had before leaving the room, saying nothing of significance but sounding as if he were trying to help explain their decisions. Finally Robbins, who had been sitting quietly, leafing through the meaningless pages of numbers, said he thought that was enough for now; that he would review the figures back at the office but that he could see there was a strong basis for the contract language that did not involve his investigation. He assured them there was nothing in their investigation that would affect the merger plan and apologized for taking up so much of their time. When he left, he did not leave a business card to help them contact him if they had any further thoughts on the matter.

As he went out the door, Buck whispered in Rich's ear, "Just you and me now." Rich sent the lawyer away and shook his head vigorously as soon as the door closed. "What the hell was that about?" His words were not loud. It was the least profane sentence he could utter at the moment. "What was in those papers?"

"Rich, that was Harley. That was the guy we fired and he does not know what we know. The papers were trash, but on page three I left him a note proving we know what we are doing."

"I thought you promised this would not come back to bite us."

"You know I am not that brilliant. I would never promise such a thing, Rich, because I know it too. I cannot promise that Mr. Harley will never come back, but I don't see any reason why he would think that is a good idea."

"Are you certain he is not a Treasury agent?"

"As certain as I can be. But it would not be bad if he were one. We have not done anything illegal; not even in the steps I took that you don't want to know about specifically." In addition, Buck thought, "That visit shows I was not overdramatizing the black side of my research."

The conversation dwindled on a little longer along these lines until Rich saw it was not getting him anywhere, so he wrapped it up for the day and went home to his wife for dinner. Buck was willing to put all the threats out of his mind in order to put Angela foremost. Or was it Keahi he needed in front? He stared at his phone. For the first time he had the contact number for both women who were troubling him and the time to call on them.

He tossed his coat on the arm of his office chair and sat on the desk while contemplating his phone. He turned it on. It rang before he made up his mind what to do.

"Damn it, Buck. You got to get your messaging set up on that phone. Or at least leave the damn phone on."

"I'll think about it, Walid. Listen, the phrase for tonight is 'it's all good'. Rich may not be entirely convinced it is apt, but I'm going with it."

"I've been dialing all afternoon, waiting for you to get back on line."

"Sorry, I should have called you, but I just got out of work. In fact, I'm still in the office."

"So Keahi's safe?"

"More than safe. She's set up with a new job. My little blackmail went about as good as it could. Maybe we should start a more ambitious operation."

"But you're in trouble with Rich for all the time you put into Keahi?"

"Oh, things are working out OK here too, in an odd way. Rich is nervous, but he'll be all right."

"Then I can tell you about Angela."

"What about her?"

"We had a talk after you left this morning. You need to talk."

"What did she say with you?"

"Let her tell you.

"That's it? That's all you have to say on it?"

"That's all."

"I'll take your recommendation into account. Give my love to Masha."

"Informed recommendation. I'll give your regards to Masha but it won't do much good. She'll need some time to cool off."

"On her worst day Masha is cool as Miles Davis carryin' a slow note at 2 am."

"She's mine. You call Angela."

Buck wanted to call Keahi. He had given her the general picture, but it seemed to need rehashing. She had not seemed amazed enough at the outcome. She might not have understood it well enough.

But now Walid's recommendation was stuck in his head. He knew Walid was right somehow, but he was not just how. He dialed Keahi's number on his cell phone and hesitated before punching the "talk" key. Nothing would be served by asserting his independence from his friend's advice, his informed advice.

It had taken a year to realize what the real lessons were from Julie. That last time together, she had asked Buck what he wanted from her. He was not prepared for the question. He liked hearing it for it moved things along very far. He answered it well on that occasion, saying he wanted from her whatever she wanted him to want. She then laid out some limits, a reasonable enough answer given the opening he provided. Except that he had not answered her well the first time. He should have laid out his limits when given the chance. Who knows when the critical moment has arrived? It seemed innocent enough; the topic was not intensely sore like a festering boil about to erupt, not to Buck anyway. The moment was long gone now and Julie with it.

Would he give a better answer next time? The question would be different, but he would need to recognize the critical time. And then, knowing it was the time, he would need to say something he could stand behind. Might he have accepted, even embraced Julie's terms? Maybe, if he had anticipated them and known what it would have been like to reject them. Paying a price is not unreasonable. A relationship must be full of compromises. Where were Julie's? She was so well prepared in her list of rules for them, she must have been thinking about them hard. The ways he was not fulfilling them-- was not likely to fulfill them-- must have irked her. It was odd, compared with what he knew of break-ups, that she had been so clear, so organized, exactly like the way he did his professional work and completely alien to his private existence. It might have been the succinctness of her presentation that silenced him rather than its composition. Who thinks of a personal relationship like that, like a contract, like a compact, like a deal between competing interests. Was he too romantic? Did he prefer the ambiguity and flexibility of an unspoken arrangement? It worked well enough in all his other relationships, didn't it? She had not been legalistic. She had not said they should make love X times a week, leaving it open whether she thought this was more than would have taken place without the contract or less. She had not said he could have no other gods before her; she accepted that he was agreeable on that point without speaking it aloud. She had not said he must help with the traditionally female chores; he had always been good about that although he was not sure that would have lasted long past the honeymoon without some carping. She had not said they needed to start a joint account and share ownership of everything; he would not have cared if she had made this a demand. Her demands, which he could not recall in detail any more, much to his surprise since they had been so clear at the time, amounted to telling him it was time to make a commitment to her; past time to woo; he had won her and now must start the part where they live as one. As a proposal, it was oddly rude, coming from the woman he was preparing to love and who professed loving him. Maybe her analysis at the time was imperfect. She seemed scared she was wasting her time; if not Buck, she needed to move on.

Buck did not want to live scared. He would take whatever lessons he had learned in some partial way from Julie and go forth. Keahi was not the one to call. She had been cared for. He had been a good guy. He ought to call the woman whose presence had stayed with him since their last meeting, the one he turned to rather than the one who had turned to him. He had consciously dismissed her as beyond his reach while unconsciously holding onto her.

He redialed a different number and reached Angela.
"Hello Angela. This is Buckminster."
...
"I'll answer to whatever name you call out."
...
"No problem with the deal for Keahi. It worked out about the way we planned. I'll monitor it and let you know if anything changes. I don't think it will."
...

"We three are in a long term relationship but I don't expect it to be very active... Not all parts of it anyway."

...

"Yeah, I just got off the phone with him. I should have called him as soon as I had the deal for Keahi but there was a crisis at my office and it took the rest of the day to work it out. I think that's OK too so now I can relax and think the thoughts I choose."

...

"No, he did not say much; just that he talked with you after I left."

...

"Sure, I wanted you to know but I also wanted to ask if it is too late to have dinner tonight."

...

"I didn't mean the café. I didn't mean a meeting of our little club. I did not even mean that we should talk over the way it came out today although it may be hard for me to hold back on that. I just meant we could have dinner together like regular people. I promised to tell you why I liked the title 'The World's Fair' so the whole adventure has this loose end that nags at me."

...

"Sorry. I was not thinking this far ahead today. How about dessert? Did you have a full multi-course meal tonight already?"

...

"I'll come to you. Is there a place in your neighborhood?"

...

"Do they have cheesecake? I love cheesecake."

There was no cheesecake in the place Angela mentioned but they met there anyway. Buck had a Danish that must have been left over from the morning but he hardly noticed. Angela had a slice of pecan pie, a silent reference to her southern roots, one that Buck could not recognize since he had not heard her story yet. They felt self-conscious, especially since Angela looked Buck in the face every moment except when she was actually finding a bite of pie with her fork. Buck considered holding his head tilted to the side that left her looking along his crooked nose instead of seeing it broadside, but it was too vain a movement to make. He felt badly for being aware of the angle of his nose and could not free his mind off it entirely, like an anomaly in one of his analytical matrices.

He suggested that they walk back to her apartment though it was several blocks. He said he had come to terms with the storm and would seek as much contact with it as he could in its waning days, for surely it would play out soon. Besides, the deli where they had met was too warm for the wintry clothes he was wearing. Angela was dressed, as usual, in lighter fabrics and flimsy shoes. In his struggle to say something, Buck nearly gave her his lecture on wearing layers in cold weather, but he stopped himself in time.

Once outside where Buck could feel more anonymous, he leaned toward her ear to begin his summary of how the Pulter case was resolved. She grasped his arm and pulled his body closer. He felt it was his duty to keep her warm and he put an arm around her. He could not get her any closer, but she could feel the pressure of his desire on her waist.

They did not speak for a long while. Angela had decided Buck should say something. She had already made herself clear. Buck agreed but could not find the right topic. It felt fine enough to walk beside her. And slowly his ordeal with Julie reminded him not to take a woman for granted. His quiet contentment may be something entirely different for her.

He spoke to himself first: "What would be possible to for me to say? That I want your elegant features on my arm to please my ego or impress my friends? Do I want your body? For a night or forever? I have no target in mind. I show interest in you because I have great interest in you. Why? I cannot know. I lack the imagination to picture us as a couple. What may have drawn me to a woman as yourself is easy to see: smart, beautiful, experienced. Frankly, there are lots of women in the world. You stand out for reasons I would not analyze. Why does not matter."

Then he spoke aloud, "In 1964, New York held its second World's Fair. Back then, a World's Fair was not a regular occurrence; it was a major public investment in the grand tradition of the Paris Exposition in 1889 for which the Eiffel Tower was built, and the 1939 New York World's Fair, symbolized by the less permanent Trylon, Perisphere and Helicline. The 1939 one fired the national imagination for a future built on new technology. The 1964 fair built on that success with telephones capable of picture images, vans that could be used like small homes, cars that could fly, and kitchens where everything ran on electricity."

"Do you find these promise you something for your future? Do you wish there was a bright hope like that now? Is that why you thought the book or the fair was so special?"

"My grandfather worked in the Boy Scout exhibit in 1939 and my father was a Boy Scout in the 1965 fair. I have their commemorative patches framed on the wall in my apartment. I would have liked, when I was fourteen, to be a Scout at the next New York World's Fair and dabble in the visions of new future. I was a Boy Scout but there was no fair for me. My grandfather's fair had been followed immediately by the Second World War. My father's fair was followed immediately by the Seattle World's Fair (the space needle), The Montreal Expo (spawned a baseball team that is now in Washington) and a long series of fairs all over the world. The first ones were so valuable, the idea was copied until any more could only be disappointing. New York simply did not bother to have another one. We can't know the future. I laugh at those glorious speculations and I am skeptical whenever the future looks too rosy."

There is one more street to cross before they reach Angela's apartment and she does not want to reach it. She is not going to ask him inside and he is not going to want to go inside. They have strolled through the night and are both too tired to start a new phase of their relationship with the dawn. There will be another time for all things.

Angela stops before they reach the last corner and leans back on the brick storefront, reaching for his hands and presses them together to feel their substance through the thick gloves. He pulls one hand away and grabs the fingers of the glove in his teeth so he can pull it off. He spits the glove onto the icy sidewalk and cups his hand onto her cheek so she can feel his warmth. The wind, it must be the wind, burns her eyes and a tear drips slowly from one of them adding a thin track of further cold touching his hand. She is embarrassed and wants to wipe it away but does not want to move away from Buck's warmth. Buck holds tight with his gloved hand and reaches into his hip pocket for the handkerchief that has awaited so many years to be used. He dabs at the glistening line. After he puts away the handkerchief, he picks up his fallen glove and puts it back on his bare hand.

Around the corner they did not quite reach and cannot see past is a dead end alley. Halfway to the back of this alley and a hundred years away a barrel is surrounded by four raw-boned men burning trash to stave off the frost. None of them wears any gloves or scarf. None of them has a woman to warm his winter. None has a plan that extends past the storm. One is wrapped in a blanket and one is eying that wrap enviously. They do not converse, their energy is reserved for staying awake which they all intuit is essential to living in the alley through this cold spell. A sudden gust sweeps past their feet, hits the end of the alley and bends back across their faces. None of them flinches; the further insult to their senses is such a tiny part of what they suffer it is not worth the effort. When the breeze dies down, one of them senses it is his turn to feed the flames. He takes only a few steps to reach the trash pile that has attracted them to this spot. He finds a large box of shredded paper, the remnants of the specialized secrets of a small firm that believes it has knowledge worth hiding. The tiny fragments burst into flames and a riot of sparks leaps upward. The men lean away from the barrel for a moment, preserving their beards and eyelashes, but not minding the brief brilliance. He shakes the box of lost information slowly for the show of it, a spectacle for his friends to bring in a new day.

"Will this storm ever end?" Buck asks Angela rhetorically.

"Buck, don't you see? It already has. The sun would be shining on us from the horizon if its light could get past these buildings. We are in a temporary shadow, standing here. See the blue coming in far over us! In a few minutes, the shadows will shrink and allow the city to show off its new costume, clean as a surgeon, gentle as a lark and fresh as a baby."

Buck raises his eyes and sees a dim blue showing through the thinning and broken clouds. It does look as promising as Angela says.

Angela is not long convinced by her own optimism. "No doubt the city is just as surely destined to soon return to tawdry as the snow melts into slush and then re-wraps us in cold mud made from filth, greed, danger, burden, sadness, poverty, violence, and, yes, for a few of us, some instants of beauty."

"But Angela, we may never get back to normal. Don't you see? It is still snowing!" With his teeth. he again

pulls off one glove to bare one hand to brush her shoulder
where a thin cloud blowing from the alley is dropping ashy
flakes. His effort to clean them away only smears them into a
thin grey paste. "Look at that! Black snow."

ᛃᛃᛃ

www.ingramcontent.com/pod-product-compliance
Lightning Source LLC
Chambersburg PA
CBHW031646100726
47898CB00006B/1991